Dance of the Goblins

Haghuf, respected elder among the unseen goblins, has only scorn for humans. Yet he is drawn into friendship with a human aristocrat by the Dance, the celebration of life that holds the goblin society together.

Count Anton - human, magician, shapeshifter – rules the human world above.

When an unwitting human wanders accidentally into the caverns, a series of events is set into motion that will lead him to betray his loyalty to his own people to avoid a war that the humans cannot possibly win.

Hunted by humans who feel he has betrayed them by his friendship with the goblins, and unwelcome in the goblin world where all humans are considered the enemy, he will be thrown into a deeper world, where even the goblins have reason to be afraid…

Dance of the Goblins

Jaq D Hawkins

International Waters Publishing
Norwich & Växjö
www.internationalwaters.co.uk

Dance of the Goblins
First edition
Published in England 1st May 2005

ISBN 1-905336-00-4
EAN 978905336005

A CIP catalogue number is available from the British Library

Cover Art Credits:
Colour Drawings by Regina Curtis
Line Art for Arch Design by Anton Channing
Graphics Design by Jaq D Hawkins

Printed and bound in England by TJ International
Padstow, Cornwall, PL28 8RW, England

International Waters
Norwich, England
Växjö, Sweden

www.Internationalwaters.co.uk

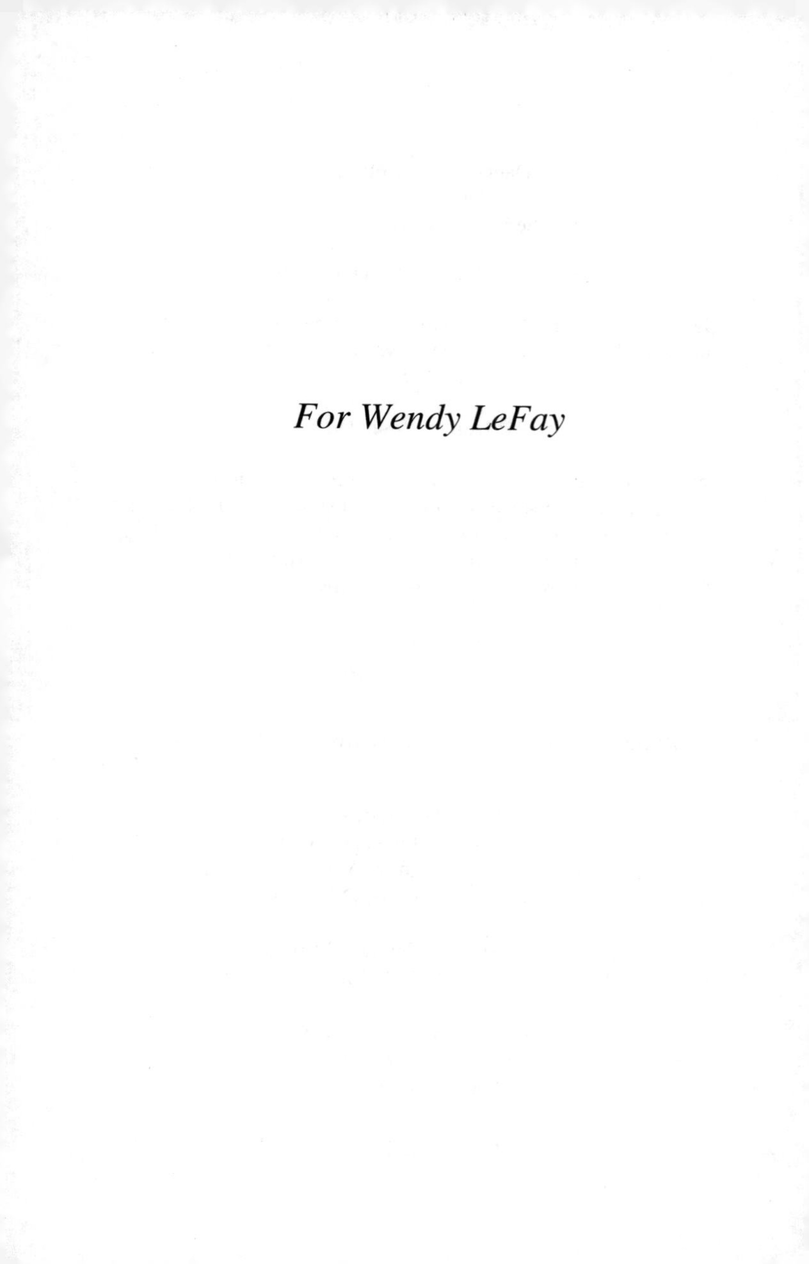

For Wendy LeFay

Acknowledgements

The author would like to thank those who have supported this project through its various stages. First of all, my early proof readers, Anton and Wendy who provided extremely valuable feedback. Also, all of my friends who have been forced to endure every change of the cover design as it developed. Clas and Kirsten, who advised that the book had potential and Karin Pasthy who made sure that most of the grammar is correct. Also, Birgitta who organised all the un-named people that offered advice and smoothed the journey from draft to print.

Special thanks goes to Nicholas Waters, for believing in the book as well as contributing tireless energy and countless hours of editorial scrutiny towards making my fantasy world come alive.

Jaq D Hawkins
March 2005

Prologue

'I don't know why we're doing this,' growled Latham. Ten pairs of eyes turned towards him as the ragged group of common men huddled within their cloaks in the damp chill of pre-dawn on the heath. Latham drew his own cloak as close as possible over his hulking frame, pulling the hood down over his dark, greasy hair. He peered at them from within his wrappings to be sure that he had their attention.

'Since when do we take orders from the women anyway? It's not like it was the first time Caleb had a fight with his missus and went off for a walk to let off steam.'

'But he always came back before,' said the younger man at his side. Latham had always liked Ranalf, but just now he was only irritated by the metalsmith's apprentice and his reasonable attitude. The boy didn't even have to be here as he had no wife yet to nag him out of his warm bed. Latham only wished they would find the missing man so that he could get back to his own. But there was no more to be done now except to keep on complaining until the others gave in and they could all go home.

'We've been walking over the heath half the night, we probably missed him in a patch of fog.'

'What was that?' The hushed voice of one of the older men had an acute sense of urgency to it. All was silent for a moment. It was Ranalf who next thought he heard a sound, almost like a voice, just on the edge of hearing. He motioned with his hand for the others to follow and crept carefully in the direction that he thought the sound had come from. He knew that sound could be deceptive in the dampness, but his intuition led him on. His trust in the odd sense that he had was quickly rewarded with another sound, like tree branches being pushed aside. The others heard it too this time and moved more quickly towards it despite the potential danger of a misstep in the dim light.

'There he is!' shouted the older man. Caleb had seemed to appear suddenly out of the side of a lichen covered hill. The man who had spotted him was almost delirious with the excitement of seeing the missing man alive and apparently unhurt, just when they had begun to give up hope. Then his face quickly changed to an expression of shock and horror.

'What is that…*thing!*' he said in an exclamation of gross disgust.

In the next heartbeat the man took in the sight of the creature that held Caleb by the arm. It seemed small and scrawny, but the muscles visible beneath its sickly green skin spoke of powerful limbs. They held as much threat as the sharp teeth protruding from its slack mouth, hanging open now in an expression of astonishment. It matched those of the humans who stood frozen in a moment of disbelief. The creature was nearly naked, wearing only a loincloth of some unknown animal skin. It was as dark as the unruly hair that hung down its back in a sweeping wave, broken only by its large, pointed ears.

There were blue marks on its upper body which looked like paint imbedded in the skin. Most mesmerising though, were the large yellow eyes that held the man's gaze for an eternal split second. Then the creature was gone. Caleb stood alone for a moment, then collapsed into unconsciousness. Ranalf leaped to his side, checking quickly for heartbeat and breath. He nodded to the others to confirm that the man was alive, then as if by a signal, the men shouted all at once in an unintelligible war cry that rang through the early morning light. They plunged through the lichen and fell on a depression that might have been an opening once, but had been freshly filled in with loose earth. Latham shouted to Ranalf to run back to the village for help, while the others called orders to each other randomly. They began to dig with their hands or any other tools they could improvise.

On the other side of the freshly filled opening, the creature ran. The others of its kind had acted quickly. Goblins learned from a young age what to do in case of a sighting. There were enough others with him to hold the wall for a few minutes at best on their own, but it would be enough. He leaped down the left hand passage, clearing the pit trap easily. He nodded with an undulation of his upper body as he said just one word to the goblin waiting just beyond the opening in the side wall.

'Sighting!'

The other goblin's eyes widened, but he reacted quickly, returning the nod briefly as he began beating a rhythm on the large drum at his side. *Now the diggers will come*, Darek thought to himself as he continued running down the passage. He stopped anyone he met to spread the message as he ran. In his mind, the young goblin retraced his movements just before the sighting, searching for any hint of carelessness. By the time he reached the deeper levels he was satisfied. There was no breach of procedure. It was just an accident of timing. But one thought terrified him.

Because of that timing, the world is going to change. Forever.

Chapter One

Haghuf woke to the familiar stench. Man-stink. His quick mind immediately assessed that the Count must be in Krapneerg. He snorted at the thought of a human in the caverns, but rose from the fur rug that served as his sleeping place. It would take some time to climb to the level where he knew he would find the visitor. His greenish flesh gleamed in the dim light from reflected water and the stones that held light. They served as the only illumination in the lower caverns. It was enough for goblin eyes which never sought to see the sunlight. Some of his kind found reasons to go *Above*, but Haghuf was content to stay underground. It was familiar here and the temperature didn't change.

He had made an exception only once, and still wondered whether it might have been a mistake. His memory of his first encounter with the Count played on his mind as he began the slow climb that would bring him closer to the stench of his old acquaintance. Then he realised that there was something different about the scent. The caverns were still and musty, some would even say airless, but scents carried on the subtle movements of the dank atmosphere.

As he rubbed the remnants of sleep from his eyes he became more aware of the spicy perfume mixed with the man-scent. He heard the first scream just as it occurred to him that it wasn't Count Anton after all. But surely a human, no doubt of that. It had been some time since one of them had explored the caverns unwittingly. Haghuf made the climb despite his disappointment, just to see what sport would be made of this one.

Realising that he was indeed disappointed that it wasn't a visit from Count Anton disturbed him a bit. None of the others had ever criticised him for making contact with the human. They had been impressed that a magician among the humans was powerful enough to attract the attention of one of their kind. Leap in particular had been ecstatic to learn that there were still some of *Those Who Dance* among the humans. There was no doubt that this breed of them had a vastly different attitude than the majority of their kind.

Still the idea of becoming so close to humans, and especially showing one of them one of the ways through the caverns, did not sit well with Haghuf. He was very old, even for a goblin. He remembered too well that they were dealing with a species that had consciously chosen to separate itself from *The Ways of Life* and to intentionally seek ways to destroy itself, uncaring as to whether it destroyed other forms of life in the process. Even now so many chose to live in the dead city above rather than to move out to the wild places where the water was pure. Many had died of their own pollutants. The species had been saved by those few who preserved the old crafts, yet more sought to start the destructive cycle over again. They were dangerous creatures.

So why had he shown Anton the way through himself? It was a question Haghuf had been unable to resolve for over five changes of the seasons of the earth.

His memory slid back to a night when the earth beat its rhythm much as it did now, the pulsing of the earth's core that would lead into the Dance. He had indeed been dancing when he had heard another rhythm mixing with that of the earth. He would soon recognise it as the rays of the soft moonlight beating their rhythm gently through the cloudy sky, and onto the surface world. The subtle rhythms met in waves of sound and vibration within the deeper rhythms of the inner core of the planet. What he heard was not light though, but feet. Feet pounding to the song of the earth as goblin feet had drummed the ground for all time, yet it was coming from above.

He knew the way, though he had never traversed it before. He had only to follow the signs as many generations of his kind had done before him. As he climbed higher, the foot beats had grown stronger. Then suddenly he was there, on the surface, and his eyes beheld the dappled effects of soft misty moonlight for the first time. Still, the sound carried him in a trance like that which the Dance begot and he moved away from the opening to the ways below. He was careful to remember the structures which he passed, so that he could find his way back. The dim light of the Moon hurt his eyes. Many times he had to stop and cover them with his arms, huddling in the shadows where none passing would notice the gnarled creature that had no business wandering about on the surface where his kind were unwanted. He knew the danger, but was compelled by the rhythm which called him.

At last he came to a wide grassy area, with only a few trees and the artificial constructs that humans were known to build in such places. The moon shone brightly onto an open area where a single figure danced and leaped about, bathed in the moon's rays as if they provided the clothing he danced without. A human, dancing naked in the moonlight. It was unprecedented, apart from in the histories written by the ancients. Humans, since the last Turning, were not often known to dance. And they did not wander about naked.

Intrigued, Haghuf sat very still in the shadow of a tree, watching. The human knew the rhythm of the earth. That in itself was an amazing discovery, but he also expressed himself through the Dance as freely as any of Haghuf's own people. That was so far beyond credulity that he couldn't help but wonder if the human was actually a mutated specimen of his own species, or if he was in fact asleep and dreaming the unlikely scene. And there was something else. A quality to the Dance that was both familiar and not so at the same time.

He shook his head and purposely brought his thoughts back to the present. There were loud voices as Haghuf approached the side cavern where the human scent drew him. The pathetic whimpers from the prisoner alternated with attempts at bravado and insistence that he must be presented to someone in charge. Both drew only contemptuous jeering and prodding with sharp instruments from his captors. One such elicited a sharp yelp from the human just as Haghuf entered through the arched rock which served as an opening to the chamber.

The man alternately fought his bindings and tried to appear aggressive to the goblins, as much as a captive with arms and legs bound might do. He puffed out his chest, shouting threats one moment and in the next he would shrink from the prodding, looking pathetic. Haghuf had little taste for such sport, and had just about decided to retreat quietly and leave them to it when the human suddenly saw him standing in the arch, quiet and still as the stone.

'You! Are you the leader here?' shouted the man with all the authority he could muster. Haghuf didn't answer right away. Slowly, he strolled towards the man, looking at him curiously as if he had never seen such a creature before. In truth, he had seen very few in his lifetime. He preferred to keep it that way.

Everything in the room seemed to stop as Haghuf examined the prisoner, crouching down slowly to look him in the eye as was the custom among goblins when engaging an enemy. The human's chest heaved with quick, shallow breaths. He licked his lips nervously, caught up in the moment of suspense while he waited for an answer. Haghuf turned his head to look at the creature sideways, first one way then the other. Then at last he spoke in his low, gravely voice, slowly and deliberately in the man's own tongue.

'We have no leader. We are all one kind here.'

The human's eyes darted from one goblin to another. His expression exposed his utter bewilderment at the concept of a leaderless race.

'But surely someone must be in charge?' he cried, almost desperately. Haghuf again took his time in answering.

'We are not like you. We do not glory in having power over our own kind.' Haghuf turned to walk away. Then as an afterthought added over his shoulder, 'or imagining that we do.'

'What shall we do with him?' shouted one of the goblins.

'Kill him,' Haghuf answered flatly just as he passed back through the arch.

Haghuf chuckled to himself as he walked out of the side cavern. It didn't matter to him whether the goblins behind him took his suggestion or not. His amusement came from the knowledge that to the human who could not comprehend non-authority, it would have sounded like an order from a superior. In fact his words carried no more authority than the shouts to strip him naked which echoed after him from the cavern in a female goblin's voice. Talla might have her own amusement with the creature before it was released.

Haghuf had learned of the ranking system among humans from Count Anton, who was himself someone of importance among his kind. Among the goblins, there was no such concept. Those who had charge of the human may well decide to throw the creature into the stew, but in fact human meat was not very palatable. Having moved so far away from the nature which gave rise to their species, humans had taken to eating all sorts of unnatural substances and processing natural foods until they lost their life force. Sometimes they even poisoned those that they left otherwise unchanged. It was far more likely that the man would be released on a hillside similar to that where he found the cavern he entered by, and left to hallucinate on black mushroom potion. This particular potion had a way of confusing the memory not only through the period of time of its effectiveness, but for several hours before. The passage where he entered would have to be closed up for a while as a precaution of course, in case he had been previously familiar with the area. There were plenty of other ways through the labyrinth of caverns that comprised their world. It would not be missed for fifty or so of the earth's seasons.

Count Anton had called the goblin society by some modern human term...*Anarco*-something. The words were meaningless to Haghuf and had no equivalent in his own language. Goblins did not need words to describe their society. They simply were. They lived among their own kind, co-operating for mutual benefit, as would seem sensible to any creature of nature. Enforcing hierarchies was for insects, like ants and bees. A few species of animals like wolves had dominant members of their tribes for breeding purposes, and others like cat creatures held territories by force. The goblins accepted these differences as things that simply *are*. The humans could have their hierarchies as well and be of no interest to goblin-kind if they didn't insist on raping the earth and spoiling nature for all beings. It was for this reason, and only this reason, that the goblins had any argument with the human species. This was also why those like the Count who fought to alert his own species to their folly were tolerated in the glades, especially when they took part in the Dance.

Haghuf continued down one of the downward passages, awake now and ready to do some work. The brief encounter with the human had made him crave the deeper places, far away from their kind. Again, his mind drifted to the rhythms of the earth and the one human dancing in the moonlight. How the pulse of the planet had given way to movement, and he had found himself caught up in the Dance, measuring beats with the strange human who must have noticed his presence in the shadows of the moonlight. Their dancing mirrored each other's movements in perfect harmony, almost like a mating dance and yet purely in celebration of life already born. It was within the Dance that Haghuf had become aware of the subtle difference in the joining of earth and sky and the magic of moonlight as it drew the human into the pulses of nature in the complete freedom of the spirit of the Dance.

When at last their eyes had met with recognition and confusion, there was none of the fear which would ordinarily arise between human and goblin in an encounter. Only trust, that of spirits in perfect harmony. They had wandered off silently together, and Haghuf had shown the human the ways to the deep places. They could not speak to each other for many visits, but still the Count returned again and again to see the things that

Haghuf would show him. The other goblins marked his passing, but did not interfere or show themselves. He was *Guest*, and that was sacred. The questions in their minds went unasked. Haghuf did not offer explanation or ask for translators from those *between* to help him communicate. Only once did he speak of it openly to a small group peering after the retreating human in the darkness of the passage to the surface. Seeing the curiosity which burned within their hearts, he said to them only, 'He Danced.'

It was after that revelation that the goblins began to go about their business and acknowledge the human on his visits. Some of the Betweeners who knew the human tongue spoke to him in passing and he began to learn their language. Over time, Haghuf learned human speech through his conversations with the Count. Eventually Count Anton was able to explain his place in the human world and that he was a magician among them. This of course impressed Haghuf even more, although it would have been no special distinction for one of his own kind. They all practised magic in their own ways. It was only that Count Anton was human that such things as magic and the Dance were so unusual, and it was this difference which fascinated Haghuf.

Count Anton had explained that there were others like him who lived within the earth's harmonies, but they were considered renegades by mainstream human society. They were forced to meet far away from the cities where most humans live, in order to be left alone to live as they would and to dance. Yes, there were others like him. The goblins had been largely unaware of them in the few wild places left on the surface, because most of the goblins themselves had forsaken the light and lived within the deep places for too many generations. It was this knowledge which had drawn

Haghuf to read the histories which had been in his charge for many years. And it was there that he had learned that there was a time, before the last Turning, when many humans danced, and magic had been known among them.

But the magicians had been far outnumbered by the authoritarians who would seek power over all of their species. They had raped the earth much as they did now, and before the Turning it was they who had kept weapons hidden in bunkers, built for survival of the predicted destruction of the planet through wars with their own kind. Though the wars had failed to obliterate them nearly enough, the planet itself had eventually moved for its own survival. The cataclysms of the Turning had cleaned much of the species and its damage from the surface.

Some of *Those Who Dance* had retreated to the underground places and would eventually develop into *Those Who Live Between.* But some had also survived above, and would learn to exist within a society of humans that sought to oppress and control all of its kind. Periodically such humans made the celebration of life itself illegal or ostracised those who kept the magic alive. They preserved superstition and idolatry, worshipping an ancient symbol, yet oblivious to its original meaning.

The histories had opened Haghuf's mind to the ancient relationships between the species, but in this he kept the knowledge to himself. He was guardian of the histories. It was his charge to keep them safe. Learning to read them had been a folly of his youth, yet in the reading he had enabled himself to pass the wisdom of the ancestors onto his people through the uncounted time of his mature life. Until he had danced with Count Anton, he had been content to read only the books of magic and wisdom that were useful to his people and their way of life. Now that he had become aware of the history of his species, he could not ignore the relationship between human and goblin. Yet he could not be sure if the knowledge would help or hinder the association between them. So with the patience inherent in his kind, he kept the knowledge he had discovered mostly to himself as he contemplated the potential effects of its general relinquishment.

The caverns above had become silent. No doubt the invading human had been given the potion as Haghuf had expected, and released with as little fuss as possible. Anything else would have resulted in more of its screams echoing through the passages. Having little forethought as to where he was going, Haghuf was only a little surprised to realise that he had wandered to the library. It was a word he had learned from Count Anton, though he had never brought him here. No one set foot in the cave where the histories were kept. The sacred office of their preservation was his alone, although a time would come when he must choose someone to whom he could pass the burden on. That time was not yet.

Originally he had only inherited the ancient histories, but he had added the books that Anton had brought as gifts and had taught him to read. It was through these gifts that Haghuf had learnt what happened after the last Turning on the surface world and of the beliefs of the humans about his people. He had also seen too clearly the dangers of the fanaticism of the humans' sterile religion. He understood why it had become so dangerous for his people to breach the surface. The humans' unnatural belief of their mastery over the earth and all that lived on it was at the root of their destruction of its resources. Had he known the extent of their absurdity without first knowing of Count Anton and the other magicians, he would have joined *Those Who Protect* in the belief that the entire species should be destroyed for the sake of the survival of all other creatures. Where the conflict between the species would eventually lead was beyond even Haghuf's ability to predict, yet he knew that he had a part to play in changes to come. The thread of chaos had begun on the night he had been drawn to the surface by Count Anton's dance.

Haghuf blamed his thoughts for his sudden feeling of unease. Here, in one of the deepest places of the earth, he usually felt calm and completely in tune with the rhythms of the planet. He had often danced in the library itself, inspired as much by the ancient knowledge he read as by the never-ending pulses of life which vibrated throughout the underground world that was his home.

But now the rhythm seemed off beat in some way, as though there was a disturbance…then suddenly he realised that indeed, what he felt was exactly that. Ignoring the natural apprehension as he began *to know* the source, Haghuf turned out of the library and climbed by the shortest route possible towards the between places, where cavern met daylight. Moving as quickly as his normally ponderous strides could carry him, he drew closer to the turbulent discordance until it reverberated within his massive skull. Then he heard the voices.

Voices raised in anger and panic assaulted his hearing. He was not yet close enough to make out the words, but he recognised many of the goblin voices. More alarming though, was that they were mixed with human voices. Haghuf strained his acute senses to identify the source, but the echoes of the underground passages surrounded him with elusive cries of indeterminate origin. Still, suspicion of the truth was already dawning in his mind as he heard the flap of goblin feet running towards him. It was Leap who appeared from around a corner, breathing heavily with the unfamiliar strain of running in haste.

'Haghuf! I'm so glad I found you!' he said between breaths.

'What is happening?' Haghuf replied, though he knew much of the answer already.

'The human was to be released, the one who wandered in…'

Haghuf nodded to show understanding. Leap had not been among those who toyed with the human, but Haghuf had a reputation for knowing much that occurred among the goblins. It was apparent that Leap had expected him to know about the incident, and he didn't waste words now on details about the current crisis as Haghuf would surely have some knowledge of it already.

'There was a search party looking for him just outside the opening. It was just a fluke, but Darek was seen.'

'How far inside have the humans come?' Haghuf asked the question calmly, assessing the potential of the crisis and what possible measures might be taken to minimise the breach of their security. Without flinching at Haghuf's instant perception of the progression of events, Leap continued.

'Only to the first stair. It was stoned shut very quickly, many had come to jeer as the human was released to hallucinate away his transgression, so they picked up every stone they could find and blocked the entrance. We hoped that would be an end to it, but they are digging! They shout gibberish and call us names. What does *demon* mean in the human tongue Haghuf?'

'So.' Haghuf replied calmly, ignoring the question. 'It begins already.'

'But what shall we do Haghuf? I came to seek your wisdom.'

Haghuf was silent a few moments as he thought. The cries he felt more than heard were blood-hunt, these animals would not be reasoned with. Outright war was to be avoided if possible. It could serve no purpose, giving only pain to both sides. If only there were a way to mislead their digging efforts long enough until the madness of the hunt grew cold in their veins, or to drug them all with the mushroom potion so that they could forget their fervour and return to their homes. But such creatures would not stop until they satisfied their superstitious thirst for blood, and no goblin could move among them so well as to slip them all a draught. Talla's shape-shifting glamour might have served, but the humans did not bring their females to battle and perceived as one of them out of place, she would surely be recognised as a succubus. They were still known in the humans' legends. Haghuf found the thought mildly amusing, considering Talla's fascination for the creatures. Perhaps she would find them less interesting now as she would no doubt be among those fighting for their lives at this very moment.

Slowly, almost imperceptibly, Haghuf began to smile. Leap knew the expression, but remained silent despite his renewed hope that indeed, the wisest of them had a plan formulating that could save the situation.

'We must send the diggers to form spiral caverns to lead them in circles,' explained Haghuf, 'and Talla can use her ability to draw them after her. They can only be distracted for a time before they realise the trick and begin using instruments to help them find direction, but it will be enough.'

Haghuf met Leap's eyes with reassurance, confident now that he spoke truth.

'We have an ally among them. He will act to avoid war.'

Leap needed no further encouragement. He ran to deliver the message to those who were now fighting to maintain the makeshift wall they had constructed. Haghuf darted down another passage, working out as he went which route would take him first to the level where supplies were kept, and then to the surface. There was no way around it, he was going to have to breach the surface for a second time to find his friend.

Leap arrived at the wall to find goblins frantically tearing rocks from the passages to reinforce the obstruction. Still the human voices rose loudly and angrily through the all-too-thin barrier as they continued to assault the wall with digging equipment. True to his name, Leap leapt about from one group to another, repeating the plan to everyone as he thrashed among the throng of goblins in near-panic. In transitional stages, the direction of the pursuit began to change. More goblins who had been summoned by runners at the beginning of the altercation arrived just in time to learn of Haghuf's plan. They began shaping the nearest caverns into a controlled route that could be alternately blockaded and opened to divert the flow of the advancement into a never-ending spiral of passages that would look much alike, and yet would give the impression of progress to the advancing humans. The ruse wouldn't hold forever, but it would buy the time needed. Meanwhile a small group of diggers worked separately to form a passage to the surface which would hopefully expel the last of the humans. It might even be used to confuse them a bit longer when they found their progress only brought them once again to the surface world they knew.

Sharp instruments began to appear through the rocks, and half the goblins fell back to begin constructing a new wall. Some of the diggers created an opening to a side passage that was now prepared for the onslaught. The speed with which they worked together was phenomenal, possible only by those who spent their entire lives working with stone. The builders finished piling boulders into a make-shift wall and began to use their magic to fuse them just as the humans demolished the first barrier. The humans might have charged forward to the newly-constructed obstruction if they hadn't been distracted by what appeared to be a maiden of their own species hailing them from the small opening in the right hand wall, which led to a new passage.

'Help!' shouted Talla in her best imitation of a human voice. With the glamour in place, they would hear a sweet female voice and see only what each of them imagined to be the most beautiful maiden alive by their own standards. Some would see a tall blond figure, while others might see a petite flame-haired beauty. It was each of their own fantasies that provided the imagery for Talla's special talent for illusion.

Talla wanted to say more, but she did not speak the human language and had learned only the one word, to be used specifically for the sort of situation they were confronted with now. It was lucky for the goblins that the humans did not take females to battle, as such illusion was ineffective with them. Talla had learned this at great cost in the times when she used to travel among the Betweeners to conduct raids on the surface world. She ducked behind the wall and ran for the next passage as the builder-goblins sealed up the opening in the hope that the humans would follow them and continue their attack on the dummy wall.

The diversion worked. The humans, on seeing what they perceived was a maiden in distress, abandoned their previous course and stampeded towards the decoy wall with much shouting and renewed rage. Leap noted that their fury would work in the goblins' favour, as a raging human had little sense of purpose or direction. As frightening as the frenzied mob was, it had become like a single organism following a chaotic path which could be manipulated to follow a course of the goblins' choosing. The simple brilliance of the plan was impressive.

As the decoy wall fell away under the onslaught, another new opening appeared at the end of the passage off to the side. A quick glimpse of the maiden guaranteed that the humans would follow the path as it was laid out for them. Talla didn't speak this time as her limited vocabulary would surely give the game away eventually. She made a mental note to learn a few more phrases from Haghuf when she got the chance. If she got the chance. There was no guarantee that whatever he had planned to do to release them from the attack would work as smoothly. There had been no time to learn what it was they were waiting for or how long the delay tactics would be either needed or effective. Haghuf was a wise goblin with a well-practised survival instinct, but nobody could predict every possible outcome.

Unfortunately the tactic didn't work for as long as they had hoped. The lack of time for proper planning prevented the goblins from mapping out the routes properly that would be most effective. The third diversion passage was dug too close to the final path they had prepared for directing the humans back to the outside. Some of the humans heard the digging through the wall and turned their attention to hacking their way through to the sound. One of the goblin diggers saw the deviation in the mob and ran ahead to tell the front diggers what was happening.

Meanwhile, the detachment of diggers working on the exit passage also heard the clang of human tools and realised that the game was up. They had anticipated that anything might go wrong, and so had done their digging from the outside in, so that no matter what happened, if the humans found this cavern sooner or later, the path would lead them out. The other diggers didn't know this as the details of the plan had been conceived on the run and only those actually participating in this detachment knew what had been decided among them. The others might work it out as it was only logic, but they couldn't know for sure.

Talla heard the shouting goblins. She knew that the others were intelligent enough to form a survival plan, yet they were certainly in danger and she had hoped that they would be able to keep the humans running in circles a bit longer. She had stayed at least one passage ahead of the humans and only showed herself when the next barrier was ready to close until now, but she had to do whatever she could to buy a little more time for Haghuf. Even a minute longer for her friends in the other passage could make the difference between life and death.

She hurtled herself towards the last opening and practically stumbled through as she called up the full force of the glamour and waved her arms to attract the attention of the diverted humans. Leap shouted to her to wait, but it was too late. Strong arms closed about her waist and pulled her right off her feet, into the protective embrace of…a human. Before she could think what to do he had sprinted towards the other tunnel in an unusual show of strength for one of his kind. He carried her over his shoulder in a position which left her upside down and feeling rather helpless. She might as well have been a sack of potatoes.

The other humans had broken through at about the same time, and she saw light as they ran as a reconstructed mob towards the opening to the surface. Her goblin eyes could see where her people had dug into the wall and buried themselves within a layer of rock, safe from the eyes of humans as they ran past. This calmed the panic which had begun to grow in her, as she realised that she was now the only one in danger and that the ruse had worked, although not quite in the way they had planned. She might well be in a position to keep the humans distracted for some time. If they were brutal enough, she might even get some enjoyment from it. She gestured towards the eyes that she knew could see to let them know that she would be alright. Let them concentrate on re-digging the passages for the possibility of a renewed assault. She could keep up the glamour for quite some time and may obtain valuable information. It would be better if she could understand their language, or had a bit more of Haghuf's talent for perceiving the thoughts of other creatures, but at least she wouldn't have to worry about being discovered or killed for being a goblin. At least as long as they did not encounter any of the human females.

Chapter Two

Haghuf had wasted no time, yet he had gathered all that would be needed for his task. Had he known the ways of the surface and the location of Count Anton's castle, he might have travelled his own paths to cover distance before going to the outside world. But he did not know and there was no time. He must go to the only place that he did know, and to summon Count Anton to come to him.

The hooded cloak he had obtained from the communal supplies had no doubt been used many times in the days when goblins would visit the surface more frequently. It was a perfect disguise, as it covered his entire body and much of his head. The hood would restrict his own sphere of vision as much as it protected his features from observation, but this would not matter as he would be effectively blind anyway and would need to find his way by other senses. Even in the between levels he could sense that the surface world was flooded with daylight now, rather than the more merciful light of the night sky.

The dark glasses he had also brought would help. His only previous journey into this realm had hurt his eyes more than enough in the moonlight. He had not only heard that daylight was far more extreme, but had seen photographs in books of the surface world turned a searing shade of yellow by the ravages of the Sun. He also saw the damage to objects on the surface, both natural and human made, that its intensive heat caused. This would be no easy task. The magic required to contact the Count would be the least of it. Perhaps it was this heat, at least in part, that was to blame for the austerity of the lives of humans. Such was the case, he mused to himself, in the depths of the volcanic realms, and those who lived there.

Haghuf had a bag slung over his shoulder which contained a quantity of mushroom potion. It was in its pure form, and needed diluting. He would have to rely on Count Anton to choose a suitable liquid that the humans would drink without question. Haghuf was a bit shorter than the average human and the weight of the bag accentuated the hump on his back that he hoped would make him appear like a wizened old man. Few would seek among the folds of his hood for the details of his face. The hood itself would help protect him from the Sun's rays. The disguise would have to be effective, there was no other choice. Haghuf had no delusions about the danger into which he placed himself.

The passages got lighter as he climbed closer to the surface. The gradual change allowed his eyes to adjust as much as they would. He waited until he could not tolerate the brightness before putting on the dark glasses. When he breached the last chamber, he stopped for a moment to look around as best as his eyes would allow and to adjust his spatial sense. He needed to remember the path he had followed to the grassy area where he had danced with Count Anton so long ago. He hoped that it had not changed much in the interim.

There were two openings from the chamber to the outside. He was sure that he had taken the left one on that other occasion and had carried on straight for a time. He moved to follow this direction, but stepped back a moment from the light which flooded through the doorway. It was harsh, even with his protections. But there was no time for indulgences or discomforts. He gathered the hood closely around his face, pushed the dark glasses as close to his eyes as possible and shut them completely. Even then he had to put a hand over the glasses to further shut out the light before he could step out into its brightness. He could only hope that there were no humans about who could observe his odd behaviour, or that they would be busy about their own business and take no notice.

He listened carefully as he walked. He knew that humans sometimes travelled in carriages with wheels which moved very fast and could be dangerous, but they were also very noisy. He heard nothing. Not even the movement of a single human out walking. He thought to himself that this must be unusual during daylight hours, but had no time to speculate why. He was just grateful for the solitude under the circumstances.

He felt carefully as he took each step. The humans had artificially flattened the land for their transports in days when there was more of such technology. He arbitrarily remembered that they called the flattened paths *roads*. He had learned more than he realised about the surface world from the books and his conversations with the Count. He remembered now that Anton had shown him a map of the roads once, pointing out the place where they had met. The diagram held little meaning for him at the time, but now it came back to him and he understood the 'aerial view' as the Count had described it. He was sure he could have found it through spatial memory, but the visualisation helped immensely. He need only walk forward for six times that the ground dipped into flattened road, then turn left and continue on until he could smell the grass growing under the trees. It was nearly as easy as following the underground passages with the help of the visualised map.

There were many smells about, most of them unfamiliar and unpleasant. Picking out anything green and growing would be easy. He heard the occasional shuffling footstep of a human as he walked further. He kept his nerves as steady as possible as he passed them and carried on walking without showing any reaction. They seemed to be content to leave him alone. Only once did he actually pass one closely on the street. It was sitting on a bench, talking to itself in a disturbed voice with words that made no sense. He thought he had learned the language fairly well, but this one seemed to be ranting in a way that he could not follow. He picked out a few words, the phrases '*demons among us*' and '*end of the world*' stood out from the gibberish. There was a tone of madness in its voice that seemed to be peculiar to humans.

As with the others, Haghuf carried on without stopping or giving any indication of noticing him. It was only a moment after that when he smelt the park. The grass felt smooth and natural between his toes, unlike the hard artificially hardened stone that the humans used for their roads and the walking paths that framed them. Such stone stored the heat of the Sun and had been more than a little uncomfortable. He was grateful for the respite for his feet. It was then that he realised that there was a serious flaw in his disguise. He nearly laughed out loud at the thought that he had got away with it anyway, at least this far. Surely as he walked, his bare feet had been visible to some extent. Yet none of the humans had noticed. He was sure he would have felt the emotional response if they had seen the greenish gnarled flesh, whether they dared say anything or not. They simply had never looked at his feet, seeing only the cloaked figure that he presented to them. Count Anton had often spoken of the fallibility of his people and how they were frequently too self-absorbed to notice details of the world around them. Haghuf was amazed that it inhibited their survival instincts to such an extreme, yet was grateful for it all the same as it had probably saved his life on this journey.

Now he must depend on this human failing for what he must do. There were a few humans in the park. He sensed them although they were quiet. One he heard snoring as he walked past. He had a strong smell about him that was separate from the smell of human. It was similar to some of the distillations that occurred in the deeper caverns, where the mushroom potion and other elixirs were made. Haghuf guessed that it was some form of intoxication potion, and this human at least would give him no trouble.

He reached the clump of trees where he had hidden on that previous occasion. That time he had left the shelter of the trees to dance in the open. This time he would conceal himself within their shadows for what he must do. He reached within the cloak and grasped the stone of the amulet that he wore around his neck. It had been a gift from Count Anton some time ago and would form a connection. Even more so for the dark blue stone, which the Count had explained was cut from the same original stone as the one he wore himself. It had been a solemn moment when the gift was presented. The matching stones were attuned to each other in a human manner that Anton had tried to explain at the time. The magician and the goblin each had their own sense of stone magic. It was the importance of such a gift that convinced Haghuf now that he could depend on Count Anton to help him with the task at hand. Despite the difference of their species, they were brothers in magic.

Apart from this, they were both dedicated to preventing the war between species that the recent incidents would make inevitable if they could not turn the unfolding pattern of events.

The shadows of the trees provided enough shade so that Haghuf was able to open his eyes in a narrow squint. The light was still severe, but he could see a little if he cupped his hands around his eyes and peered out through a narrow tunnel of vision. There were very few humans in the park. Haghuf didn't know if it was normal for them to avoid the one piece of natural landscape that existed in their concreted world, yet he was grateful for the sparse population in the present circumstances. The one he had passed earlier looked to be asleep on a bench, holding a flask of some sort clutched in his hand as if it were of value. A few others were gathered close together some distance away, their heads close together in conversation. A female of the species was walking away from his direction with a small creature on some sort of restraint. None of them took any notice of his passing. They were apparently completely oblivious of his presence among the trees. The question was whether they would continue to ignore him when he began to dance.

There was nothing for it, he had come here for this purpose. If he was to be discovered, then at least whatever transpired as a result would be the result of his attempts to bring peace between the species again. Haghuf remained in the deepest shadows as he began to project his consciousness into the earth. Through the layers of all that was buried and the caverns that he knew so well, he projected inward, to the very heart of the planet until he began to feel rather than hear the rhythmic throbbing that would lead him to the Dance. As his feet began to pound the ground in response to the beat that matched the beating of his own heart, he clutched the amulet and focused his mind on a mental image of his friend, and of their first dance together.

He had no sense of time, and as the Dance continued he also lost his sense of space and of self. There was only movement, rhythm, the throbbing of the earth, and the Dance. As he finished, he noticed the amulet still clutched in his hand. Then he opened his eyes a little, suddenly realising that he had closed them without noticing. He was still in the shadow of the trees and his eyes had adjusted somewhat to the light. He began to focus on the human figure standing before him.

'What were you doing?' asked the high-pitched voice of a female child.

Haghuf peered at her through the hood, held closely now around his face. Surely one look at him would alarm the child, and her mother would likely be nearby to respond to the screams. The trouble was, he dared not answer her. His voice would sound gravelly to a human and that too might frighten her. But his silence would seem odd as well and at any moment she might call for her mother to solve the puzzle for her. Haghuf bowed to her, to delay the awkwardness of the moment, and didn't see the taller figure approach.

'He was doing magic child, run along and do not interfere in the doings of wizards.' The smooth, deep voice sent relief flooding through Haghuf's veins as the child scampered off to find other amusements. He rose to his full height, letting the hood fall back just a little as he looked up into the starburst rainbow of colours that characterised the eyes of his friend.

'Well met Count Anton,' Haghuf said calmly. He gave no indication of urgency in his speech or movements. One might think he was making casual conversation as he continued to speak.

'There is trouble afoot.' He listened expectantly. Count Anton would surely know the events which had brought him to such desperate action.

'As it happens, word was brought to me of trouble at Nodgnirraf,' replied Count Anton. 'I have a carriage to travel there. But we have a problem. I can hardly take you with me so far and so close to danger, but leaving you here to find your own way back to the opening to Krapneerg does not sit well.'

'There is no other way Anton, I must come with you,' said Haghuf in his usual steady voice. 'I know the ways underground and Nodgnirraf is not so far that it would take a half days walk as you count time. Besides, Nodgnirraf is near Nacibrab and I wish to visit someone in that place. We can part company before we get very close to the trouble.' Haghuf looked up again at his friend. 'Do you know how to find the way to Nacibrab?'

Anton hesitated a moment before answering. It had been unspoken between them, but they both knew that Anton had explored the ways of the caverns far beyond what most goblins would consider acceptable for an outsider, a human. If he were ever to betray them, his knowledge would be dangerous to them. Knowing that he possessed the knowledge brought him danger of its own, as many of the goblins found it difficult to trust any human. The problem of his overactive curiosity could easily be solved through an 'accident', something that would be all too easy within the caverns where there were many traps against invasion anyway. He was lucky to have avoided falling into one of them already by a genuine misstep.

'Yes Haghuf, I can show you the opening.'

Count Anton's honesty in the dangerous circumstances reinforced Haghuf's confidence in his friend's co-operation. They walked to the carriage at the edge of the park quickly, saving further conversation for the privacy inside. Haghuf entered the vehicle as if it were a natural thing to do. He was aware of its nature and workings and had even seen photographs of earlier versions of the transport devices which depended on fuels no longer available to the humans. Haghuf wondered how many of the sun-powered carriages like Count Anton's still travelled the ancient roads. With a signal, the driver started it up and Haghuf tried not to show his unease at the sudden and unnaturally swift movement. As soon as he had settled into the feeling of motion, he pulled the potion out of the bag on his back and handed it to the Count.

'You know what this is?'

Count Anton examined the flask a moment before answering.

'This will be the mushroom potion you give to humans to make them forget.'

Haghuf nodded, remembering a moment of folly long ago when he had explained the potion to Anton. It was after that explanation that he realised that he had said too much of goblin survival methods. It was then that he had become more cautious in their conversations. But now, it was a time to speak plainly.

'It needs dilution, one part to fifty in any liquid. A couple of swallows is all that is needed.'

Count Anton smiled slowly, suddenly looking a bit like a satisfied cat.

'And what if one drinks a larger quantity? Can it be dangerous?'

'It will not poison them if that's what you mean,' Haghuf answered, 'but I would not recommend trying to operate a device like this one we are riding in after drinking it, not that they will be awake long enough to get very far into mischief.'

'Good!' Count Anton chuckled. 'I know just the thing. It's just as well that this happened on the Sabbath morning, the streets are clear and we're making good time. Still, we have a little while before we will reach our destination. It's good to enjoy your company again Haghuf.'

Haghuf noted Count Anton's words. The Sabbath morning. The way the humans went about marking time was still much a mystery to him, but he recognised the term. It was something significant to their religion. A religion that he knew was of little taste to Anton and the other magicians. Yet it permeated the culture of the humans in ways that were unavoidable. The magicians simply found ways to work around the disruptions that this day of observance imposed. Apparently it had actually been to their advantage on this occasion, as the austerity of their rituals required that few humans were wandering about in comparison to other days.

'Still, I would not have you captured as a result of my pleasure in your company,' continued Count Anton, 'you must allow me to see you safely on your path before I carry out this task you have brought me…' Count Anton smiled at his own words, 'to betray the trust of my people and spoil their fun.'

Haghuf was accustomed to Count Anton's wry humour, and enjoyed the joke with him. He was right of course, that was precisely the task he had brought for him to do. The fact that it was of mutual benefit to the species didn't change that simple truth. He was pleased that the Count's quick mind had understood the intention without further explanation.

'As if you did not enjoy the sport of bending the will and purpose of others of your kind,' replied Haghuf, hiding a secret smile of his own within the protective hood. Anton roared with laughter in response.

'You know me too well! Twisting these weak-minded fools from their pack hunting may be little sport, but it does amuse me in its way. A proper hunter, after all, only preys on what it can eat. I can hardly imagine these superstitious cretins eating goblin.'

Haghuf chuckled at the analogy. Anton's affinity with wolves had long been a fascination for Haghuf, and it made him seem all the more like one of his own kind. He had actually seen him begin to change once, when he had walked with him as far as the between places and almost to the last level. A little moonlight had spilled into the passage. The transformation had been subtle, yet promising of the phenomenal effect of its completion. He had wondered at the time if he would like Anton after the shape-shift.

'Not that we would be any less dead for the wasted massacre they wish on us,' Haghuf replied.

'I was already travelling to the site when I heard the beat of your call,' Anton mused. 'Your potion is no doubt just the remedy we need for this situation, but I worry about you Haghuf.' Count Anton flipped his long black hair behind him with a movement of the head and looked serious. Haghuf recognised the concern, and the affection behind it, but he had done only what needed to be done. Surely the Count could see that?

'Why do you take such risks?' asked the Count.

'Because I never want to forget that I am alive,' answered Haghuf. 'That is what makes us different from them. They sink into the decline of routine for the sake of a safe and comfortable life, yet it is one without adventure, without that spark which makes us what we are. They seek comfort in materialism because they have forgotten what they were meant to be, creatures of magic, who perpetuate the chaos as we do. Now they are nothing. Parasites! They destroy all on the earth without thought for any species but their own because they have sunk into the depression that should have led to their extinction centuries ago, and they refuse to die because they have too much intelligence to allow it to happen. They invent ways of continuance, and entertainments to give it some meaning, yet waste their potential in everlasting toil and the pursuit of an illusory dream of leisure which they deny themselves for the very sake of working towards its possibility. They haven't worked it out yet, but they have condemned themselves, all of their species, to the perpetual Hell of their own mythology.'

Count Anton looked thoughtful at his friend's words. He knew that they were true. He recognised Haghuf's resentment of the folly of humans, based on their common ancestry. The two of them had enjoyed many philosophical conversations in the past which determined much the same opinion, but the direct way in which Haghuf expressed it now effected him in a way that made him feel a little uncomfortable. On the one hand, he enjoyed being human, because he knew the potential of his species and did everything in his power to live as humans were meant to live; for pleasure, for the moment, and for magic. But on the other hand, he also recognised the pattern that the non-magicians had fallen into. It was one that had occurred before in the history of his kind, more than once, and which had destroyed their civilisations every time as a result of the arrogance that was inherent in them.

'Haghuf my friend, we both know the nature of my people. Yet there are some of us who manage not to fall into the patterns of greed and self-destruction that plague the ages of human history. Surely there must be a way to teach them to live in harmony with the earth, to feel the Dance?'

Haghuf thought a moment before answering.

'For that, you would have to teach them magic. You, and your magician friends, satisfy your lust for power through your talents in the sacred art. The weak humans, those who have no sense of internal power, seek it through their austerity and authority over others. You know this is true. Those who most seek power in your social structure are those who are the most lacking in a sense of self-worth or significance. They are nothing, and would perish easily without the assistance of others. So they seek to rule among your species and to find those who will serve them. There are always many who will consent to this slavery in the hope that they will rise in the artificial hierarchy they support. They, like the people in the highest authority, fear any form of self-sufficiency. They are not survivors.'

Anton sighed deeply. There was nothing in Haghuf's words with which he could argue. In any case, there was no time for further conversation. The sign for Nacibrab caught his attention, and he signalled the driver to stop.

Haghuf saw the sign and sat up quickly in alarm, suddenly shaking free of the languishing dizziness which had been creeping up on him as a result of the heat and the relief of turning the potion over to Anton. The sign was identical in design to one he had personally removed from the opening to Krapneerg.

'What is the meaning of this!' he demanded of Anton.

'It is one of those things I have been meaning to discuss with you for some time,' answered the Count. 'However, we have no time now. If you go through the opening below the sign, then travel down the steps, you will find your way safely. Don't worry, only magicians recognise the signs. To other humans, they are no different from the other signs from before the Turning. Now go! And trust me.'

Haghuf realised that he did indeed trust Anton completely. Even glancing at the driver as he climbed out of the carriage, he knew without doubt that Count Anton would only allow such a position to be filled by someone who was trustworthy beyond suspicion. His glance was more one of curiosity, as the concept of keeping servants of one's own kind would always remain a perplexing notion to him. As much as he would have liked to examine the sign for a bit longer, he knew that the Count would not continue on to his task until he saw Haghuf safely enter his own realms.

'Visit soon!' he called through the window of the carriage.

'I will!' replied Anton, 'I promise!'

Haghuf quickly walked through the opening and hid within a cool shadow for a moment as he listened to the wheels of the carriage roll away. His part of the mission had been successful, it was up to Anton now. The deep, cool places called to him. In a few moments, this scorching heat would be behind him and with luck, he would not have occasion to breach this world again in daylight. Meanwhile he positioned himself within the shadow to see the sign just outside, clearly giving away the way to his world. And then it occurred to him that such signs might exist at other openings. It would have to be investigated.

For the moment though, he would seek the cool caverns and visit the creature whom he had come here to consult. Then, perhaps, he could convince the goblins of Nacibrab that it would be a good idea to come back in the moonlight to remove this sign. Magicians or no magicians, leaving such a trail for humans was simply not safe.

He turned and hopped quickly down the steps, following his instincts to take him deeper and deeper into the coolness of the caverns of Nacibrab.

Chapter Three

Talla hadn't been ready for the sudden daylight that assaulted her senses as the human carried her into the outside world. Her abrupt scream was half a whimper as she threw her hands over her eyes to shield them from the sun's glaring rays.

'Latham!' shouted a man's voice. 'Stop a minute and put her down, there is no pursuit. Can't you see that her eyes have not adjusted to the light yet? She might have been a prisoner in that dark hell for years for all we know.'

She felt herself lowered to the cool ground and a lightweight garment of some sort was thrown over her. It had a hood. The more gentle man who had spoken arranged it to shield her face. She had not understood his words, but the kindness was apparent. She was grateful for the covering for another reason besides her eyes. She was not sure how well she could hold the glamour in this heat! It seared through her consciousness and made her drowsy, interfering with the focus that the magic required.

'The others will keep the blasted demons busy a while,' replied Latham. 'Ranalf, do you think she may be someone of importance? A kidnapped princess or some such?'

'I don't know,' said Ranalf, who had spoken first. 'The legends say that the caverns of Hell extend throughout the world. She might be from another land, I think we would have heard if a local princess had been kidnapped by demons. And I know I've never seen her before.' He knelt down and tried to peer through the hood into her eyes as he spoke to her. 'Miss, do you understand us? Can we help you?'

Talla, still did not understand him. It was clear that they were discussing her, and that one of them was speaking to her, but she could not reply in their language and so only shook her head and buried her face in her arms. She was beginning to wonder if she had allowed herself to be carried off to her doom. If the humans didn't discover her deception, the heat of the sun might well kill her. She tried to think how she might escape, but no plan immediately came to her. She would have to remain alert and look for an opportune moment.

'I think we should take her to the women,' said Ranalf decisively. 'They can take care of her properly.' He gently stroked Talla's head, trying to comfort her in whatever way he could. The illusion he had seen when he looked at her was of a beautiful maiden from his deepest fantasies as would be the case with any man who gazed at her while she radiated the glamour. He felt a tenderness towards her and sympathy for her plight. Latham, for his part, also saw a woman from his own fantasies, but his protective instincts towards her took a different turn.

'It would take too long to take her to them and explain everything, and they would probably fuss over her until she lost whatever reason she still possesses after her ordeal with the demons. I know a place nearby where I can take her and she can sleep in peace for a while. We need all hands at the battle. You go back and I'll look after her until she sleeps. Then I'll lock her in safely and join you.'

Ranalf didn't like the plan, but it made sense. The women of their clan would certainly make a fuss and would probably be jealous of her beauty as well. What bothered him was leaving her in the care of Latham. He was a good man for his part and loyal to the clan, but his concern for the woman didn't ring as true to Ranalf as would have made him feel comfortable. Still, he could hardly accuse Latham of having bad intent, even though the man had a well-known history of being less respectful to women than was expected of the men of their clan. There was a rumour that his wife had been seen with bruises on her face more than once, but the woman had made no accusations. She even gave excuses for the bruises to the other women blaming her own clumsiness. Ranalf had no reason to believe that Latham would strike a woman who was a stranger and possibly an aristocrat. There was no time to wallow in self-indulgent judgementalism, they must return to the battle as quickly as possible.

'Alright Latham, you look after her, but get back as soon as you can. We need every man!' Ranalf didn't know what he hoped that urging him to return quickly would accomplish, but he knew that he would feel better knowing that Latham was not with the maiden. His own fascination for her beauty had affected him in ways that he dared not consider at that moment. It was entirely possible that she may be too high born to take notice of the attention of a common labourer like himself. And of course princesses only married their rescuers in stories. Worse, Latham had more claim to the position of rescuer than he had himself, although Latham already had a wife and was not free to marry the girl as Ranalf was.

With one last look at the beautiful maiden, he turned and ran back towards the battle. Talla felt his touch in that last glance. It stirred something in her, but there was not time to think about what it was as she was being dragged by the hand by the other human in the opposite direction. She wished that she could have understood their discussion about her. She wanted to know what plan had been made regarding her. The large man pulled her down pathways which were lined with buildings, all much alike. She did not know what they were for, but looked around in curiosity as they passed. Her eyes were better able to tolerate the bright sunlight than Haghuf's had been. She was a Betweener and had often encountered daylight spilling into the upper passages, although not directly as was the case now. However, the shade of the hood helped to shield her from the direct glare.

Latham dragged her to the door of a building and let her hand go just long enough to shoulder the door open. The structures were obviously very old and had been unused for some time. The lock broke through the rotted wood easily. The buildings had decorative carvings around the windows which gave the impression that they might have been very pretty when they were new, but now the faded paint and worm holes in the carvings confirmed what Talla believed about anything the humans made - that it was doomed to decay into ugliness as the natural contours of the deep caverns never would. Even the world of the Betweeners was subject to this decay, as there were parts of it which had once crossed over into the realm of humans.

Latham grabbed her hand again and pulled her into the building. It looked like a dwelling, with furniture for sitting on and many objects around, for what purposes she could not guess. Some of them appeared to be merely decorative. There was a musty smell which spoke of the decay of many of the furnishings. She would have liked to examine the room in more detail, but Latham was dragging her from one doorway to another until he found what he wanted. Suddenly he pulled her into another room and threw her onto a large, soft mattress. It bounced comfortably and the playful part of her wanted to jump up and down on it. However, this was not the time for such distractions. The man was fumbling with the fastenings on his clothing and immediately his purpose was clear. He meant to ravish her.

Rather than fear, she reacted with fascination. She had often fantasised about the tales she had heard among her people, tales of the succubus who came to humans in the night and seduced them. It was said that they were more easily able to breed with humans and that the succubi had replenished their species in this way for a very long time between two Turnings. It had become too dangerous now. It was a betweener tale, although her own fascination for humans had earned her the epithet. Most of the deep ones knew little of the tradition and simply accepted the low birth rate of their kind, saying that their long lives warranted little procreation.

Since her maturity, Talla had speculated on the dangers of breaching the human world and on what pleasures she might find in coming to them in the night. She had been told that the old method was known to the humans now and that rather than succumb to pleasure they would call her evil and kill her for her gift. So far, that had kept her from defying the warnings and seeking out a pretty human. Now here she was, about to be ravished willingly by one of them. She would have preferred the other one, he was far more pleasing to look at, but this one would do. She sat up on the bed, feeling more confident now as the building was far cooler than the outside world and she could focus her will on the glamour. She pulled the dress she wore over her head, revealing to his illusioned eyes the most beautiful naked woman that he would ever encounter.

The man stopped in mid-motion, visibly shocked by her nakedness and the willingness in her eyes. Her entreating arms reached out to him, inviting him to come and claim his prize. She moved seductively, rotating her hips gracefully as she stood from the bed and walked towards him. Her open arms motioned for him to come to her. The would-be ravisher was about to become the ravished. His mouth hung open in disbelief, women simply did not behave this way. As she moved closer to him, he took a step backwards and croaked out a single word.

'Succubus!'

The glamour flickered for a moment as Talla, taken aback, suddenly sucked in her breath. The word was the same in both languages. She regained her composure as well as the illusion, but it was too late. The man had stumbled out of the room faster than she would have thought he could move and flung himself through the door of the building, running back the way they had come. Talla was alone.

For a moment she was confused. She understood what had happened, but instead of attacking her and killing her the human had run away. Probably back to join his comrades in trying to kill her people. She wondered for a moment what plan might be in progress even now to prevent that. Goblins were survivors, there would surely be something clever afoot. She had done her part as a diversion.

But now she was alone in the surface world and it began to occur to her that she didn't really know how to get back to her own familiar caverns. She couldn't stay where she was, the man might return with others once the shock of seeing her as she was for a moment wore off. It hadn't taken all that long to get here. She knew that she must leave quickly in case he came back immediately. She put the dress and hooded cape back on. It would be needed to maintain her disguise as well as protecting her from the light. Her sense of direction had always been keen. She would have to rely on it in unfamiliar terrain now.

On a whim, she jumped on the bed and bounced on it a few times. Dust rose, but the potential of a new fun toy to play with appealed to her goblin nature too much to pass up a chance to give it a go. Then she leapt off the bed and returned to the larger first room, the one with the odd assortment of objects. She knew that she must not dawdle, but a few moments to look around would surely do no harm.

The purpose of some of the furnishings was obvious. There were items to sit on and tables to place things on. Less obvious was a cube-shaped object with a reflective surface on one side which was placed in a corner facing the sitting furniture as if it were meant to command attention. Next to this was a recession in the wall which contained very old ashes. This was no doubt a place where humans would have made fire for cooking food. She examined the structure and shuddered at the thought of how hot the room would have become when they did this. A shelf just above the fireplace was lined with small objects that seemed to serve no practical purpose, yet some of them were pretty. One in particular drew her attention. It was hardly bigger than her hand, yet it resembled a dragon from legend. It was an iridescent blue and green colour with a white jewel set into the place between and just above the eyes where the psychic sense emanated from in her kind. This intrigued her, as she knew that humans were completely unaware of this significance. Yet the artificial stone with which the object was made was obviously of human construction.

She kept hold of the little dragon statue as she turned and walked outside. Her senses were telling her it was time to leave. She was completely lost in a strange world, but she turned the opposite direction from that which the human had gone. Common sense was enough to work out that running into him and any help he might bring as he returned to deal with her was a bad idea.

* * *

Latham was out of breath from running. He had hardly broken his pace all the way back to the battle site. He needed to tell someone what he had seen as quickly as possible and perhaps gather a party to go back and kill the succubus. His thoughts were scattered in all directions and as he hailed familiar faces in the crowd, he was confused by the relative calm and change in atmosphere that had come over the angry mob that he had left with the woman - the succubus - slung over his shoulder not so long ago.

Suddenly Ranalf was at his side.

'Latham! Is she alright, is she safe?' Latham was still out of breath and unable to speak clearly so he nodded his head. He could see that Ranalf was ensorceled by the evil creature, no doubt he thought he was in love with her. Such were the ways of evil spirits. Before he could think, Ranalf continued: 'Count Anton is here! He has called everyone to a meeting to decide what to do. We can organise properly now with one of his clever plans to guide us. We've been chasing our tails so far, and Jerrold seems to have completely lost his reason. He started ranting about demons and how we were all going to die and be eaten by them because of some prophecy. I've never heard of such a prophecy, but he ran away and we've had to get on without him. I'm so glad you're back, there are hardly thirty of us here and we don't know how many of *them* there might be.'

'Have - you - sent - for - help?' gasped Latham between breaths.

'Not yet, I was about to go myself when Count Anton arrived. He said to wait and gather everyone who was involved in the chase so that we could have a planning meeting. He said everyone was panicking too much and we had to co-ordinate our efforts or we would be picked off one by one. I found out just afterwards that Jerrold had run off, but I haven't had a chance to tell him yet.'

'Must - speak - with - him.' Latham was still labouring for breath as he tried to speak, but it was enough.

'Come with me,' answered Ranalf, 'I'll explain what happened with the woman and you can tell him whatever it is you need to.' Latham nodded vigorously in agreement. Then Ranalf turned and looked at him with concern. 'Latham, you did say the lady is alright didn't you?' Latham nodded again. He would ask Count Anton what to say to Ranalf. The Count always had an answer for any problem. He had saved their people many times over with his wisdom and Latham had no doubt that he could put his trust completely in this man, as a person even more than as an aristocrat. He followed Ranalf to a table where the Count had set some people to preparing food and serving beer for the men.

Ranalf was a somewhat audacious young man, and strode up to the Count as if he were a noble himself.

'Count Anton!' he called in a clear strong voice. 'A man here must speak with you.' The Count turned and handed them each a mug of beer. Latham was still panting, although less desperately now.

'There was a woman,' continued Ranalf. 'We saw her being held captive when we were chasing the demons through the caverns. Latham grabbed her and we rescued her, but we don't know who she is yet. Latham took her somewhere safe.'

The Count looked at the panting Latham expectantly. He saw before him a very common man. Big, probably not too bright, with scraggy brown hair and dull grey eyes. He hadn't shaved that day and the sweat from his morning's adventures did him no favours in either appearance or smell. He was a contrast to the smaller man who had introduced him. This man looked neater and was probably more intelligent. He was young, not more than twenty. Apart from the grime of a morning of hard digging, he might have been one of Anton's own page boys.

'What are your names?' asked the Count. Ranalf beamed at the interest that such a man would take in common citizens.

'I am Ranalf, and this is Latham.'

'Well Latham, what is it that you must speak with me about?' Anton's voice was calm and smooth, even enticing in the impression of complete control that he radiated with every word. His steady eyes seemed to have an almost magical command to them, which made the men feel that they must obey him for more reasons than his authority as their ruler.

'Private,' croaked Latham under his breath, glancing sideways at Ranalf.

Count Anton could see that something important had occurred, but that the big man felt a need to keep it secret even from his young companion. He glanced around at the proceedings, and with a sense of satisfaction decided that the timing couldn't have been better.

'Ranalf, go and tell the stewards that they are to serve the men now and to be generous with the beer. They are not to taste any themselves yet, as I do not want them drunk. You men however, need the fortification. Run now!'

Ranalf complied, bowing to Count Anton first as he had neglected to do on his introduction.

'Come Latham, sit over here and tell me your story.' The Count led him to a comfortable looking patch of grass, keeping an eye on Ranalf the whole time. As he had hoped, the young man had performed his task and delivered the message before beginning to quaff the mug of beer in his hand. He sat down opposite Latham so that he was facing the main crowd and Latham had his back to the other men. Latham had recovered most of his breath and didn't wait for an invitation to begin speaking.

'It's the woman sir, I was just finding a safe place to leave her so's I could come back to the battle. You know, a comfortable room in one of those old terraced houses in the middle of the city.'

Anton knew only too well and could easily guess Latham's real intention for taking her to that desolate place.

'I started to leave her by the door of one of the bedrooms, you know like a proper gentleman would do...' Latham's eyes were darting everywhere, except where they might meet with the penetrating gaze of Count Anton. He began to feel a little embarrassed, but then covered it with righteous indignation.

'I was just going to leave, I swear it! And suddenly she took off her dress and started coming at me, singing some sort of hypnotic song. I knew what she was right away, and when I said the word...she changed for a moment. She was one of those demon creatures, and she changed right before my eyes back into the beautiful woman! It's evil sorcery those demons use sir, pure evil!'

'But you ran away,' stated the Count reassuringly.

'Yes sir, I'm a married man you know. A real woman coming at me like that would make me run, but when I saw what she was, I didn't stop running until I got all the way back here! We need to get some men and go capture it and kill it before it gets away sir! And Ranalf, he doesn't know. I think he's fallen for the woman he thought she was. I don't know what to say to him.' Latham had worked himself into a frenzy of panic as he related the events in his own way, especially his concern for the young man.

'You've done the right thing coming straight to me, Latham,' said the Count calmly. 'I know just what to do, and I'll take care of Ranalf as well.'

'Oh thank you sir!' gushed Latham. 'I knew you could fix everything!'

'Of course I can fix everything, Latham. Just leave it to me. You deserve to relax a little, drink your beer and let me worry about these problems.'

Latham took a big swig of the beer and seemed to let his breath out completely for the first time since the demon woman had tried to seduce him.

'Oh thank you sir.' He took another swig. 'I feel much better now.' The mug was upended.

'There was one more thing I meant to tell you. Something Ranalf said…'

'What was it, Latham?' the Count asked quickly as he tried to pull the man back into a sitting position. He had slumped over, and Anton's efforts were of no use. He had passed out. Whatever the additional piece of information was, it would be lost forever in the stupor of the potion. Count Anton hoped that it was something that would resolve itself as a result of the collective memory loss that all of the men were sharing now.

He looked around at the field of sleeping men. The two stewards he had assigned to distribute the drugged beer looked bewildered, but Count Anton rejoined them and assured them that nobody would suffer permanent harm. The potion would wear off, and the crisis would be forgotten. The stewards, like many of Count Anton's staff, were magicians. They had known about the goblins all along and wondered what the Count was going to do to resolve this situation. As understanding sunk in, they both began to laugh.

As soon as they had recovered, he explained the attributes of the potion and gave them instructions to use his carriage to transport the men back to his castle. They would have to take a few at a time, but the laborious task would be worthwhile. After adding some further instructions for preparations for the re-awakening, he set out on foot to locate the woman. Count Anton had no doubt from Latham's story that she was a goblin. He was sufficiently aware of the effects of a magical glamour to guess the rest. The goblins had been clever to lead the men where they wished in this way, but now the female may well need help finding her way home.

He wasn't sure of this. If she were an experienced succubus she might know her way around the city very well indeed. However, to the best of his knowledge, the practice was disused and she may be completely lost. There was no hope of contacting the goblins through the nearby passage. It was completely blocked up. The nearest possible opening was at Nacibrab, but it may not be wise for him to wander brashly into goblin territory this close to the trouble just now. Back at Krapneerg, he was well known and felt reasonably safe. Here…he couldn't be sure.

It didn't take a much searching to locate the terraced houses. Anton was familiar with all parts of the city and expected that Latham would have travelled in a fairly straight line. His deduction paid off quickly when he examined a row of houses that looked like the sort of places that a man like Latham might take a woman for 'privacy'. His eye fell on a door which he could see had recently been broken and stood partially open.

As he entered the dwelling, the fresh footprints in the dust confirmed his expectations. He followed them to each room that Latham had examined and into the bedroom where he had taken the goblin woman. The bed was rumpled as if someone had been jumping on it, but otherwise there was little disturbance in the room. There obviously hadn't been a struggle. At least that part of Latham's story rang true. He probably had actually turned tail and ran the minute the woman stopped looking like a victim and returned his advances. The Count chuckled to himself, imagining the sudden change of heart that the ignorant man would have had as he found himself confronted with a demon out of legend. He probably thought she was preparing to suck out his soul as in the stories he would have heard.

The footprints doubled back, so she wasn't anywhere in the house anymore. They deviated to the edges of the room. On the mantelpiece an empty circle surrounded by dusty shelf suggested that she had taken one of the decorative objects that had been there. He wondered what it might have been as he examined the other fantasy figures of elves and unicorns. Then he walked back outside, turning once to look at the house, trying to imagine what it might have been like once. The houses in this row had been expensive in their day, a place that only the very rich could live in. He wondered for a moment if his own ancestors had ever set foot inside any of them.

Goblins were generally more clever than humans. Count Anton tried to think what he would do after the man ran away if he had been a kidnapped goblin woman lost in the human world. He might be able to follow her spirit trail a little, but he didn't know her so it would be difficult and he would have to rely more on his good sense. The man would have run to the right from the house, so naturally she would go left to avoid running into him. Then what? He began walking quickly, trying to see his world through a goblin's eyes.

The small side street soon led to a much larger street. He stopped to contemplate what this would mean to a goblin. In the underground caverns, the larger passages of the deep places generally led somewhere important. Even in the between places, tunnels acted as thoroughfares while side passages led to more private areas. But which way would she go? He sniffed the air, looking for a hint of her trail. He couldn't pick up any sense of her, but there was something else. Water. The river was to the south. He guessed that she would have smelt it as well and moved towards it, keeping his eyes open for anything that would attract the attention of a wandering goblin.

All creatures needed water and the cool spring air must seem very warm to the goblins in comparison to the cold and dank conditions they lived in naturally. The daylight was beginning to fail, which would make her trail harder to follow if there was some physical sign of her passing. Anton began to worry that he actually might not find her before nightfall. He tried to think of a way to get some help. The goblins might be able to search in the dark better than humans, but he dared not try to contact those who could be found nearby. Humans were unlikely to be welcome in the caverns after the day's events and even Haghuf had limited influence among those who resented the freedom with which he explored the caverns. He had tried to be unobtrusive, but the goblins could always sense his presence and some of them radiated resentment all too loudly, although these never spoke to him.

As he walked, Anton continually tried to sense any hint of the woman's presence, but there was no perceivable trace. In itself, that meant nothing. The abilities of the goblins were still something he knew far too little about. Their magic was similar to that of his own group of magicians, yet they seemed to have individual talents that were indeterminable by an outsider. He had overheard enough conversation to be aware that they knew and respected the unique abilities of each of their kind, but the extent of these abilities could only be guessed at. Anton thought that he probably knew Haghuf well enough that he would be able to follow his essence. An unknown woman however, and a succubus to boot, might well be able to cloak her passing or even do it automatically without realising. He knew magicians who could do it intentionally, himself included, although it never shielded him from the prying eyes in the caverns.

When he reached the riverside, he was more bewildered than ever. The river was far too wide to swim across and he couldn't imagine a goblin attempting it. Especially one wearing a dress. She might have continued in either direction, if she had come here at all. He looked around the river bank for any sign of someone passing. He could be a pretty good tracker when he tried.

The river was reasonably clean, although the old histories told of a time when it was far too polluted to swim in or to drink from its cool waters. There was concern that such a time could come again as current technology imitated the mistakes of the ancient past. Anton inspected as far up and down the river as he could see, hoping vainly for a sign of movement.

Then something did indeed catch his eye. His own castle, a fair distance away but still visible by the riverbank downstream. Would she go there, knowing he would help her? Her glamour would not have an effect on the women of the castle and she must know this, but goblins have their ways of stealth. Anton didn't know all of them despite his best attempts to learn everything he could about them. There had been times in the caverns when a goblin was simply *there* when it hadn't been a moment earlier. That was in their own terrain of course, how well one of them would fare in the surface world was anybody's guess.

He took a few steps downstream, then hesitated. He couldn't be sure of his direction. She may have gone somewhere else entirely. But what else could he do? He sat for a moment on a large rock to think. Out of habit, his eyes scanned in all directions seeking awareness of any living thing that might be nearby. Then something glittered near him and he turned to see a small object sitting right next to the rock he was sitting on. It was an odd thing to be sitting outside on the ground next to a rock. Anton picked it up and examined it. It was an iridescent blue and green figurine, a depiction of a fantasy dragon from the old times. A small jewel was set into its forehead where the third eye would be.

He turned it over and examined it, brushing some dust away from the edges of the bottom where it had apparently been torn away from cobwebs fairly recently. The object was just the right shape and size to fit the empty spot on the mantelpiece back at the house where the woman had encountered Latham.. He was just getting up when he saw the indentation in a spot of mud near the rock. It was unmistakable, the heel of a goblin footprint. It was too wide and knobbly to be anything else. Anton stuffed the statue into an inside jacket pocket and started walking quickly towards the castle.

Chapter Four

Haghuf felt the beat of the Dance as soon as he entered the surface levels. He felt no surprise in this, goblins entered into the Dance spontaneously often enough. He wasn't so far from the site of the day's events that he could expect the news not to travel. Any reason might lead them into the Dance, he would have been more surprised to find the caverns quiet during this visit. If nothing else, the *Kol'ksu* would know that he was coming.

The music became louder as he travelled lower, far beyond the between levels to the deeper places where his own kind preferred to keep their celebrations lest the surface dwellers should hear and be drawn to that which they wouldn't understand. Solid rock was a good insulator. Soon Haghuf began passing goblins at various amusements, some playing instruments of different sorts, others dancing to the natural beat of the earth. Haghuf's passing was noted, but unremarkable. He was well known among his kind. One young goblin, busy playing a flute-like instrument, nodded an acknowledgement without interrupting his tune. Haghuf did not respond. It was not expected.

Haghuf knew these passages well as he had visited on occasion. That he should come when there had been misfortune was all but expected. More goblins acknowledged him in various ways as he drew nearer to the centre of activity and the concentration of the population grew denser. Some nodded as had the musician, others waved or even spoke polite greetings. A sudden left turn and a narrow passage along the wall brought him to his first destination, a round spacious room within the caverns which served as a central meeting place for *Those Who Dance*. It was a natural hollow within the earth, or so it seemed. Whether goblin magic had shaped it so conveniently was a matter for speculation. The goblins, for the most part, didn't bother to dwell on the matter. They simply came there to dance.

Haghuf was immediately caught up by the blast of music as he turned through the twisting passage that blocked much of the sound from the earlier levels. It was completely in tune with the natural rhythm of the planet itself, reflecting and complimenting the heartbeat of all of life with drumbeats and high-pitched melodies from the reed and bone instruments that goblins favoured. He felt at one with himself and all that existed as his centre of gravity floated in tune with the harmonies and crescendos of the music which moved him. Hardly conscious, he gave himself over to the *heka*, the creation principle which reverberated along the spine of sound and vibration that was the Dance.

He didn't know or care how long he danced, but he became conscious of his movements once again when he felt himself being pulled along by the arm. Opening the eyes that he didn't realise he had closed, he looked on the familiar countenance of a goblin he knew well. He made no attempt to speak, he would not have been heard. Instead he followed the goblin through another side passage and along various small pathways until they reached a part of the caverns which was sufficiently shielded from the thundering music to allow conversation.

'What news, Haghuf?'

'Surely,' answered Haghuf, 'you will have heard of events at Nodgnirraf.'

'Naturally,' the other goblin continued. 'We suspect that it may have been the vibration of our own music that drew the human into the caverns.'

'What disturbs me is that he travelled so far,' said Haghuf. 'Surely he must have been seen and watched from the time he entered the between levels?' Haghuf sat on a rock, realising for the first time that it had been this thought that had been working its way around in the back of his mind since the incident first occurred. It was this that had put Count Anton into his mind so acutely.

'He was watched of course. But he did not pass beyond the between levels for many hours. He found the main passage that leads between your grotto and ours in the north. The betweeners are always reluctant to be seen as you know. He was followed until he reached Krapneerg. Then he tried to explore one of the passages to the deeper places, and you know the rest.' The goblin was one of the deep ones, like Haghuf, so his knowledge of the details of the events was not surprising. Haghuf was well aware that his companion shared his ability to track the vibrations of living creatures through the rock itself. It was this ability which would have caused him to intercept the human personally, had he not been sleeping at the time.

'Our music, as you can hear, plays loud and reaches long.' The goblin looked Haghuf in the eye as he conveyed a significant meaning through his words. 'We dance to celebrate. And to mourn.'

Haghuf understood. He got up and walked randomly about the enclave as he spoke.

'The child was born dead?'

'No,' answered the other goblin. 'It lives still. But it will not survive. It is deformed, and witless.'

Haghuf felt genuine sorrow, although he did not know many of the goblins in Nacibrab closely and probably had never met the mother.

'So few of us are bred, fewer still survive,' he stated flatly. 'What of the mother?'

'She takes comfort that it was only a male,' answered the goblin. 'Some speak of the old ways, that the child could be switched as a changeling.'

Haghuf knew the custom well. A goblin child, doomed to deformity and death by nature's law, could be changed for a human child, one which would live and improve the breeding stock. Like the ways of the succubus, the practice had been abandoned in times when the wrathful humans sought to hunt out and obliterate the entire goblin population. Enough generations of the humans had passed since then and the old ways had become only stories and legends among them, but the goblins remembered.

'It is not a good time to stir the humans by stealing their children,' Haghuf speculated. 'Perhaps if it were a female...we have so few of them.'

'I was on my way to visit the mother when I saw you in the Dance. Haghuf, will you come with me?'

Haghuf hesitated before answering.

'You know that I have come to visit Le-ina?'

The other goblin's eyes widened a moment, then he regained his composure.

'I might have guessed. It is not just my old bones that would bring you so far. For a moment, I thought it might be the events nearby that drew you here and just a convenience visit. I think some part of me knew, but did not want to acknowledge that it had come to this. Our paths coincide, will you come with me and offer what comfort you are able, before you take the path to the *Kol'ksu*?'

Haghuf nodded. It was custom among the old ones for visitors to offer comfort to a bereaved mother. He had assumed that she must have been a betweener as they were able to breed more often, but the other goblin's suggestion indicated that, in fact, she was a deep dweller like himself. It would be negligent to pass through her realms without offering his sympathy.

He followed the other goblin through a labyrinth of small passages which took him further and further away from the music. He did not know these passages, but could feel himself moving deeper into the earth with every step. The throb of the planet became stronger, stirring the unity with life and its cycles within him stronger as the sound of the music faded. He found himself walking in the rhythm of the Dance. It was as though he were caught up within the heartbeat of all of existence in which he played an essential part.

The distant drumbeats mixed with the corresponding earth pulse, ringing in his ears and his consciousness in tribal passion as he was brought into the presence of three goblin females, one holding a small bundle. She was bent over it where she sat, letting tears drop as the other females sang condolence and farewell songs with her. The goblin who brought Haghuf went and sat among them, joining in the song. Haghuf stood silently, waiting. After a moment, the song reached a natural end, and the females all looked up at Haghuf simultaneously. They recognised him at once, although he did not know any of them.

'I offer my respects to a lady of the deep dwellers.' He spoke formally, bowing deeply in the way that was reserved among their kind for special honours. 'And also my condolences.' There was no more to the formula. Nothing more could be said to console the grief of child loss.

'He has come to seek Le-ina,' whispered his host. The women all flinched, sitting more upright with eyes widening, much as the other goblin had reacted at the mention of the name.

'So,' began the mother, 'such times as bring you to see the prophesier have come. Perhaps it is better then, that he will not live to see them.' She seemed to harden, no longer tearful, accepting the loss with the stoicism that a race which does not breed easily must develop.

Haghuf observed the bundle. It squirmed slightly, living still. He speculated how much more difficult such a one must be to release than one born already dead. The mother stood up resolutely and walked towards Haghuf. The others stayed still, guessing her purpose and remaining silent to show respect. For just a moment her eyes met Haghuf's. She had the wide, golden eyes which were considered most attractive among their kind. Even blackened with tears, their hypnotic gaze drew him in, making him a servant of her will as was in the nature of the few females of goblin kind.

Then she dropped her gaze, and placed the bundle at Haghuf's feet. She turned her back to both and walked the customary three steps, showing her rejection of the non-viable child.

'Take it to the *Kol'ksu*,' she stated flatly, 'as a gift.' Then she sat again among the females, her back to Haghuf and the child.

The other goblin slipped out of the opening quietly, waiting for Haghuf so that he could guide him back to more familiar paths. Still silent, to show respect for the solemnity of their custom, Haghuf picked up the bundle. Bowing once again to the female's back, he re-joined his companion and left the females to themselves.

They walked without speaking, the heartbeat of the Dance still reverberating throughout both their consciousness and instincts. After a few moments they reached a larger tunnel. Haghuf knew his way from here. The other goblin turned and nodded slightly to him, then walked away silently as was proper for the rite that Haghuf had been asked to perform. For just the flicker of a moment, Haghuf spared a thought for Count Anton. There was much in the customs of the deep dwellers that he knew nothing about. Haghuf wondered what he would think of the ways of nature as they were practised much deeper than any realm the Count had been allowed to explore. He turned and walked the downward path, moving closer towards one of the hidden realms that he had never felt he could talk about to the Count. Some secrets were hidden very deeply indeed.

The caverns grew darker even to goblin eyes as Haghuf descended to nearly the deepest of them all. A side passage to the left that would have been missed by anyone who didn't already know it was there, led to a natural stairway of rock, descending still deeper into the bowels of the planet. In this winding space, complete darkness ruled. There was no hint of light to catch the eyes, and no direction for sound to travel. The echo of Haghuf's breath reverberated from all directions, confusing the senses as the walls seemed to close in claustrophobically. There was nothing but the heartbeat of the earth, still vibrating its rhythm for those who could hear, and the touch of the next step for cautious feet to feel carefully before shifting body weight onto the foot that might stumble too easily. At the bottom of this stairway was a straight passage. At the end of that was the faintest outline of grey light that promised an opening to another realm. One which knew light of sorts.

Haghuf didn't know how long it took him to traverse this labyrinth. It had been a very long time since he last came here. Somehow he always managed to forget the terror that this path raised even in him, a goblin of the deep places who should be well accustomed to darkness, close passages and unsure walking ground. There was something else that guarded the passage, a thing of unseen force which challenged all who would pass to the realm of the *Kol'ksu*. In the time of Haghuf's long memory, no other besides his mentor had tried. A few youngsters would occasionally challenge each other, but none passed beyond the top of the stairway before fleeing back to more familiar paths in stark panic. Haghuf himself did not visit the *Kol'ksu* lightly. Those he had told of his intention had reacted with alarm because they knew the dire warnings that must have precipitated the decision. Haghuf sensed a time of chaos, an eruption of tumultuous change about to come.

The grey luminescence grew no brighter as Haghuf approached. A turn to the left and then to the right as he passed through the monoliths that guarded the entrance brought him into a spacious cavern which was dimly lit by iridescent stones. These were encrusted among the stalactites that overhung a lake which took up much of the space in the cavern. The black water reflected this meagre light, bright to Haghuf's darkness-adjusted eyes, which created a flickering sensation throughout the cavern. It might have been a trick of the reflection which gave the impression that little glimmers of light occasionally shot out from the lake itself. Haghuf had never thought of a better explanation.

The rocky shore which surrounded the lake also shimmered in an eerie sort of iridescence. The shapes of the rocks themselves appeared black in the dim light, but with glowing edges of blue and green, shifting to violet as Haghuf's eyes moved over the terrain. In this alien cavern, the rhythm of the earth seemed to beat differently, as though to a subtly different timing than the ordinary world. Haghuf always felt as though he could hear song within the walls, the sonorous voice of a woman singing just on the edge of hearing where he couldn't quite follow the melody.

The lake rippled with movement, revealing the presence of its inhabitants. Haghuf didn't know how many water-goblins lived within its depths. Those beings so much like his own kind, and yet different, which they called *Kol'ksu*. Legend said that all of their kind held the gift of prophecy, yet only one would come to the surface to deliver her gift to the land-bound seeker. Haghuf had visited Le-ina twice before. The first time was only an introduction, though it sent shivers down his spine to remember that first encounter. The second had been when he inherited the task of keeper of the histories. On both occasions, he had been given predictions without asking for them. They had been true to an uncanny degree. And now his unease at the events which had befallen human and goblin brought him here to seek prophecy for the first time, in order to best serve the interests of his kind.

He bent down and searched by touch more than sight for a small rock to skim across the surface of the pond to draw attention to his presence. On both occasions that he had visited before, this had been the method used that would bring Le-ina out of her watery home to share her knowledge with the land dwellers. Like all goblin kind, she gave freely of her gifts for the benefit of all. She expected no payment, but Haghuf knew she and the others would appreciate the gift he brought.

He had learned to throw the stones from just the right angle so that they would skim rather than sink, potentially hurting an underwater swimmer. He was just bending to position himself to best advantage when he heard a deep, whispering yet melodic female voice from behind him.

'Surely Le-ina will have felt the disturbance in the balance of the world, and will know of your coming.'

Haghuf stopped in mid-movement, chilled by the tone more than the surprise of the words coming from the rocks behind him. He turned slowly, straining his eyes. Remembering his charge, he used the presentation of the gift as a pretext for moving closer where he might see her better.

'Le-ina.' He acknowledged her respectfully, slightly bowing before approaching her. 'I bring you a gift, freely given by one who had the right of choice.'

He handed the baby goblin to her, unwrapping it from its cloth first so that he presented only that which would be of interest to her. She took the infant, instinctively holding it close to her chest in a maternal gesture. Haghuf took the opportunity to look at her more closely than he had ever dared to before. In many ways, she looked much as any goblin, except that her naked flesh was covered with scales, and her milky eyes were larger. Her hair was completely white, yet reflected the light of the many colours that surrounded her. Haghuf speculated that humans would easily have mistaken her for a mermaid from one of their own legends, but for her scaled legs. They were not a fishes tail, but two limbs much like his own, only wider and streamlined for swimming, ending in large webbed feet. Sitting demurely with her legs together on land, it would be easy to mistake them for a single fishtail. The webbing between her long fingers wrapped the child securely, though it was not the comfort that kept it from crying. It simply had not the breath.

'Your people breed not easily Haghuf. My sympathies to the mother of this damaged creature.' She held it tenderly to her, as if it were her own young. She began rocking slightly in her place, keeping rhythm with the pulse that pervaded all things. Without further preamble, she began to speak of the future in the same abrupt manner which had characterised Haghuf's previous visits to her realm. The dim coloured light reflected from her long pointed teeth as she formed the words. They reminded Haghuf of his fear on their first encounter when he had first fully realised that this was a flesh eater that in other circumstances, may well consider him fair game.

'The time is upon us when much that has been hidden will be revealed. Human and goblin together will decide the fate of both races. You know more than any how closely entwined they are, and how delicate the balance lies between them when all of the truth shall be known.

If ignorance is chosen, all will die. The races will pass from the earth and the lands will be ruled only by the small creatures that survive until another Turning shall bring renewed evolution for sentient species. If the knowledge comes too early, only one species will die, and if too late, perhaps both will perish. Yet some will survive to start the cycle again.

One will come between the worlds to convey the secrets wisely, and another will come in the next generation who will challenge all that we have known of life, when the superstitions rise to plague the races once again. One spark, and all will wither again in the flames of ignorance. Yet hope remains so long as the one moves with the tides and rhythms that he has learned to know. A female plays a part that would seem to destroy all that has been accomplished. Yet it is she who will salvage something from the ashes of devastation.

You, Haghuf, play a part in all that comes to pass. Like the butterfly, you bring the tiniest of fluctuations to the changes in the winds of events. All that you touch is chaos, and it is in trusting to chaos, that the world may be saved.'

She stopped speaking as suddenly as she had started, and stopped her rocking motion, looking more closely at the baby now that it had settled comfortably within her embrace.

'Haghuf, look at this.'

Le-ina's look of surprise as she examined the infant dismayed Haghuf. He had never seen her lose her perfect composure before. Le-ina who knew all, simply could not be surprised. But she had reacted unmistakably with astonishment at something she had found. He obeyed immediately, approaching the baby and actually looking at it for the first time. The deformity was apparent. The breaths were shallow, they would not continue for long. Not only had it been born improperly formed, but also internally undeveloped to an extent that it was beyond any hope of independent survival. But there was something else. Le-ina turned the infant and ran her long webbed fingers over the shoulder blades of the creature, being careful not to cut it with her razor-sharp talons.

Haghuf opened his mouth to speak when he saw what she was directing to his attention to. The small protuberances from the shoulder blades were not part of the deformity. They were indisputably the beginnings of wings. He moved his mouth as if to speak, but no words found their way through his ordinarily astute mental processes. The rarity of the event was beyond the normal expression that words could provide. For the first time, tears welled in his eyes for the tragedy of the loss. Gently, almost possessively, Le-ina took the infant back into her arms.

'Tell the mother of this one, that his brother will live.'

It was a statement of fact, of prophecy, expressed without emotion despite the furrow on her brow that had appeared with the discovery. Clutching the infant tightly, she sprang from the rock and dived into the water. Haghuf saw several glitters of movement converge below the spot where she had entered the lake, followed by the rapid bubbling and chopping of water that indicated a feeding frenzy. He had intended to be gone before she took the meat to the other *Kol'ksu.*

He turned and left through the dark passage as quickly as possible. The dark stair seemed not quite so black on returning, perhaps only because he knew that more familiar passages awaited him beyond it. The light seemed to grow quickly as he climbed higher and the beat of the earth to regain its familiar, even rhythm. He wanted to dance. The flow of life pulsed within him strongly now, all the more alive for his close proximity to death on his journey. He wanted to join the others in the main cavern, to lose himself in the Dance and leave remembrance of the prophecies for a later time when he could think more clearly on their meanings.

The more intimate prophecy of the *Kol'ksu* rang in Haghuf's memory. There was no choice but to deliver the message personally, and to accept the implied command behind it. For one who carried the blood of the winged goblins in her veins, no healthy child could be expected from the seed of those too close akin. All in Nacibrab would be at least cousin to the woman. It would be for Haghuf to provide the seed of its becoming.

He entered her private cavern quietly, respectfully. He found her going about her business, chatting with the other females as though nothing had occurred to disrupt their ordinary lives. They turned as he entered, obviously surprised at his return.

'I have a message,' he said in explanation. The woman nodded silently. It would be a bit awkward to explain the details of his encounter. A mother who sends her child to its death does not await a report on the morbid details. Haghuf only repeated the exact words that Le-ina had spoken about her next child. One of the other females touched the mother gently on the arm, suddenly smiling broadly and lighting up the room with the joy in her eyes.

'Joy sister!' she exclaimed excitedly. The other woman made a similar gesture.

'And perhaps a daughter the next time,' she said, then kissed the woman gently on the cheek. Both women scurried out, feet flapping excitedly on the stone as they ran to spread the news among the others. Haghuf was left alone with the female. He observed her for a moment, wondering. The rhythm of the Dance grew louder in his consciousness as he beheld her, and the moment. Still, there was one thing he wished to learn.

'You knew?' he asked.

The female hesitated a moment before answering. It was not customary to mention a newborn after its death and the proper mourning rites. She struggled a moment with the conflicting impulses within her being. The Dance called her, the wellspring of life, and yet she was confronted with death. The rhythm held within it a cycle of birth and death that was never ending - a spiral of creation and destruction, each dependent on the other in a balance of forces that was calling her to its unconscious embrace. Yet there was a question to answer, and she must honour the one who would seed her next child for the short time of his purpose, though he would be as nothing to her or the unborn a moment afterwards. At last she answered in a strangely emotional voice.

'Any mother examines her newborn. I knew. I found the wings a moment after he first breathed the air of life.' She looked away then, suddenly ashamed of her weakness.

'It may have been cowardly to send it to the *Kol'ksu*, but how could I kill it myself? It would have been better if it had been born dead, or not born at all.'

'But you carry the blood,' said Haghuf in his matter-of-fact manner.

'Yes,' she said quickly as she spun back to face him, 'And the prophesier has said that the next one will live. Did she also say what that will mean in the world unfolding before us? With the humans bringing death to us once more?' Her sudden vehemence took Haghuf aback for a moment, conveyed as it was against the backdrop of the passion raised by the drum beats and the urge to join the Dance. He took a careful breath before answering.

'I am not sure. She said many things. I have not unravelled them all yet. But you know the powers of those of the blood. I believe your son has a part to play.'

'So be it then.' she said, and the vehemence turned into an intense ardour as she flung herself into Haghuf's embrace, moving with him in the resounding rhythm of the Dance of Creation.

Chapter Five

Talla looked upon the castle from a safe distance, or so she thought. She hid within the shadows of an artificial outcrop of human making. She could not guess its purpose, but had more important matters to decide for the moment and no time to speculate. Human eyes were weak in the dark, and it was indeed becoming as dark as the surface world was likely to do in the glow of the rising moon. Yet even in moonshadow she felt vulnerable, exposed. She did not know how many humans might inhabit the castle, but some of them would surely be women. She continued to focus her glamour, knowing that it would be ineffective if she were seen by one of them. At least if a man happened upon her, she would have that protection.

She was used to walking long distances in the underground passages, but the artificial rock that the humans paved their roads with was hot and had hurt her feet after a time. She had soothed them in the river, but the cooler night air was very welcome.

Talla stayed very still in the shadow as she tried to think how she might locate Count Anton without being discovered by the women. This was the sticking point on which none of her people would be able to advise her. The layout of the castle and its grounds was unknown, even to Haghuf. Of course if she could find Haghuf, she would not need to ask help of the human Count. She smiled to herself, realising that in fact she was glad of the excuse to seek him out. She had seen him many times of course, but never close up, and never in a situation where she might speak to him freely. Fear and excitement intermingled as she contemplated the fact that unless something drastic happened, she would certainly have to speak to him now.

She had nearly made up her mind to try scaling the wall and hiding within the shadows inside the courtyard. There she could wait until she could find a man unaccompanied who might give her the information she needed to find the Count. But before she had taken a step she heard a human voice behind her.

'You! Miss! Are you alright?' A large human male appeared from behind her, closely followed by another of similar size. They wore identical clothing, and radiated an air of authority. Unable to comprehend their words or to respond, she backed away, pulling the cloak closer around her and keeping her focus on the glamour.

'You don't know how glad I am to see you move lady, you were so still I thought maybe you were dead.'

She only shook her head helplessly, unable to understand.

'She looks frightened Garth, I wonder if something has happened to her,' said the other man.

'I dunno,' replied the one called Garth, 'but we can't leave her out here to freeze to death. I think we should take her to the women. Maybe she'll talk to them.'

'She ain't talking to us,' said the other man as he reached to take her arm.

Talla pulled back instinctively, but the guards rushed forward and each grabbed an arm.

'Hold it little lady, we won't hurt you. Poor thing is frightened to death.' The one called Garth tried to stroke her hair, to comfort her, but she pulled her head away and contemplated biting him. Thinking better of it, she began to cry instead. She knew this would make them think she was weak and might make them careless if she should need to free herself of them. The men continued to hold her arms tightly as they pulled her towards the castle.

Remembering her earlier experience of Latham, she wondered if all human men just forced their women to go where they wanted them to go and to do what they wanted them to do. As fascinated as she was with humans, she was glad that she was not one of them. She would never receive so little respect from one of her own. At least there was a possibility that these men would take her to the Count. She knew that among humans, those in authority were consulted for all decisions. It seemed an odd practice to a race of beings who consulted whoever was best qualified to provide information or instruction according to the need. It might serve her purposes now if she was brought into his presence. But what about the castle women?

There was a walled path which led around the castle and eventually took them to an opening into the courtyard. Talla felt the panic rising as she was dragged closer to the open gate. Her eyes darted everywhere, looking for any sign of danger. It was quite dark now and she wouldn't be spotted from a distance easily, but her natural skin would glow green in the moonlight all too clearly to those who were unaffected by the glamour if they came close enough to see her.

Instinctively, she began to struggle a little harder as they pulled her towards a door. One of the men shouted something as he struggled to hold her and a crease of light appeared as the door slowly opened. A figure emerged from the opening, impossible to see clearly with the light streaming behind her. The silhouette was wearing a dress. Talla screamed, reflexively twisting first one way and then the other so that the handholds on her were shaken loose for just the moment she needed to get away. But there was nowhere to run to. She was trapped within the courtyard unless she decided to go over the wall in a manner that would betray her disguise completely. She huddled into a shadow, drawing the cloak closely around her and pulling even her feet and hands within the folds of cloth which concealed her. The hood she brought as far down over her face as possible until she couldn't even see past its protective layers.

The man called Garth was talking with the human woman, obviously discussing her in their unknown language.

'I don't know who she is, we found her just wandering loose outside the castle. Thought we'd best bring her in for protection.'

The woman walked calmly over to Talla and stroked her head through the protective hood.

'Poor little thing,' she said. 'Frightened near to death by the look of it.'

Talla rocked back and forth on the soles of her feet, searching instinctively for the pulse of the earth beneath them until it began to come to her, and she could take courage from the rhythm of the Dance. She reached her consciousness deep into the earth and it began to come to her. The woman's voice continued to speak.

'God knows what she's been through that would leave her out in the cold. Lost and probably hungry. Might have lost her wits completely. The Count will want to know about this.'

Talla caught the word, the woman was speaking of the Count. She knew then what she must do. She would have to brave it out, let this woman take her to him. She reached her senses through the concealing layers to examine the woman. She was not very tall, but rather round. The hand that stroked her was rough, one that knew work unlike the Count who had such smooth baby-like flesh on his unspoiled palms. She must be one of his servants. Allowing her to take charge of the situation would surely result in coming to him. She couldn't stay as she was forever. Sooner or later, the men would no doubt decide to drag her along again, and then her disguise would be breached the moment a single hand was pulled from its sleeve.

Still huddling within the cloak, Talla stood up carefully, crouching just a little to ensure that the cloak did not reveal her feet. She kept her hands wrapped in the sleeves and the hood draped across her features. Then she laid her head gently on the woman's shoulder to indicate that she was prepared to trust her.

'There, you see Garth?' said the woman triumphantly. 'All she needs is a little gentleness. Dragging her along like a prisoner probably scared her more than being lost and alone! You leave her to me now, I'll look after her.' Laying a gentle hand on Talla's arm, she led her through the brightly lit doorway, and into the world of the humans.

* * *

Count Anton looked on his own castle in the shadows of the newly darkened sky. His senses were more keen now, as the shape-shifter instincts began to tune into the strands of electromagnetic force that permeated the earth and all that happened upon it. He could feel the thrumming of the deep places, probably enhanced by the goblins and their own recognition of disruption from the day's events.

The castle seemed quiet, there was no sense of alarm as would accompany the capture of a goblin. Yet he was sure that she had come this way. It was a tentative connection, but the statue in his pocket, one which she had touched, gave him a faint impression of her. He wondered a moment if perhaps she had recognised the way to Lirrewot which was nearby. Creeping stealthily through the shadows by habit, he came to where the opening had always been and immediately noticed that the sign was gone. The opening itself seemed unchanged, but if he had not known exactly where it was, he could easily have walked right by it without noticing.

He dare not venture far inside. The goblins here would know of him, but they didn't know him as Haghuf and his lot did. Haghuf had warned him long ago not to enter these particular tunnels. Apparently there was strong anti-human sentiment here at the best of times. Placing his hand over the bulge in his pocket where the dragon statue was concealed, he tried to reach out for any trace that would tell him that the goblin woman had come this way. He found none. Yet he had found it difficult to follow her from the beginning. He couldn't be sure that it wasn't just his own inability to catch the scent.

He explored the area a little, looking for clues and sniffing the air tentatively. He was just beginning to wonder where his guards were when he saw someone sitting on a wall. It was a man, a commoner. Count Anton didn't know him, but he could see that the man was drunk. He swayed uncontrollably in his attempts to maintain his sitting position, and the stench of stale alcohol lay on the air in his vicinity. For a moment Anton wondered if it might be one of the men from the altercation, having wandered away from the 'festivities' he had prepared for them. Yet it seemed unlikely that they would be awake so soon, or would be able to just wander off. He hesitated. Should he make himself known or would it be better to slip away and go straight to the castle? He must look in on the situation with the others very soon, regardless of his other pursuit.

The man solved the dilemma by looking up at that moment, directly at the Count.

'Count Anton, Sir!' The man emphasised the term of respect in his loud and drunken voice. 'I come looking for you, but s'a long walk from Nodgnirraf.' The man swayed drunkenly, obviously struggling to retain consciousness. Nodgnirraf. The Count needed any information that might relate to the day's events. He indulged the man a moment, hoping it wouldn't be some unrelated trivial matter that brought him so far to seek him out. Eloquently, with the smooth melodic voice he used for dealing with diplomatic situations, Count Anton addressed the man as if he were the most important ambassador worthy of no less than his full attention.

'It isn't every day that a gentleman from Nodgnirraf appears on my castle doorstep to seek me out. Tell me sir, what brings you so far?'

The man blinked several times, visibly confused by the unfamiliar honourifics used towards him. After a moment, he regained his train of thought and continued with his intended message.

'Demons sir! Lots of 'em. They were coming right outta the ground and folks was doin' battle with 'em. Then when I ran to find help, I got a bit lost and somehow ended up on the other side of the city, and there was another one walking down the street just as bold as you please! It had a cloak thrown over its head o'course, but it was one of 'em. Its big green flappy feet was paddin' down the pavement like it had a purpose, no hesitation. I tried stirring folks up to help me catch it, but there was no one about, it bein' the Sabbath and all folks was in Temple, apart from those what was lookin' fer one o'the lads.'

The man stopped speaking a moment, apparently straining to remember what came next. Anton seized the opportunity to glean a little more information about what had happened in Nodgnirraf.

'Why were people looking for one of your men?'

'He had a fight with his missus in the early hours when most folks is asleep, they fight all the time them two. Never shoulda got married atall, but 'course its too late now and they just have to make the best of it. Anyways, he went storming outta the house God knows where, and when he didn't come back she got worried about him and started goin' door to door asking for help to go look fer 'im. We got some of us together and went lookin'. Found him too, maybe just a bit o'luck but we come across him in an old part of the city, and damned if there weren't a demon draggin' him right out of a hole in the ground! The light weren't up yet but it was a demon bold as brass, its skin shinin' a glowin' green and its pointed ears and those big hungry yellow eyes they got. And the flappy feet o'course, like that other one.'

The man stopped again. He was swaying drastically now, and looked ready to pass out any second. Anton was fitting this account into his own knowledge of the morning events. There was one more thing he wanted to know if he could get any more sense out of the drunken man. He sat beside him and gripped his shoulder firmly, shaking him slightly to help him maintain consciousness.

'What happened to the man you found?'

'We figured they drugged 'im or sumthin.' The man's speech was rapidly becoming less distinct. 'He made no sense, ranting 'bout unicorns and such and hardly able to keep 'is eyes open. You know what folks are like when they're about to pass out drunk.' Anton suppressed a laugh, as the demonstration was all too clear. 'We laid 'im down outta the way and went after 'em, and then....' The man hesitated at the point where he had panicked and ran. 'I went for help sir. An' I come to find you and tell you after I saw t'other one.'

Anton speculated as to whether it would be wise to take charge of this man and bring him into the castle with the others, but his memories of the morning were probably too clear and too long past to erase even with the goblin's potion. He needed to get inside and to check on the situation, but this man had obviously left the site before the others had been drugged and may turn into a real problem. Where had he seen another 'demon'? Anton remembered Haghuf walking in the morning light to the park. Could he have seen Haghuf? He was about to ask the man where he had wandered to, but the man was out cold.

Well, at least that solved the immediate problem. It was time he dealt with those other men, and the first of them may well have awakened by now as the goblins would have drugged him well before the others had consumed their potioned beer. He trusted his chosen men implicitly but there were a lot of men to look after. Plus his own talent for making the story he was planning to tell them believable was essential to the plan. He would have to send some guards to collect this man as soon as he got a chance. Anton laid him on the grass as comfortably as possible and started towards the castle.

The night air was comfortably cool. In other circumstances, he would be enjoying the walk after dark and perhaps even letting his wilder impulses run freely, but for now he was needed for more urgent matters. He strode confidently up the causeway and into the main courtyard as befitted the Master of the castle. He continued to wonder about the lack of guards, speculating on whether it might be a good idea to post more than just a couple of men on either side of the grounds. Few people were about at all, and there was no likelihood of trouble of any kind, but a complete absence of any challenge hardly seemed fitting for what was after all, meant to be a fortress.

The Count passed a couple of servants who greeted him respectfully, welcoming him home. He took the trouble to acknowledge them politely, but did not stop his steady pace towards the banquet hall. His elite guard, the magicians, would be there. All the while he continued to wonder about the lost goblin woman. Had she found her way home through the opening at Lirrewot? Was she still skulking about in the streets? Had he walked right past her, perhaps hiding from the steps of a human, without realising she was there? He touched the ornament in his pocket again and tried to sense some trace of her. No other living being had touched the item for a very long time before she had picked it up. The abandoned terrace houses where she had found it were avoided in general, considered taboo by the others of his species although the plague that killed their previous occupants had died out long since. Some memories lasted a very long time. The sense of her was strong on the statue, and there was a tension within it that spoke of fear, confusion. All was not well with her, and he was sure that she was nearby.

Anton reached the banquet hall and entered without ceremony. As he entered through the massive oak door, he forgot the goblin woman for a moment and a smile spread across his face into a mischievous grin. Everything was exactly as he had ordered it and he couldn't deny that he was enjoying this little ruse as if it were only a prank rather than a crucial deception meant to avoid a war.

The room was decorated for an elaborate party, one that had seemingly occurred the night before. The stewards from the campsite at the battle were now dressed as befitted servants at a diplomatic occasion, and the men from the battle were all sleeping peacefully in positions around the room which suggested that they had been socialising before passing out where they sat. Some of them were leaning on the large colourful cushions that decorated the room, others hunched over tables laden with the remains of rich food and drink.

The smell of a strong liqueur reeked in the room, especially from the mouths and clothing of the men. Many of them had empty pewter wine cups in their hands with traces of the drink clinging to the inside as if it had once been quite full. Now, the only tricky part was going to be to convince them that they had indulged in the festivities freely, when it would not have been in their nature to do so. Count Anton had gone over his story in his head many times, filling in the details that might be questioned. In the end, he knew that they would accept his word over their own better judgement, yet he had no experience of this potion and couldn't be sure how thoroughly the memories would be erased.

He wondered about the first man, the one the goblins had captured and set free. He didn't know the man's name, or have any description of him. He could be any one of them, but theoretically he would wake first as he had been drugged hours before the others. But then, he didn't know what doses the goblins would administer, or how it compared to the amounts he used to spike the beer. The stewards grinned conspiratorially at him as they went about their nearly finished preparations. One of them motioned to the Count that he wanted a private word, out of hearing of the unconscious men who showed some signs of beginning to stir. The Count followed him to a side room where they could speak freely.

'They might wake up any minute sir, one of 'em already did and Jerak took him down to the kitchens.'

Anton contemplated the idea of going to speak with the wakened man first, but he needed to be present when the others reached consciousness. He tapped his fingers together as he contemplated what instructions to give.

'It is probably the one the goblins set free. He was drugged long before the others. He must not speak with them before we have had a chance to plant the story we decided on into his mind, did he say anything yet?'

'Not much sir,' answered the steward. 'He was confused, asking where he was. Jerak was telling him the story you said to as they walked off. He was thirsty, said his mouth felt like an army had marched through it in mid-summer with the dust flying.'

'That may be an after effect of the drug,' the Count speculated out loud. 'Dani, see that the kitchens send pitchers of fresh water here, and spread the story among the other servants that I've been entertaining during the night.' The order was given perfunctorily, as from one who was used to issuing orders to servants and expected obedience. Dani would of course run to fulfil the command, although the role of servant was one the magicians played by choice rather than station. In circle, the dynamics between them would be entirely different.

'And Dani,' the Count continued, 'tell Jerak that somehow he must keep the man away from these others until I speak with him.'

'Yes sir,' replied Dani, then he bowed slightly and ran to carry out the commands.

Anton settled himself in for a long night. With luck, the men would not fully wake until a late enough hour to make his story more plausible. He poured himself a small amount of the liqueur and sat beside the fire, enjoying its comforting warmth. He raised his hand to his pocket again, realising that he hadn't removed his long coat. At least it was the light velvet one and would not seem out of place at a diplomatic banquet, even the imaginary one he had concocted for the occasion. He had just begun contemplating trying some fire gazing to try to learn something of the missing goblin woman when Dani came rushing back in, one of the kitchen women at his heels.

'Sir, I think you should speak with this woman.' Dani gave him a significant look as he spoke, something was afoot.

'By all means,' Anton replied coolly, 'do come in and tell me what the problem might be.'

'Sir,' began the woman, remembering to curtsey. 'It ain't a problem so much as a curious situation. The water you ordered is being prepared and should be here shortly.' She curtsied again, looking just a bit anxious. It was clear that she had more to say, but hadn't quite formulated the words yet.

'Surely sending water is not so curious? I think there is something else you want to tell me,' the Count prompted her. Her eyes widened in surprise. Anton had to suppress a chuckle as he noted that she was completely unaware of her own body language and had jumped to the conclusion that he had read her mind, a common assumption among some of the simpler people. It added to his mystique, so he let such situations go unexplained. It didn't hurt to let them have just a little fear to augment their respect for him.

'Sorry sir, I was just gettin' to it,' she went on. 'The guards found a strange woman out in the grounds, sir. They say she's real pretty and noble like, although me and the other women ain't seen her proper 'cause she's terrified and keeps herself wrapped up in her cloak.'

The Count was suddenly very attentive. He carefully guarded his own anxious reaction and his eagerness to hear what had been done with this woman. Patiently, fighting his own pounding heart to maintain his calm exterior, he pulled two chairs forward and placed one conveniently for the woman to sit on while taking the other himself. He met Dani's eyes a split second, enough to indicate that he would take care of the situation but that Dani should stay nearby in case he was needed. Dani busied himself checking the breathing of the sleeping men that the woman seemed to take no notice of in her haste to convey her story.

'Anyways, we put food in front of her and she wouldn't take it, until we would get distracted and then she seemed to grab it quick like inside her cloak and ate everything she could get her hands on. Musta been starvin' the poor thing!'

'What did you give her?' asked the Count. Despite his need to hear the full story, his curiosity about the eating habits of goblins had tormented him for a very long time. Whenever he had asked Haghuf what they ate, the only answer he had received was a cryptic, 'Whatever comes to us.'

'Well, I give her some cake first, and then there was some roasted meat and vegetables left over from dinner so we put that out for her and it disappeared when we weren't looking, just like the cake. And there was a small loaf of bread, I swear sir I never seen a woman pack away so much food in me life!' The servant looked positively scandalised by the unladylike greed of the woman. Once again, Anton had to suppress a smile.

'Go on then, continue your story. Where is the woman now?' He wanted her to get to the point, and to tell him the whereabouts of the goblin woman without getting too distracted with details now.

'Well sir,' she continued, 'She got real upset when we tried to pull her cloak away from her face so we could at least look at her when we talked to her. Just screamed and cried and such like and pulled the thing closer, so we thought she might have lost her senses. God knows what happened to her. So we reckoned we needed to keep her safe until we could tell you about her.' The woman stopped a moment, seeming to collect her thoughts. She looked a little nervous about finishing her tale.

'And?' prompted Anton.

'Well,' said the servant tentatively. She began wringing her hands together. She was obviously expecting the Count to object to some aspect of her actions. 'I could only think of one place where she could be locked in comfortably.'

'The Tower,' said the Count, quickly understanding.

'Yes sir, she seemed to respond to the mention of your name, so I coaxed her along and she followed every time I said it. When we passed your private rooms, she stopped like she knew where she was and started sniffing the door like an animal. It was real creepy sir, I never seen anybody act like that in me life. I think she wanted to go in but I called her up the stairs the rest of the way, saying your name over and over and she followed and went in like she was real anxious to see you.'

'And you locked her in,' he finished for her. She nodded to indicate that she had done so. Anton noticed that the woman looked as if she was expecting a whipping, although he had never treated any of his servants badly. Other servants were beginning to appear with the pitchers of water that he had ordered, placing them strategically on tables with fresh goblets so they would be ready when the apparently drunken guests required them. Anton smiled at the woman to put her at her ease.

'You've done well in a difficult situation, I'll take care of it now,' he reassured her. She breathed a sigh of relief and stood to curtsey to the Count.

'Thank you, sir.'

Anton had no time to exchange further pleasantries, He gestured to Dani who had stayed within hearing distance, although he had heard some of the story from the woman before he had brought her to the Count.

'Dani, are my guests likely to wake very soon?' Anton asked quickly.

'I think not sir, they're fitful but they breathe evenly, like the drunk often sleep.' Indeed, the sound of snoring was clearly heard from several of the sleepers.

'I'll return as quickly as I can, I must see to this woman. If anyone awakes, give them my apologies.'

Dani understood. The Count needed to be in two places at once, and even his magic couldn't provide that. Dani and the others would have to employ delaying tactics if the men woke before the Count's return. Also the kitchen woman needed to be sent back to her own business so that no word of this wandering woman reached the ears of these men.

Anton sprang up the steps two at a time. Whoever this goblin woman was, he admired her courage and resourcefulness. She had managed to get past a kitchen full of women and even to get hold of food without revealing herself. With what he suspected of her earlier ordeal with Latham, she had experienced rather a lot of challenges for one day. But goblins were survivors, it was in the most basic quality of their nature. Thus it was no surprise to Anton when he flew through the Tower door to find the room empty.

There were signs that she had been here for a time. Nobody came here, it was forbidden. That was why the kitchen woman had been so nervous and why his own quarters were directly below this cell. It had in fact been used as a prison sometime in history, but there was no need of that now. It made an excellent confinement for humans because there was only the one door, and a long straight drop outside from the only window. It was considered inescapable, for humans. Goblins had their own ways of getting in and out of places. It was one of the things he wanted to learn about them, but on some subjects Haghuf could be less co-operative than on others.

He used the Tower for the ancient books, some of which he had copied for Haghuf. And like Haghuf, there were some that he had chosen to keep secret. There was much that they shared between them, but the habits of many generations did not die easily. One of the most secret books lay open, carefully placed to avoid any unnecessary disturbance of the pages by the breeze through the window. It would appear that the goblin woman could read. It was another thing he knew little of, how many of them did? He did know enough that he could surmise that she knew the importance of what she had found in the book, yet she had not taken it with her. This too, he found curious. Goblins were notoriously inquisitive and loyal to their own kind, and he would have expected such a find to be immediately taken to Haghuf. But here it lay, treated with respect yet left in its place.

The anomaly perplexed him, but the urgency of the situation pervaded his speculations. Anton realised he needed to follow her. She hadn't been put here so long ago, therefore she couldn't have gone very far. He could not guess how she escaped from the Tower. He had no choice but to take the usual route down the steps. Some instinct drew him outside of the courtyard, back the way he had come and towards the place where he had encountered the man who had escaped the potion. His wolf senses urged him on and he broke into a run, sensing extreme danger. Not for himself, but for her. He didn't stop to analyse how he knew, it was just something in the feel of the air, and the vibration of the earth that pulled him towards the impression of danger.

Chapter Six

Talla was tired. In her own world, her people slept when they were tired with no consideration of day or night on the surface world. The sun had come and gone during her day among the humans, but it was the fatigue itself that told her she was past due for some rest. Still, she must not sleep among the humans. She had been careful among them making sure no part of her, not the slightest finger had been visible to them at any time.

She knew they were only trying to help her when they offered food, but she could not reach out and allow her goblin hands to give her away. So she ignored manners, and snatched the food when she felt their attention drift elsewhere. She could not look out of the hood without risking that they would see her white-irised eyes, and that alone would reveal that she was not one of them. At least she had eaten well. She had only consumed a couple of fish by the river before that, since the altercation began. The *Kol'ksu* had been only too glad to offer them as she cooled herself from the heat of the unaccustomed sunlight. It had perhaps been risky to pull off the dress and dive in, yet it was so refreshing that it had been worth the danger - and of course the *Kol'ksu* kept watch for any sign of humans. They would always look after her in whatever ways they could.

She had begun to pick up a few words of human speech, but not enough to follow a conversation. She read them by their actions which had seemed kind until they had locked her in the tower room. She believed them to be taking her to see the Count. The woman had kept saying *Count Anton* as if that had been her intention and had lead her up a long stairway. They had come to a door which she was sure must have been where he was, she recognised his scent from his visits to Haghuf. She had lurked nearby on many such visits, more than either the Count or Haghuf could possibly sense. It was a skill she had learned from her mother's people.

Then the woman lead her further up the stairs, to this room. Trusting perhaps too much, Talla had entered as the human woman lit a candle. But there was nobody there. That was when the door was shut and she heard the turning of the lock. Goblins didn't use locks of course, but she knew what they were. She knew rather a lot about humans. She had also seen the locks on the dwellings where the human man had dragged her off. It didn't worry her greatly, as there was a window and therefore an escape.

She wandered around the room for a few minutes, observing her surroundings. She wondered if the humans would send Count Anton to her here, but one could never be sure of the behaviour of humans. Her instincts fought the idea of forced captivity of any kind. She looked out of the window, noting the straight drop to the ground. Then she tested her fingers against the stones of the outside wall. They were a rougher texture than the passages of her underground world, but the fingers stuck securely. She could leave any time she wanted to.

The room intrigued her though. There was a decorative bookcase with symbols drawn all over it. Books filled its shelves which were very old, yet the books were neatly dusted and cared for as if they were read frequently. There were large cushions here and there in rich colours and a table and chair which looked like a comfortable place to read. There was also a small desk near the window. This was where the candle stood. The rest of the room was filled with wooden boxes of some sort. She speculated that Count Anton might keep important treasures here. Humans were given to collecting such things.

She went to the books and examined their titles. She had expected them to be written in the human language, but she could read them clearly. This surprised her more than anything else, yet the books themselves were impressive. They were books of ancient magic, the sort of thing that Haghuf would take a healthy interest in if he were to see them. She would have to bring him here when things were calm again. She took one of the books down from the shelf, laid it on the table and opened it at a random page. She began to read, still amazed at the script in plain goblin language. She was sure that Haghuf had never had this book in his care, or even seen it. It had no scent of goblin anywhere on it, not even faintly as it would have if one of the ancients had handled it. Somehow, it had come directly to humans.

The thought of Count Anton reading the book reminded her of the other chamber, the one that held his scent. She left the book where it was and returned to the window, leaning out far enough to see the wall below. She immediately found what she sought, another window just far enough down to belong to that other chamber. She cast herself over the window sill and crawled head first down the wall. Her sticky fingers and toes pressed into the stones where they fastened themselves securely, sucking the stone itself into the circular membranes that were meant for the purpose. She moved one limb at a time, creeping down the wall like a spider under the cover of the night's darkness, despite the awkwardness of the dress which slid up to her waist, or rather down to her waist from this angle.

When she reached the top of the window, she first listened carefully, then sent her other senses forward. There was no impression of anyone there. She swung herself deftly through the window and landed gently on a soft carpet, sending the folds of her skirt cascading back around her legs where they belonged. The scent of the Count was overpowering. The room was quite dark, and therefore all the easier for her to see the rich surroundings. It was clearly his sleeping space. A large, soft bed dominated the room. It was unlike those she had seen in the other dwellings. This one had a post rising from each corner, which supported a structure above the bed where curtains of embroidered tapestry hung decoratively, tied to the posts to allow a view of the sleeping space. She sat on the bed, bouncing a few times to test it for comfort.

Resisting the urge to jump on it as she had done on the other bed earlier, she looked around at the other furnishings. There were tables and storage chests with drawers which pulled out. Talla quickly investigated and found that they were filled with clothing and other human objects. Count Anton seemed to have rather a lot of clothing. To Talla, this was a puzzle. Goblins dressed simply and although they were prone to decoration, they were quite happy to wear the same clothing until it wore out and change its decorations as the impulse arose.

Several ornaments sat on shelves and on top of other furniture. It reminded her of the dragon statue she had picked up before. She couldn't remember now what she had done with it, but she didn't have it anymore. There were also paintings on the walls. They were elaborate images of fantasy creatures, including some of goblins. She was sure she could see Haghuf in one of them. Talla was fascinated with the extent of decoration that humans collected. It had never occurred to her, or apparently to any of her kind, that they could easily paint the walls of passages in their own realm. But then the walls were moved often enough that it probably wasn't practical.

Suddenly she felt something. There was a disturbance somewhere. The vibrations seemed to travel from the ground right up through the stones of the Tower so that the floor of the room was nearly as alive as a cavern floor during the Dance, but with the wrong energy. Within this vibration was a certainty that someone was coming. She smoothed the bed with her hands to disguise the impressions which betrayed her presence, then leapt for the window and back over the edge. She crawled swiftly down the wall this time, leaping onto the ground when she was near enough. Then she ran as quickly as she could out of the castle grounds. She didn't know where she would go, but she decided that coming among the humans had been an act of madness. Still, she knew that she would return in time. Now that she knew where to find Count Anton alone, she could do it without the danger of encounters with other humans. She would just have to come when they all slept, as surface dwellers tended to do according to the light cycles.

She hoped to find a safe area to hide until just before the sun would rise. This seemed to be a safe time to find them sleeping. It was an odd thing, that humans timed their sleep according to the darkness, yet did not actually sleep when it became dark. Perhaps it was the soft light of early morning that relaxed them.

Keeping her senses alert for the men who had found her before, she climbed over walls and travelled paths that humans would not find easy. There didn't seem to be any of the creatures about. Still, having been captured once was enough to make her more wary. She understood now why the old practices had been abandoned. Any contact with humans was risky, they had too much of a tendency to try to control the movements of others. She wondered how Count Anton managed to free himself of prying eyes long enough to make his visits to her world.

The *Kol'ksu* had not been able to advise her on how to find her way back to her own world. Their ways to the river were long and all under water. She had no gills to breathe through their passages. She would have to use her own senses to find a way. It was easy enough to feel the thrum of the Dance beneath the earth, but finding an opening to travel there was another thing. She was not a digger and one goblin alone could not form a whole passage where there was none.

She began to wonder if she should have hidden herself within Count Anton's chamber and awaited his return. The room had many places of concealment; cupboards, shadows, and a large space beneath the soft bed that appeared to be unused apart from shoving shoes underneath. But it was too late for that now, unless she hid somewhere outside and returned when she was sure that all of the humans were sleeping. There were only the guards to consider, as they seemed to stay awake at night to look after the others.

She stopped to listen for any sound on the night breeze. There were many things to be heard or felt for those who could listen. Small creatures moved in the undergrowth and birds flew among tree branches. These would be the night hunters, as the smaller birds slept like humans in the darkness. She could smell pigeon among the array of scents that came to her as she concentrated on her sensory awareness. It was a very familiar smell, as the birds were particularly easy to lure into the between places and bred quite freely in the surface world. There always seemed to be plenty of them to augment the food supplies.

Thinking of this brought back the memory of the food she had eaten among the humans. The vegetables were familiar enough, although they seemed to have cooked them far too long so that they were soft and slid down the throat with hardly any chewing at all. The meat had been particularly good though, of a sort that was unfamiliar. The cuts appeared to come from an animal much larger than the swine that were occasionally herded into the caverns. She made a mental note to learn more of human food habits when the opportunity arose. The other thing they gave her, a sweet, sticky substance that they called cake, was a real curiosity to her. It was pleasant, but unfilling to the deepest part of her being that looked for the nutrients in the other foods. She would have to learn its purpose.

The smell of human was strong, but that much she had expected. This place was human territory, and to be avoided. She continued to listen, straining to filter through the ordinary night sounds, and then she heard them. It was a faint sound of a voice, most certainly one of the men who had captured her before. Then it was answered by the other familiar voice. They were well away from her, walking further with each step towards the other side of the castle. A human wouldn't have been able to hear them at all.

Still, the scent of human reeked, and was mixed with something else, a strong and unpleasant smell. Suddenly she spun round just as the sound she thought was her own breathing changed rhythm and identified itself as coming from another being all too close behind her.

'Demon!' shouted the man, as he leaped towards her and pinned her against the wall with his hands tightly gripping her upper arms. The ferocity of the attack panicked her and the slam against the wall knocked enough air from her lungs to elicit a squeal from her throat. Then her defensive instincts simultaneously called the glamour to her and raised her right leg to kick the attacker squarely between the legs.

'Witch!' he shouted, and from his crouched position as he held his injured parts, his arms swung in a spin that brought the back of his hand across her face in a blow that knocked her off her feet. She crumpled into a heap, fighting for consciousness and for the power to keep the glamour in place.

'Don't try your sorceress disguises with me demon witch, I've seen you for what you are,' the man growled. In that moment two things happened simultaneously. Talla felt her eyes narrow, knowing that even the glamour could not disguise the milky white iris and slightly elongated pupils, and her lips pulled back from her sharp teeth in the way that could mean only the hunt. This man was meat. As her awareness accepted the change, another creature flew out of the darkness, striking the man from the side at a speed she wouldn't have thought possible from a land dweller.

At first she had thought it was a large wolf, black and fierce. She was sure that she had heard a very different sort of growl in the ethereal air that had settled on the scene from that which any human was capable of issuing. But all at once it was speaking to the man, fierce in anger but certainly human.

'Damn it man, what are you doing? You don't strike a woman within stones throw of my own castle!'

Talla recognised him at the same moment that the other man did.

'I'm sorry sir, but don't be fooled by her sorceries, it ain't no woman! Count Anton, sir, it's a demon, I swear it!' The man grovelled on the ground where the blow to the side of his body had toppled him.

Count Anton's demeanour changed so suddenly that for a moment, Talla wasn't sure if he was the same man. A sly smile pulled at the corners of his mouth as he transformed into the very picture of placation.

'Of course, you told me of them before.' He flicked a glance and a wink at Talla as his smooth, even voice drew the trust of the injured man in, artfully in a way that she couldn't help but admire so much that she stayed completely still, watching the scene with fascination.

'I knew you'd see reason sir,' the man babbled on, 'they say you know how to defeat demons and all sorts.'

'Of course, I'll take care of everything.' The Count moved towards the man, taking something from his pocket that gleamed in the faint light of morning. Talla thought it looked like a metal bottle of some sort, what the humans in the kitchens had called a flask. 'Here, you need a drink after taking on a demon alone, I'll take care of everything now. You can relax, rest a while.' He supported the man with one arm while putting the flask to his lips.

'Thank you sir.' The man gulped greedily from the flask. 'I knew I could…count...on…' He dropped from mid-word into a deep, drugged sleep.

Talla's eyes widened. Where had Count Anton obtained mushroom potion? Surely nothing else could have worked so quickly.

Count Anton laid the man carefully on the ground and turned his attention to Talla, looking directly into her eyes and speaking to her in her own language.

'Do not be afraid, I am a friend of your people. A friend of Haghuf.' He did not recognise her, which almost surprised her. She had lurked in the shadows during his visits and observed him so often that it seemed odd to her that he wouldn't recall her at least by familiar sense, but she was particularly adept at the art of all forms of concealment in her own realms. Her obvious lapses in the surface world told her that she would have to learn to move within different shadows if she intended to return here.

'I know you Count Anton,' she answered. 'I am of Haghuf's clan.' It was the closest word she could use to describe her connection to Krapneerg and Haghuf, that the human would understand.

'I have been looking for you, I know what happened in Nodgnirraf. You dropped this.' He pulled the dragon statue from his pocket, extending it to her. This amazed her, as she had forgotten the ornament again. She remembered now, she had put it down when she had disrobed to swim among the *Kol'ksu* in the river, to seek food and advice. In her hurry to move on, the thing had slipped her mind. It was, after all, only an object. She had only picked it up in the first place because she had thought it pretty.

'Keep it,' she said, 'and think of me when you look at it.' It was only then that she noticed that the dragon's eyes, although a different colour, were much like her own. The Count looked at the statue as if he were seeing it for the first time. Such baubles were of course meaningless to goblins, they lived a totally non-materialistic life that could take and leave such things with no thought of ownership.

'What is your name?' he asked.

'I am Talla.' she stood up now, brushing herself off and regaining her dignity.

'Talla,' he repeated, 'very pretty.' She smiled at the compliment, suddenly realising that she had entirely forgotten the glamour. He was seeing her as she was, green and alien to him, yet he was responding as if he were speaking to a woman of his own kind. She looked directly into his colourful starburst eyes, seeing them more closely now than she ever had before. He was a pretty one indeed and she found her fanciful attraction to him was becoming a very real desire, yet one that she dared not reveal in so delicate a situation.

'I came here to seek you out, Count Anton.' She dropped her eyes now, a little embarrassed to admit her ignorance. 'They say you know the ways to our world, and I have not the knowledge of the surface world to recognise the openings even if I were standing next to one.'

Anton's smiled, almost laughing at the admission.

'Actually, you nearly are. Come.' He gestured for her to follow, then led her just a few steps down and around the outcrop where they had stood. There, as clearly as could be, was a passage to the goblin realms.

'I had anticipated that you might come to me when I found the statue by the river. As far as I know, goblins don't swim.' Talla had to pull the cloak close around her face to conceal her own smile at his words. Apparently he did not realise how many times he had bathed in the river among the water goblins. She knew for a fact that more than once, he had been within arms reach of the *Kol'ksu*. They would not molest him, but he was closely watched. Another human might well have disappeared within the river currents, leaving no trace.

'The signs are gone now,' he continued, 'I think your people have taken them because I told Haghuf how the magicians recognise the ways. This one is very familiar to me, as it is so near my own castle. This is the way to Lirrewot.'

Suddenly she gripped his arm and spoke very seriously.

'You must not come through this passage, Count Anton. There has always been anti-human sentiment among the goblins there. Now may be a bad time.'

'I understand.' Again, his eyes met hers as he placed his hand gently over hers. 'I will come through Krapneerg in a few days. Tell Haghuf.' Her eyes drew him in, hypnotically. Something in her touch disturbed him. It took all of his self control to pull away from her, touching her fingertips gently as their hands slid slowly apart.

'Speak well of me, Talla. Tell Haghuf I will come very soon.'

'I will tell of your deeds at Storytelling in Lirrewot,' she said seriously. They must all know that you are goblin-friend.'

The Count leant forward to bestow a chaste kiss on her cheek in farewell. She allowed it freely, taking note of the proximity of the castle to the cavern opening as she offered the side of her face for the touch of his lips. She would return to see him again. She turned then, and scurried back into her own world.

Anton turned reluctantly from the passage. Automatically, he touched the place on his arm where she had gripped him. She was stronger than any human woman, but that in itself was not surprising. What bothered him was that one spot on his arm hurt a bit, as if it were bruised. He rolled his sleeves up and found a perfectly round spot that looked as if a tentacle had been sucking hard on it. Once again, his face broke into a self-satisfied smirk. He had worked out one of the goblin puzzles.

He walked back to where he had left the unconscious man. He would have to remember to send someone after him this time. Unfortunately, there was no other option, he would have to be detained away from the others.

Distractedly, he took the dragon statue from his pocket once again, looking closely at the eyes. A little white iridescent paint, and they would look much like hers. He contemplated once again the total detachment from material objects that was normal life among the goblins. Then, as he glanced again at the drugged man, he remembered the urgency. He had to get back to the banquet hall as quickly as possible. He pocketed the ornament again and broke immediately into a run.

There was no one left awake by now to observe his passing. The few guards he kept were more for formality than anything else. It kept them employed and provided back-up if there might someday be need of it. The Count slowed a bit as he approached the banquet hall, regaining his breath so that he could make a dignified entrance. He swooped through the door with his usual aplomb, grinning widely at the hungover men who appeared as though they were just waking up.

'Welcome back to the world of the living gentlemen, lovely to see you up and about.' His voice boomed through their befuddled minds, familiar and yet foreign in their confusion at waking in completely unexpected circumstances. Some looked around uncomfortably, while others fought the fog of semi-consciousness for some anchor of normality to convince themselves that they weren't lost in some unknown dream world. The stewards suppressed their own smiles as they busied themselves clearing up the liqueur goblets and empty plates that would not be needed any further. One man overcame his obvious embarrassment at the realisation that he was within the Count's castle and managed to speak.

'Please sir, can you tell us how we came to be here?' he asked. The Count immediately seized the opportunity to test how well the memory-loss qualities of the potion had done their work.

'You don't remember?' He looked about the room, making eye contact with as many of the men as possible. 'Do any of you remember the banquet?' Several men shook their heads, while others only tried to look as insignificant as possible. The man who had spoken provided an answer.

'I remember setting out to find a missing man from our clan, and everyone getting all excited about the hunt…and then waking up here. That's all.' The Count laughed with amusement and looked around for any sign of anyone showing more clarity. He spotted Latham among the crowd. He was a big man and the potion might not have affected him as much as some of the others.

'What about you Latham,' he called above the heads of the confused men. Calling him by name would reinforce the impression of unremembered events that Anton could supply as he saw fit. 'Do you remember anything about yesterday or last night?'

Latham started at the sound of his name, surprised that the Count would know it.

'Not much sir,' he answered after a moment, 'only settin' out to find 'im and then some evil dreams…dreams of demons and monsters and the like.'

'I dreamed of a beautiful maiden,' exclaimed Ranalf from beside Latham. 'She was the most incredible thing I ever saw, and such eyes!'

'You best get yerself married Ranalf. Soon,' said Latham, drawing laughter from some of the other men who were beginning to relax a little and exchange snippets of similar 'dreams'.

'Count Anton, sir,' called Ranalf above the growing din after a few minutes. 'Can you tell us what happened here? And how we came to be here in the first place?' The Count had been enjoying the stories of dreams far too much, as well as listening carefully for any hint of potential trouble. The deception seemed to have worked perfectly.

'Your friend came to me about...a personal matter,' he began to explain, knowing that they would remember the argument with his wife that had caused the man to storm out of his home a full day before. 'As it happened, I was entertaining and so invited him in to share the festivities with various nobles, whom I expect are still sleeping peacefully.'

At the mention of nobles, some of the men began to look nervous again.

'Then your trail brought all of you here as well, it's as simple as that, and here you are!' Anton gestured around the room, taking in the men as well as the remnants of the imaginary banquet with the sweep of his arms.

'Sir,' began another man nervously. 'Are you sayin' we was here with nobility, getting drunk?!' This time Anton laughed heartily.

'My good man, you were here among drunken nobles, who probably mistook you for angels or wenches for all I know. This liqueur is deadly stuff, and bad for the memory as well, as you can see. They've probably forgotten you were ever here.'

The finality of the words put an end to their discomfort. At least it did until someone mentioned their wives and Anton informed them that they had been away for an entire day and night. That put them into action, and soon Count Anton had arranged to have some of the more anxious of them transported by his own carriage, with the idea that they would let the other families know that their men were well and on their way home. The carriage would make several more trips, taking them all back as it would be a long walk otherwise. Breakfast was being provided in the meantime for those who waited long enough. Anton breathed a sigh of relief when all was arranged so that the men would not leave the banquet hall until they were taken home. He then took Dani aside.

'What have we done with the other one?' Anton's tone had turned serious so quickly that the steward blinked a moment as he remembered whom the Count meant.

'Oh him,' he remembered at last. 'Jerak left him with that young kitchen wench that old Peg complains about so much. He was drooling over her so he reckoned he didn't need to worry about him wandering back here, but he told her to keep him entertained anyway.'

'Good,' Anton replied, looking unconvinced. 'I'd better see to him, he's no doubt forgotten his wife completely and they'll think I'm running a brothel. The last thing I need is people watching my movements right now.'

Distractedly, he left Dani and made for the kitchens. He needed to know what this man remembered, or had been told. Lack of sleep was fuddling his own mind. It had been a long night, after a long day, and there was a danger that he would confuse his stories if he had to keep this up any longer. However, when he did find the man, his attempts to question him proved that he needn't worry. The man was inherently stupid and absent-minded. He didn't remember the argument with his wife, or anything else that had happened. He was astonished to learn that he had come to Count Anton to discuss whether there was any way to free himself of his marriage.

The wench had disappeared as soon as the wife was mentioned, probably to find some obscure corner to skulk in to avoid getting saddled with any kind of work. The Count personally led the man who had started all the trouble to the carriage to be taken home immediately, on the pretext that his wife would be the most worried of them all. In truth, he just wanted the idiot out of his castle.

As he climbed the stairs to his private bedchamber, Count Anton couldn't help thinking that there may have been less trouble if the goblins had gone ahead and eaten the dolt. He undressed, thinking of the goblin woman…Talla. He knew she would be alright with her own kind, yet wished there was some way to know for certain that she had got home to Kraapneerg. He lay on his bed, and immediately recognised her scent on the coverlet. As he drifted into sleep, he convinced himself that it was not wolf senses, but imagination and wishful thinking that brought her image and scent to mind in his fatigued state. Some part of his distant mind nagged that there was something awry in thinking of the woman in this way. She was not a human, and not to be desired. Then he slept.

Chapter Seven

Three days passed before Count Anton felt sure that all had settled down sufficiently that he could risk a visit to Haghuf. Rumour of the people at Nodgnirraf came to him from his own sources. Their wives had been at first frantic for their husbands' safety, then livid that they had stayed away for so long. This was followed by a gamut of jealousy and forgiveness when they learned that they had been entertained by the Count himself. Some of them contrived excuses to try to keep their husbands under the eye of the Count in the hope of receiving invitations to future festivities at the castle. Ranalf, one of the few single young men of the clan, was recruited to run messages between Nodgnirraf and the castle.

Count Anton was amused by the intrigues and even considered at one point the idea of throwing a party just to invite the commoners and give the poor henpecked men some relief. But then he remembered some of the individuals among them, and abandoned the idea. He just couldn't bring himself to spend an evening among bigoted, ignorant men and a roomful of shrewish women, some of whom would no doubt begin throwing their teenage daughters into his path in the hope of a beneficial marriage.

The only really interesting man among them was the young man, Ranalf. His occasional visits to bring the various trumped-up excuses for communication with Nodgnirraf provided a bit of intelligent company and a good game of chess. Count Anton felt that the lad showed potential. It might even be worth considering whether the other magicians would take an interest in him. Those who lived in the castle certainly noticed his quick mind and common sense. It wasn't long before Ranalf admitted to them that he had allowed himself to be used as a pawn for the village wives to send their messages because he actually enjoyed the respite in better company.

It was just after the first of these visits that Anton decided it was safe to visit Haghuf again, at least in the between level. Whether the goblins in the deeper places would welcome him was another matter. Ranalf had appeared, displaying his familiar mixture of brash façade mixed with an endearing shy approach, and had been brought into the presence of the Count. His news of the village was invaluable, much more than he could possibly know. So Anton invited him to a game of chess, beat him mercilessly, and enjoyed a pleasant evening drinking and gossiping with the lad. He then sent him on his way with messages for his people and invited him to come back freely when the women plotted another approach.

The following day, the Count travelled to Krapneerg. The sign was gone, as were others he had observed throughout the city. He knew many of the places well though and this one most of all. He wandered into the opening, listening for any sign of movement. There was none. This in itself was not unusual. The goblins were often occupied in the deeper levels. He listened carefully, reaching for the thrum of the earth. He felt it rise throughout his being, steady as a heartbeat, but not augmented by the stomping of feet or the music of the Dance. The world of the goblins was very quiet indeed.

Anton followed the familiar paths down to the betweener levels, keeping both eyes and ears open for any sign of movement. The place seemed to be completely deserted. But of course in the realms of the goblins things were not always as they seemed. Despite the familiarity of the passages, he began to feel a little nervous. He would have been happier to have been accompanied by Haghuf on his first visit to this world since the troubles of the other day. Haghuf himself made no secret of the fact that he had no use for humans and teased Anton that he wasn't sure why he tolerated his company. Anton knew why of course, but he couldn't be sure that it was enough to maintain their friendship through a war between the species.

He crept quietly, still listening as hard as he could as he approached the narrow passage that would take him to the deeper levels. He was startled by a sudden clattering of rocks behind him. Turning instinctively into a defensive position, he just caught the sight of a ginger tail disappearing behind a pillar. Letting out the breath he hadn't realised he was holding, he crept around the other side of the pillar to get a better look at the small animal before reaching for it. As he had surmised from the quick glance, it was only a cat. The animal looked as though it intended to back away, yet when Anton extended his hand it relaxed and came forward and brushed itself under his hand to be stroked. He picked it up, grateful to have an ordinary living thing appear in order to break the tense silence of the apparently deserted cavern.

He walked back to the passage, but released the cat before stepping through the opening. As he put the creature down, the words echoed in his mind, '*Whatever comes to us.*' Immediately he tried to shoo it further away from the passage, but it slipped past him and scurried through the opening. Anton tried to follow, but the cat ran too fast and disappeared into one of the labyrinthine corridors that branched off from the initial passage. He had no choice but to give it up for lost.

He followed the familiar path, still looking for any sign of goblin. He knew that his scent would travel quickly through the dank atmosphere. Haghuf had complained about man-stink often enough. He expected that his friend would come to meet him before he reached unfamiliar paths. That was what usually occurred. The other possibilities were pushed down in his consciousness, not to be examined now that he was here. Turning back was not an option. Goblins were too prone to make sport of frightened humans and he was suddenly not so sure of his immunity.

He reached a fairly open cavern, one which Haghuf had often met him in. He knew the way to Haghuf's accustomed sleeping place from here but thought it might be rude to go that far. He had just about made up his mind to sit and wait when he heard a scuffling behind him. He turned, saw nothing, then turned back and found himself nose to nose with a goblin. It wasn't Haghuf.

Neither spoke for a moment, it was impossible to read the goblin's mood. Then, as his heart slowed a bit, Anton realised that he had seen this goblin before. He had even spoken with him more than once.

'What news, Leap?' said Anton. His eyes deliberately traced a path up the wall, across the ceiling, and down behind him where he had heard the scuffling. He turned back and smirked at Leap. A mischievous smile spread across the goblin's face. They both knew that Count Anton had worked out how the goblin had walked across the ceiling and popped up in front of him so suddenly, though neither referred to it.

'Much is afoot, Count Anton,' the Goblin replied. Talla has returned of late, spreading the story of your rescue of her from one enclave to another. She is at Storytelling now, regaling us with your prowess in battle once again.' The goblin glanced behind and to either side of the Count. 'Where is Haghuf?'

Anton's smile disappeared.

'I had thought to find him here,' he answered. 'I promised to visit him as soon as possible when I left him at Nacibrab.'

Leap looked thoughtful for a moment.

'Nacibrab...,' he said absently, and then to Anton, 'you saw him enter the passage?'

'Yes, I waited until he was safely inside before I went to deal with the humans.' Count Anton often spoke of the humans as if he were referring to another species than his own. Leap nodded, accepting the confirmation.'

'Haghuf would have me welcome you in his absence. Will you join us at Storytelling?'

Anton had to conceal his excitement at this invitation, as well as the trepidation. Haghuf had never invited him to attend Storytelling, although he had explained its nature. He had the impression that it was too much a part of the inner culture of the goblins, or that Haghuf would not want him to hear some of the tales. Despite their close friendship and the information they shared between them, both were aware that the other kept a few secrets still.

'I would be most honoured,' Anton replied formally, bowing slightly to Leap. He was not sure if the formality was quite appropriate, but the goblin turned and led him down a passage he had not travelled through before. In fact, despite many visits, he had not even noticed the entrance to it before. Some of the ways of the goblins appeared to the casual eye as another wall, yet held openings to the most secret places. He hoped that Haghuf was alright and that he would not be angry. The other goblin seemed to be satisfied as soon as he learned that Haghuf had gone safely underground. It seemed that the only danger they perceived was that presented by humans. Accidents and natural disasters just didn't seem to occur to them.

Anton was led to an expansive cavern that was filled with far more goblins than he realised actually lived in all of Krapneerg. It was no wonder that the other levels seemed so deserted, they had all gone to Storytelling. From what Haghuf had told him of Storytelling, it should have been no surprise that it was so well attended. It was more than an entertainment, but a central news gathering where goblins learned the histories and science of their kind as well as hearing stories of current events. Legends and tales that they made up themselves would be interspersed randomly with the sort of information that human children would learn in schools and even with lessons in the use of magic for the young ones.

There were noticeably few of these. Anton could not see the front of the crowd clearly, but apart from two youngsters who seemed to jump up and clap at all of the exciting parts of the story that was being told, it appeared that the room was filled with adult goblins. The actual age range was impossible for him to determine. Younger adult goblins, like Leap whom he had heard described as such by Haghuf on a previous visit, looked much the same as the older ones like Haghuf himself.

A few heads turned as they entered the room from the back. Anton imagined that he saw some disapproving expressions and a couple of exaggerated sniffs from goblins he didn't recognise, but they quickly turned their attention back to Talla, who was at the front of the room telling the story of his rescue of her. The sight of her thrilled him in an odd way, one which he found a little disconcerting. Another goblin appeared from beside them, pushing roughly made bowls of food into their hands. Leap motioned for him to follow to a vacant place where they could sit and listen. Talla was just finishing her tale, but she stopped for just a heartbeat and turned suddenly in his direction before speaking the last few phrases, as if they were for him alone.

'And the goblin maiden saw beauty in the face of the human as he held her eyes with the magic of his own.' She spoke the words slowly and seductively, sending them into the soul of every listener as if he were there to witness the event. She was an accomplished storyteller.

'He gave her a kiss and with an unspoken promise that they would meet again, she descended safely back to her own realms, to meet him only in dreams until such time as she could return.'

There was a hand gesture which appeared to be a signal that the tale was finished. The goblins shouted and stamped their feet to show their approval. Anton joined in, taking his cues from those around him, although he had heard only the last few words. He wondered how much of it had been a fanciful version and whether she knew of the dreams he had been having of her since that night.

She sat somewhere in the front and another goblin came forward and started telling a story about the last Turning. Anton examined the food he had been given. His natural inclination was to assess its nature carefully before putting anything into his mouth. He felt some conflict between his curiosity about goblin fare and his reluctance to find himself with a mouthful of cat...or worse...which made him cautious. There were fresh vegetables which surprised him as they couldn't have been grown underground. He started munching on a carrot so that he would not seem impolite while he tried to determine the nature of the meat. There was no bread or other baked goods which was unsurprising. It appeared to be a very healthy combination of meat, vegetables, and some sort of nuts or grain ground up and cooked into a porridge which was at the bottom of the bowl. Anton glanced at Leap and saw that he had nearly finished his own meal and was using two fingers to bring the porridge to his mouth like a spoon.

He imitated the motions as best he could, but could not help taking a careful sniff of the meat. It smelled and looked like roast pork but he could not be sure. He had heard that human flesh had a similar smell and texture. Suddenly a large flat hand descended heavily on his shoulder and a voice was whispering in his ear.

'It's swine, nobody you know.' He turned and saw an unfamiliar goblin grinning at him, enjoying his discomfiture. Anton smiled back, and took a bite. He hoped the goblin was telling the truth. At least he knew he was safe from anything worse than this good natured teasing, as Leap had invited him to the Storytelling and therefore he was *guest*. Just as he was about to turn around and give his attention to the story being told, something else caught his eye, a patch of ginger fur at the back of the room. The cat had wandered right into the one place that was packed with goblins.

There was nothing he would be able to do to rescue it now. Its scent drew several pairs of eyes around to look straight at it. He tried willing the creature to run for its life, but the cat caught sight of him and stupidly started running directly towards him instead. The cat leaped at him and he raised his hands to catch it, hoping that the goblins would extend guest immunity to it when they saw that it had befriended him. But the cat didn't land in Anton's arms. Instead, it settled squarely on the shoulder of the goblin who had spoken to him. Anton guessed that his own expression must have been one of shock and horror judging from the laughter of several of the goblins who were near enough to witness the little drama playing out. The goblin next to him didn't react to the cat, but turned to Anton, grinning at him once again.

'This is *Lucky*. We don't eat him either.' The goblin reached to stroke the cat on his shoulder as he spoke. From behind him, another goblin leaned forward and spoke.

'That's why we call him *Lucky*!' He said through his laughter. All of them seemed to be amusing themselves by watching his obvious concern for the little cat.

Count Anton caught on that in fact the cat was a pet of sorts. It was probably a wild one, but it was obviously well known to the goblins and came and went unmolested. He joined in the laughter at his own expense. Then they all quieted again to listen to the speaker at the front of the cavern. He seemed to be giving a lesson in history with his tale, possibly directed mostly at the younger goblins in the front.

'It was before the time of the second Turning that the magic books were placed between the paws of the great beast.'

A child goblin interrupted from the front of the crowd.

'What exactly is a Turning?' He called loudly to the storyteller.

'Just as it says,' explained the speaker, 'Each time the humans bring such pollution and damage to the earth that it seems as though the planet must die of it,'

Anton thought he detected a subtle glance in his direction.

'The planet itself turns over, changing its field of force so that the land changes. Mountains fall and ocean beds rise to become new mountains and the surface is devastated. Most of the humans die, although a few are always left to start the cycle again.

'There have been many Turnings, we don't know how many. That is why we count them backwards. The last Turning was the most recent. The second Turning came before that, and so on throughout all of time.'

The storyteller then seemed to change direction from his intended tale, speaking of the legends of which Anton and Haghuf had often shared knowledge and sources of information. The goblin's tone altered, seeming to take on an ethereal quality as he spoke reverently of the ancient tale.

'In legend, the Ancestors lived mostly on the surface. Some dug into the ground to mine metals and stones of value and other substances. But even they returned to the surface when the light faded, where they made their homes. Some of them studied the sky and the stars and learned many things about the movements of planets. Unfortunately, they were steadfastly naïve about the movement of their own.

They saw the signs, they read the legends that came before. The scientists understood the polarity of a magnetic world. Evidence was in plenty that the planet had shifted before, yet still they were unprepared when it happened again. Yes, the earth itself shifted poles, as it had done many times before, and many of the ancestors died in calamities too horrible to describe. Yet as always in the history of the world, some survived.

Most of the survivors were just in the right place at the time. Those few who saw the shift coming and prepared shelters had no better or worse chance than the others. When the ground itself swallows up your protective box and rearranges the ocean over it, you still don't survive. But the earth is constant in its patterns.

Enough land always stays above the surface, or resurfaces, to leave room for the living creatures to thrive once more. In the process of change, new caverns are formed. Some connect with the surface, some do not.

After the second Turning, some of the ancestors found themselves deep within the planet. There were no known paths to the surface. Yet there was air to breathe, and there was water that was probably more pure than any they had drunk in their chemical infested lives on the surface. The earth has a way of cleansing the water before it reaches the underground streams. Those who lived near the streams learned that they were places of power and once they had managed to work out their basic survival and to recognise their freedom to live as they would, they began to develop their magic.

Others among the ancestors did find paths to the surface. Not at first of course. The ways were difficult. Those who were able to reach the surface easily did so and threw their lot in with the other surface dwellers. But those who became like us and then found their way above many generations later found that they had changed, as had the surface dwellers. They were no longer the same race, though still the same species. We know this kinship was preserved between the races because there were some who bred with the surface dwellers, coming to their women at night. They made legends of the visitations and developed superstitions about us all, so that it became dangerous to go to the surface anymore. They even killed some of the infants, calling them 'changelings' and imagining that the ancestors had stolen their own young. And sometimes, they did.

Still, the ancestors had become adventurous and they learned to dig tunnels. They mined metals like the elder ancestors had once done. Contact with the surface dwellers became too dangerous and slowly, slowly they learned to keep hidden and to guard the ways. Eventually, those who lived 'between' broke through a barrier to the deepest realms where our kind had survived, and we found that our two cultures were very different, almost as much as our physical attributes.

You see, much time had passed as all of this happened. The deep dwellers did not record time, but we worked out that it must have been thousands of changes of the earth's seasons while we lived deep within where there are no seasons. Where there is little light save that which reflects from the glassy surface of a molten pool of rock or the foam of the underground streams. Our eyes were too sensitive to the light to go very close to the surface, but slowly, over many generations and cross-breeding with the 'betweeners', two races became one and the betweeners of the second Turning became deep dwellers themselves.

Their cultures mixed well despite their differences, as did their magic. The dwellers of the deep had learned the Dance from the rhythm of the earth itself and danced to celebrate life at every turn. The betweeners had fashioned musical instruments from stone as well as collecting some from those on the surface and imitating their designs. So although they too knew the Dance it had a different character, one that was lighter and held a sense of freedom.

And so the combined races of goblin left the surface more and more to the humans who would eventually drive the planet again to turn with their destructive ways. The goblins meanwhile developed skills to shape the earth and some became diggers, while others developed other abilities to contribute to mutual survival. It was those who practised the art of finding water to drink who eventually uncovered the deep dwellers from an earlier time, perhaps several Turnings before, who had mastered the ways of the underground streams and pools. They had developed the skill of prophecy, but it was some time and many died before we were able to communicate with the *Kol*…'

'Enough!' boomed the voice from behind, echoing the command throughout the cavern walls. The speaker had frozen in mid-word, and all eyes turned around to the source of the interruption. Anton turned as well, recognising despite the unfamiliar tone the voice of Haghuf. He felt a mixture of trepidation and relief. His friend was safe, but he was clearly not pleased with the scene before him. Haghuf walked slowly through the sitting crowd to Anton's side. He spoke slowly and deliberately, in the way he did when choosing his words carefully.

'I think this tale may be long for the ears of our *guest*.'

Anton admired the diplomacy. It was clear that the tale was taking a direction that was giving him more information than he was meant to hear, yet the sacred tradition of *guest* would be preserved through the art of phrasing the objection as a consideration for his own benefit. Had such a technique been used by a human, he would have pleaded his interest and encouraged the tale to go on. But there was something very final in the way that Haghuf had expressed himself beyond the words. A line had been drawn. Count Anton had the wisdom not to challenge it.

'Count Anton,' continued Haghuf directly to the guest, his demeanor changing quickly to that of an indulgent host. 'Perhaps you would like to tell a story of your own people, and how you came to be a *respected one* among them.'

The goblins immediately stamped and shouted, encouraging Anton to tell a story. He chuckled to himself, as he did indeed have a story of his family inheritance that Haghuf had never heard. One which he expected would be amusing to the goblins with their love of ridiculing human society and its false hierarchy. He was about to assent when he noticed the marks on Haghuf's shoulder. The wounds were not dangerously deep, but they looked decidedly like bite marks from something with goblin-sharp teeth. And there were a lot of them. The Count's face dropped, suddenly full of concern. The subtle shake of Haghuf's head told him that it wasn't something to speak of while others might hear.

'Perhaps another time,' Anton called loudly to the assembled listeners. 'But now I must speak with Haghuf, and then return to the surface. I thank you for your hospitality.' He bowed to them all and retreated to the passage behind them, pulling Haghuf along with him by the uninjured arm.

Haghuf allowed the familiarity just long enough to get out of the immediate hearing of the group, then pulled away. He once again looked angry.

'How came you to be here?' Haghuf demanded.

'I invited him,' said Leap's voice from behind him. Anton and Haghuf both turned to regard Leap. 'I'm sorry Haghuf, I was only welcoming him in your absence.'

Haghuf opened his mouth to reply, but just then Talla appeared in the passage.

'Haghuf, I would speak with you.' Her eyes focused on Haghuf, taking no notice of Anton. There was something in them, some meaning that passed between one goblin and another that the Count could not fathom. He felt disappointment that she did not look at him, yet could see that some matter of importance to her required

Haghuf's attention. Haghuf looked from one to the other of them. After a moment he settled on a solution.

'Leap, take Count Anton to the library. I will follow soon.' Haghuf turned, gently taking Talla's hand, and led her through another passage. She turned just before they disappeared, giving Anton the full benefit of her smile as her eyes met his, then she was gone. In that moment, he could not imagine why goblins were considered ugly by the humans. Although most of them were not to his taste, in fact the finely chiselled features and pointed ears, large eyes and full lips suited some of them very well indeed.

'Come,' said Leap, motioning for Anton to follow him down yet another passage, 'it's this way.' Anton turned obediently and followed the goblin. There was nothing else he could do.

Haghuf led Talla well away from other ears before stopping to listen to her questions. He had already guessed what news she would have from him. At last a suitable spot was found and he sat on a rock and waited patiently. She made herself comfortable before she looked into the eyes of the other goblin and asked what she wished to know.

'It is said that you have been to Nacibrab.' It was more a statement than a question, but Haghuf nodded his confirmation. She hesitated a moment, choosing the order of her questions carefully.

'You sought prophecy?'

Haghuf closed his eyes and sighed. There was no doubt now that his guess about the direction of her questioning had been correct. He nodded again.

'What did she tell you?' asked Talla, unrelenting. This at least, Haghuf could answer without hesitation.

'War comes. In this generation and the next. The details are couched in allegory as always, but that much is clear. I have written her words. I may well consult Count Anton as to their meaning, though I have a strong aversion to revealing their source. Magician or no, he is still a human.'

This time it was Talla who nodded, understanding the customs that were meant to protect their kind. Whatever fascination she might develop for the beauty of a human, this loyalty must always come first. Again she hesitated, and Haghuf braced himself for the question he knew must come next.

'How does my mother?' she asked at last. Her eyes spoke of the longing that never left her, of a mother she couldn't know as she wished.

'Le-ina fares well,' Haghuf replied cautiously. 'But I think her arms are still empty.' He remembered the *Kol'ksu* holding the doomed infant so lovingly, as if to mother it herself, before she took it to the others for the feed.

It was a difficult subject between himself and Talla, an unheard-of situation. A mother would never fail to nurture her own young among their kind, unless it was unviable and had to be released to death. But Le-ina's child had been born without scales and without gills. Rumour had it that she had been seeded by Haghuf's predecessor, but neither Le-ina or old Anknor ever confirmed or denied the whispers.

Talla had been a healthy infant, and a female. She could not breathe in water or survive among her mother's people, yet as a land dwelling goblin she was a healthy specimen and could not be given to death as a sickling. In the end she had to be turned over to a bereaved mother for nurturing and Le-ina had never had the luxury of grieving for her lost child. Instead she had lived with the knowledge that her child yet lived among strangers.

Worse, the available mother was a betweener. Talla would not learn the old ways of the deep dwellers unless yet another would take responsibility for some of her teaching and that too was unheard of. It was unlikely that the substitute mother would agree.

But as she grew, Talla developed her own curiosity and because of the Storytelling, she knew of her origins. She had been told never to seek out her mother because the pain would torture them both, yet she had been looked after by the others of her mother's people, the *Kol'ksu*. They came to her in places of water, always, and helped to guide her in the ways that they were able. It was they who had taught her to listen to the wisdom of Haghuf.

There was nothing more he could tell her now. She took leave of him, thanking him, and sought out her own places of solitude. She was in no mood to try to speak with the human Count. He was waiting for Haghuf anyway. She knew where to find him when she was ready.

Haghuf regretted that although he could feel some of her pain, there was little he could do to erase it. He wondered at such times if the separation caused more cruelty than it prevented. There had been no precedent and it was the *Kol'ksu* themselves who recommended it when the decision had been made.

Clearing his mind of the unsolveable problem, he took the path towards the library.

Chapter Eight

Count Anton was reading a sheet of parchment when Haghuf entered the library.

'Humph.' Haghuf snorted. 'I might have known you would waste no time finding that.'

'It was lying out with the ink hardly dry, I couldn't have missed it,' replied Anton absently. 'Where did you get this?'

'Doesn't matter.' Haghuf's tone had that note of finality that told Anton that he would get no information about the source of the words, at least not at the moment.

'Where did you get those injuries on your shoulder?' Anton looked at the marks on Haghuf with concern, speculating that some sort of altercation with other goblins might have caused them. They were about the right size to be goblin tooth-marks and there were a lot of them.

'That doesn't matter either,' Haghuf replied flatly.

Anton wasn't one to accept Haghuf's uninformative mood easily. He might have apologised again for taking advantage of the invitation from Leap, yet it would have seemed impolite to refuse at the time. Haghuf would have done the same in his place. In fact, Haghuf had a special talent for gathering information which Anton admired. It was one of the things that earned him the respect of the other goblins. They sought his wisdom in situations of crisis because he usually had answers, not because of any official position. Anton earned a similar respect in the human world, yet his position as a leader among them held a certain responsibility to obtain solutions to problems even when he had none. There were times when he envied Haghuf the freedom his society allowed him.

'I have been receiving frequent messages from the people of Nodgnirraf, usually about trivial matters.' Count Anton tried coaxing a more talkative mood by ignoring Haghuf's grumpiness and using his natural charm. The goblin often responded well to the smooth tone of his voice that Anton used for diplomatic conversations, even though he knew the trick.

'Some of them have complained that ground dwelling rodents have been digging in and taking vegetables.' Anton stole a glance at Haghuf, just catching the hint of a smile that played at the corner of his mouth. Anton held the parchment up and read aloud the first few lines of the prophecy.

'The time is upon us when much that has been hidden will be revealed and human and goblin together will decide the fate of both races. You know more than any how closely entwined they are and how delicate the balance lies between them when all of the truth shall be known.' Anton's penetrating eyes caught Haghuf's like those of a snake about to swallow its prey.

'So, these words were spoken to you by someone with the gift of prophecy?'

Haghuf didn't answer. He turned his back to Anton and allowed him to read on.

'If ignorance is chosen, all will die. The races will pass from the earth and the lands will be ruled only by the small creatures that survive until another Turning shall bring renewed evolution for sentient species.' Anton stopped a moment. 'Haghuf, where do you get parchment?'

'We make it of course,' was the quick answer. 'Surely the fate of the planet hardly depends on our use of simple crafts.'

'Parchment making is a difficult skill and the flax it is made from is hardly going to grow underground.' When he didn't receive an answer, Anton pressed on. His words became more impassioned as he spoke. 'The goblins could hardly dig enough vegetables from the gardens of Nodgnirraf to feed them regularly at every Storytelling, or whenever else you eat. Haghuf, why do you keep me in the dark about such ordinary things?'

'Would you have me tell a human, even you, every detail of how my people survive?' Haghuf turned now, meeting Anton's vehemence with his own. 'I tell you of our history and you ask for information about our food supplies. Is it so important to know the lives of goblin gardeners or where the tunnels lead to places where we can grow food unmolested by humans? You know there was a time when the deep dwellers had little more than rats, underground creatures and mushrooms to eat. Can you guess how they learned which mushrooms caused hallucinations or death? We are a survivor species. We do not continue that survival by giving every detail of such information to the species that hunts and kills us. Not even to you Anton.' He stopped a moment and took a deep breath, his fingers unconsciously fingering the blue stone amulet that he wore round his neck. Then he repeated, 'Not even to you.'

He took a few steps away from the Count, thinking what he would say next.

'I had Leap bring you to the library because I wanted you to read this.' He indicated the parchment in Anton's hand. 'It doesn't matter where it comes from or what we eat, ignorance of much more important things threatens to destroy both our species. I need your help Anton.'

'My questions are not intellectual curiosity this time, Haghuf.' Anton spoke more calmly now. He could see Haghuf's position and how his own questions would look to him. 'We have a problem, and it concerns all of this.' He waved the parchment to indicate that it had some connection to what he had to say.

'When I used your potion to drug those men, one of them had already left the camp. I think you passed him on the way to summon me.' Haghuf listened attentively to Anton's words. The memory of the human ranting about demons came back to him, although he had completely forgotten about it until now.

'On his own the man would probably be ignored and assumed a madman, but there are humans south of the river. They have a Temple of their own in Tebmal. They have always believed in a more extreme version of the religion of the non-magicians. They believe that the world is destined to have a war between their sterile god and an adversary god of the demons. Usually they stay within their own communities and stir themselves up with a form of Storytelling that speaks of battles and glory far in the future, when their god and his angels will defeat the adversary and all the demons. Like the others, this religion is based entirely on faith and so they need no evidence to back it up. They teach it to their children and propagate a mass delusion that keeps them in a constant state of battle preparation.'

The Count paced a few steps before continuing.

'Perhaps we should have eradicated the beliefs centuries ago, but the religion was based on control of the masses and one of the defences the originators put into it is that the beliefs include one that says they will be persecuted. To attempt to dispose of this religion in any way would look as though their predictions were true and cause rebellion. The magicians have been better able to exist alongside these people by ignoring their religion and allowing them to believe that we are somehow in accordance with them.'

Anton turned, meeting Haghuf's eyes.

'Most of the people of Nodgnirraf have written the man off as a lunatic, so he has gone to the others across the river. He is telling them that he actually saw the demons, that they came from the ground. Their belief is that these evil creatures come from a place called Hell, which is underground, and that they will come from the deep places to eat their children.'

'Humph,' snorted Haghuf. 'Maybe that isn't such a bad idea.'

Anton's mouth twitched, but he controlled the urge to laugh.

'I'm being serious, Haghuf, one of the other men had dreams about your people. Half memories that escaped the potion. He is half ready to believe the stories himself and only stays quiet because the others would think him mad as well. Don't you see Haghuf? They see your people as those demons, because of your pointed ears and other features. If a single goblin is seen above ground, it will be evidence that it isn't all tales. There would be panic, and war. We only escaped it the other day because the man is a drunkard. He was trying to find his way to the river, to go for help. By the time he found it, it was dark and he came to me instead.

'I meant to do something about him, but I forgot. I left him unconscious, passed out on the very grounds of my castle. I've been told that he went back to the clan after that, but when they rejected his story and told him they had all been cavorting at my castle instead, he disappeared. I heard later that he was stirring up the fanatics across the river.'

Haghuf looked thoughtful for a moment, then reached for the parchment in Anton's hand.

He read carefully, 'If the knowledge comes too early, only one species will die, and if too late, perhaps both will perish...one will come between the worlds to convey the secrets wisely...Yet hope remains so long as the one moves with the tides and rhythms that he has learned to know...and it is in trusting to chaos, that the world may be saved.' Anton paused a moment.

'We must trust our instincts, and move as the tide of events takes us,' he said, his eyes still on the words. Then he looked up, his old amused smirk back in place.

Haghuf met his eyes. The bond between them was unchanged by the argument. His own usual humour was returning.

'I would very much like for you to tell me that story sometime, the one that made your eyes glint at the Storytelling.' Haghuf took the parchment from Anton and walked to a shelf, placing it carefully above a row of books. An unmistakable feeling of rhythm had begun to grow in the room. Both Haghuf and Anton were becoming aware of the spell of the Dance. The Storytelling would have finished and the music had begun. 'I will tell others of the danger that grows on the surface. Anton, do you know where your loyalties lie?'

Anton felt the heartbeat of life from the planet and all that existed on it, hypnotic in its steady beat. It drew him into itself and he had no wish to resist.

'I abhor stupidity of any kind.' The Count made a sour face as he answered. 'Ignorance is a choice. This is why I keep apart from the fools of my species.'

'You may have to make difficult choices before another season passes.' Anton read a warning in Haghuf's words. The goblin often predicted trends of things to come, but there was no use in trying to squeeze details from him. He knew from experience that Haghuf would be unable to define his impressions any more clearly. The Dance called to them both. Whatever the future had in store, this was at the essence of both of their beings.

They left the library, saying nothing more of the affairs that threatened this peace of perfect balance and harmony. They met the others in the main cavern to join in the Dance. Anton looked occasionally for any sign of Talla, but could not see her anywhere in the crowd. It was within the rhythm of the Dance that the first warning came. A subtle disharmony of tension grew somewhere in the south. All who danced were aware of it, but only Haghuf and the Count could guess its cause.

In Tebmal, on the surface world among the humans, a very different sort of gathering was taking place. All of the people of the south had been called to a special night meeting in an old, deteriorating building that they only ordinarily used for the Sabbath celebrations, if one could call it celebration. The people sat stiffly on chairs, accustomed to rites of an austere nature where obedience to a higher power was at the centre of their faith. All was created by their invisible god and happened through divine will. Except of course, the demons. Demons were sent to destroy mankind according to their beliefs. They were servants of the adversary who was evil by nature and took pleasure in torture and destruction.

The southern cult was shunned even by other humans, despite the fact that they believed in a similar religion. Their extremist beliefs that any form of pleasure such as dancing, music, eating beyond what was needed for survival, making love to their wives for more than procreation, was considered to be sinful ways. Demonic ways. They would not drink beer or indulge in any form of intoxicant. They wore simple clothing without colour which covered their bodies completely, especially the women, as all things of flesh were considered to be temptations to pleasure and the ways of evil.

Anton was well aware of the cult, but normally left them to themselves and their delusions of rewards in the afterlife as payment for their austerity on earth. He found it facetious that they thought that pleasures considered sinful in earthly life would suddenly be allowed in the afterlife by the sort of god who would demand such denial of all that gave life meaning. He also knew the history of this cult which had grown from the ashes of the last Turning. There had been similar cults which had existed before it. The mind-control techniques of religion had been studied by others of his own kind in the previous age, but too few were aware of them now to prevent the rise of man's greatest enemy to himself.

Brother Paul prepared to address the assembly. As he laced the perfect knot in his tie, he convinced himself that it was not pride that led him to emphasise his own name every time he introduced himself. He was named after their prophet for a purpose. He believed that the reason he was blessed with the name was that he had been chosen by the Divine to lead his people to righteous ways in the Lord. He was convinced that the battle with the Adversary was destined to happen in his lifetime.

He resented the fact that the large temple in the city, named for that same prophet, was run by those who had such limited vision and faith. The northerners were sinful people, given to vanity and pleasures of the flesh that were not right in the eyes of the Lord. It was because of such people that the adversary grew strong in the world, always tempting the younger people with time-wasting amusements when they should be studying The Book.

A part of him liked to believe that he was in some way descended from that first Paul, although he knew that such a holy man would never defile himself by touching the filthy flesh of a woman. It was a spiritual inheritance of a sort, one that did not require sin to propagate the line. His teacher had been of that line as well, though he had not been so blessed as to be actually named for the prophet.

Today's meeting would prove Paul's claim to the name, as well as the truth of the beliefs behind all that their faith had required of them for so many centuries. Keeping the faithful in line had been his life's work. It hadn't always been easy when the temptations of the flesh constantly distracted the young people. Too often they had asked for some proof of the divine and had to be reminded of the penalties for questioning the faith itself.

But now he had the proof. The man Jerrold, from one of the lukewarm northern clans who indulged in all manner of fleshly pleasures, had come to him to witness that the actual demons of Hell had been seen. Not just by him, but by many of his clan. Unfortunately the others had lost their memory of the experience through drink and carousing at the castle of the decadent Count Anton.

Paul frowned at the thought of Count Anton. The man was clearly an unbeliever and indulged in all manner of pleasurable pursuits at his whim, yet he held the respect of the people, even the faithful, who went to him at the slightest hint of crisis when they should be praying to God to deliver them. Paul could not help but believe that the hereditary position that the Count held might better have gone to someone like himself, who could lead the people to righteousness and who could show a stronger presence to the leaders of other settlements, rather than coming into their land to indulge in all manner of sin at the legendary parties at the Count's castle.

Paul believed that these foreigners would come to invade someday and that the people should be battle ready. But weapons were scarce, and all of his missives to Count Anton to arm the people in readiness had met only with flippant responses that showed no concern whatsoever for either their physical or spiritual protection. The man had even had the audacity to invite Paul to one of his parties, an obvious attempt to lead him away from his righteous and sober path.

The warm-up speaker was just finishing. Brother Harrison had a knack for getting the faithful excited about salvation in a way that worked well with Paul's technique for putting the fear of the Lord into the flock. The crowd was shouting praises in one moment and then became totally silent as Brother Harrison made the introduction.

'Brothers and sisters, we all glory in the love of the Lord, and his prophecy tells us that we will be called to Him to engage in battle with the adversary. Now I want you to listen carefully to the words of our leader, named for the prophet Paul who warned us of the end times coming when the demons would come from the earth, bringing fire and brimstone to destroy the faithful. That's you and me brothers and sisters. May I introduce the man who will lead us into battle with our enemies and into the glory of the Lord, Brother Paul!'

There was no applause, but only tense, rapt attention as the congregation waited patiently for their leader to walk slowly onto the stage. His eyes looked about the room, hard and cold, one might even say accusing. If there were any among them that did not hang on every word of Brother Paul, they would not dare to let it show under that piercing gaze. The tension mounted, until at last the voice boomed out with the authority of one who had been commissioned by God personally to lead them all to salvation.

'We are all sinners!'

All sat in silence, awaiting the next missive.

'But we can be saved.'

The eyes traversed the room again, seeking out any hidden scrap of sin in the hearts of each individual there. He had them entranced, their full attention focused on his every word.

'My brothers and sisters, we, the faithful, have always known the truth of the prophecies. We have kept ourselves free of the sinful behaviour that is not pleasing to the Lord, unlike our northern neighbours across the river.'

Another pause, for dramatic effect, then he continued, pointing an accusatory finger in the general direction of the river.

'Now the northern sinners are paying the price for their folly, as the demons rise from the ground to fulfil the fortellings of the prophet Paul, as we have always known would happen in our lifetimes! My brothers and sisters, I tell you now that Brother Jerrold has come to join us today,' he slowed his speech, using the technique of speaking one word per heartbeat to emphasise his words, 'and he has seen the demons with his own eyes!'

Gasps came from the audience, their belief in the words of Brother Paul was absolute. An undercurrent of fear began to grow as Paul paused again to let the weight of his words sink in, and then choosing just the right moment, he captured their attention once again.

'But you my brothers and sisters, know that the prophecy says that you will all be saved, and that we will be victorious in the battle to come.' The cold eyes darted here and there, ascertaining that the faces of the faithful showed the reflection of the renewed hope that he bestowed upon them. 'And here, to testify in person, is Brother Jerrold who has done battle with the demons himself, and lived to tell about it. He is here to bring this message to all of you, the faithful, that we can win. We will win. And the Lord will smile on the chosen.'

He gestured to Jerrold to come forward, noting the looks of excitement on the faces of his flock. This would be the one difficult moment, as the man Jerrold was a drunkard and varied in coherence. Paul had done everything in his power to keep him well away from drink and believed that he had been successful as such vile brews were not so readily available south of the river as they were in the north. But the man's hands shook, and his eyes were dull. He appeared to be possessed by demons himself and had actually curled up on the floor and begged for just one drink that very morning. Paul's ability to control the man was limited, although he was sure that a little time among his flock would lead him to compliance.

'Brother Jerrold,' boomed the voice of Brother Paul as he took the man's elbow and guided him up onto the stage, 'tell us, in your own words, how you encountered the demons!'

The man looked frightened, but it added to the image that Paul wanted to portray of a man shaken by a very real ordeal from which he had survived unscathed. Jerrold stuttered a little at first as he spoke.

'W-we were l-looking for a missing man and we found him on a hillside, bewitched by some foul magic, and they were dragging him along like they were taking him somewhere. Then when they saw us they ran away, back into the ground.'

Somehow the story had grown in Jerrold's mind so that the one demon that had actually been seen had become many. Paul's coaxing when he had first related the story seemed to have clarified such details.

'Back into the ground!' Boomed the voice of Paul, repeating the words for emphasis. 'And you and some other men chased them right back to Hell from whence they came!'

Paul thought it best to finish the story for Jerrold, as he was shaking more and spoke too weakly to stir the flock to action as was Paul's intention. Yet he had one more question to ask Jerrold, hoping that he would repeat the same answer that he had given to Paul in their private discussion.

'Tell us, Brother Jerrold, what did these demons look like?'

Again Jerrold's eyes darted from face to face, expecting disbelief as he recounted the same description which had earned him only ridicule from his own clan. He spoke slowly, unsurely.

'They were green, sort of a glowing light green, and they had pointed ears. They had big yellow eyes that reflected the light, slanted like cats eyes that looked right through you. And they had a woman held captive...'

This was better than anything Paul could have anticipated, that he would mention the woman just at that moment. He had recounted the entire story to Paul earlier of course, but this was the best opportunity he would ever get to exploit the episode.

'A woman,' boomed Paul's voice. 'One of our own, held captive by foul demons! I tell you, brothers and sisters, we have a moral duty to dig these vile creatures out of their fiery haven and to release all human prisoners that they may be holding! How many daughters of men have gone missing among us? I call on each and every man among you to take to the boats with me this night, and set up a camp where Brother Jerrold saw the demons. At dawn we will dig them out of their loathsome refuge and reclaim our own children!'

Shouts of approval followed this impassioned speech. The men began to organise into a vehement mob. Paul felt both satisfied and a little guilty for bringing the missing girls into it. He knew as well as many fathers among them that several girls in recent years had run away, crossing the river on their own to escape the marriages that their fathers had arranged on their behalf. They had been sinners, women who were weak and craved the pleasures of the flesh that the northern girls enjoyed rather than being grateful for the righteous husbands that their fathers had chosen for them.

Some of the mothers tried to excuse them because of their youth, as marriages were arranged as a girl entered puberty. This was part of the reason that it was customary to marry them to mature men who could teach them to be obedient and useful wives. Most of those who had run away had never been heard from again. Some were presumed dead from drowning during the river crossing. Their mothers were forbidden to cry for them, or even to speak of them within hearing of their husbands. They were given up for dead, regardless. The men believed that the girls deserved whatever torment came to them in the end for their sinful ways.

The men were sparked by the thought of recovering their lost daughters. Paul had whipped them up into a fervour for a holy war. The men, led by Brother Paul, gathered all the weapons and digging equipment they could find and took to the boats. The women were left to prepare medical supplies and food for their victorious return.

* * *

It was not possible to discern night or day in the deep places. Talla knew that it must be night on the surface because Count Anton would have visited by day and had been gone now for some time. She had slept, but only lightly as the rhythm of the Dance had invaded her solitude. She had chosen not to join the others. It was habitual that the Dance would follow Storytelling and she was usually among the first to give herself over to the pulsing sensations of the earth which would be joined by the musicians and led into the Dance.

She had been acutely aware of the rhythms as she lay resting, entertaining fanciful thoughts. Many of these involved the human, Count Anton, goblin friend, rescuer.

Many seasons of attending the Storytelling had provided much information about the movements of humans, along with the history of her own people. There were lessons of various sorts, and even fanciful stories which served no other purpose than entertainment. She had told many stories of her own and had thoroughly enjoyed relating her adventures on the surface and the gallant rescue by Count Anton. The goblins would have known that the rescue had probably saved the drunken human's life, but the intent was unchanged. Anton himself had seen only the maiden in distress and had obviously not considered the sharp teeth and claws that a goblin, even a maiden goblin, would use to defend itself. Still, the rescue had made a better story and she had allowed his interference on her behalf partially because the romanticism appealed to her.

Then suddenly he had appeared as she told the story again. She had travelled to several goblin enclaves and joined their Storytellings to spread Count Anton's reputation as much as possible. Here at home it had been the first opportunity and as she told it she had caught his scent. When Leap appeared with the Count at his heels as she was speaking, she could not resist the urge to tease the human with an exaggerated portrayal of the fair goblin maiden who saw beauty in the face of her human rescuer. But was it exaggerated? She did find beauty in his features. It was the image of him in her mind as she lay feeling the pulses of nature calling to the deeper part of herself where all sensation arose that drew her to the decision to visit him this night.

Procuring the same cloak that had protected her so well before, she made her way upwards, to the between levels where she would be able to confirm the changing of light and darkness to her satisfaction. She told no one of her plan. She could feel the disturbance that the others felt in the Dance and knew the advice that would be forthcoming. There was something afoot, but that was far to the south. She, more than most goblins, could predict that no harm would come of this single excursion. She was, after all, of the direct blood line of prophesiers. Sometimes, like when she had allowed herself to be carried away by the humans, she just *knew* that the end would turn out alright. She trusted entirely to the natural rhythms of chaos.

She followed the easy paths of the between levels for what seemed like a long time, hoping that the timing would be right. She met few other goblins, as even betweeners tended to go to the deeper places once a Dance had started. Those she did meet minded their own business as was the way of goblins. They were very unlike the humans she had encountered who seemed to think it was their task to interfere with her movements. She would watch carefully for them this time. She walked for a very long time, running part of the way as was the habit of goblins. Eventually she came to the now familiar enclave at Lirrewot. She passed a couple of goblins playing a game with stones as she made her way to the opening. They seemed a little familiar, though she did not know them well. She nodded as she passed them and they returned the polite greeting without interrupting their game.

As she looked out of the opening to the surface world she reached out with her senses to determine if any humans were about. Her experience with the drunken one before had impressed her of the very real dangers that she risked by coming to their world. She listened intently and thought she could just hear a scrap of conversation distantly, but another sound drew her attention. Splashing, coming from the river. But not a natural splashing as of the *Kol'ksu* playing in the moonlight, it was a rhythmic splashing that spoke to her senses of disturbance, the disturbance in the Dance that they had all sensed.

She crept from her hiding place to a high vantage point, grateful for the darkness of a moonless night, and focused her eyes on the source of the sound. There were boats on the river, boats filled with men coming from the southern side of the city. Talla knew about boats from the stories about her mother's people from another age. She also knew that there had been a time before the last Turning when the river was crossed by bridges which afforded easy access from one side to the other. She was grateful now that Haghuf had kept the books secret that told of their construction. The boats moved slowly, powered only by men rowing. It would be a while before they could reach the shore, time enough for goblin runners to spread the word.

She turned and ran back to the two goblins whom she had passed earlier. She told them of the men coming across the water and the connection to the disturbance in the Dance that she felt so strongly. Knowing her by her white hair and eyes, they reacted quickly without further question. She might have been amused if she had known that this far from Krapneerg she was sometimes referred to as 'child of the prophesier'. Those she knew well always treated her as one of themselves, yet they were always reminded by her colouring and features that she was of the *Kol'ksu.*

Talla returned to the opening, reaching out again to sense any change. In the depths behind her, she could just hear the blowing of a goblin battle horn. Somewhere the Dance continued, the pulses of the earth thrumming the rhythm that matched her own heartbeat and warmed her blood. She felt no panic. The boats would still take some time to cross and humans were known to always attack at dawn. They would be tracked, although it was easy to guess that they would go straight to Nodgnirraf. There was time yet, she convinced herself, for her reason for coming here. And besides, Count Anton must be told of this. But first, the calling of the life forces must be satisfied. Then the morning would see her safely underground.

She located the position of the guards again and this time ascertained that there were no other humans about. Then, rather than following even the safer paths she had found before, the night's darkness saw a solitary cloaked and hooded figure climb directly over the outer wall of the castle. After a quick sniff to confirm that the courtyard was empty, she climbed head first down the other side, sprang off the wall near the bottom, and ran towards the tower. She leapt up again onto the wall of the Tower and climbed quickly. She easily found the window again. Memory for the shape of a place was strong in those who lived underground.

She climbed inside silently, still clinging to the walls to avoid knocking over any items that might be near the window. Then she stopped for a moment to look and listen. She had seen clearly that there was a figure sleeping in the bed as she came through the window, now she listened closely for his breaths. They were deep and even, those of a person deep in sleep. She moved carefully around the walls until she found a place to climb down without dislodging any paintings. Then she walked silently over to the bed and looked more closely.

It was indeed Count Anton. The coverlet was pulled partially over his face, but enough of his features were visible that there was no doubt of his identity. He slept deeply. His black curls were spread carelessly across the pillow and over his bare white shoulder. The long black eyelashes fell across his fair cheeks like those of a sleeping child, making him look young in the relaxation of sleep, almost like a boy. Some faint freckles that she had not noticed before added to the illusion. She nearly giggled as she noticed them.

The fine beauty of his features, at rest now rather than animated with his usual air of lively humour, drew her to him with an instinct that she knew had lain dormant in her kind for many long seasons of the earth. Her dress and cloak fell to the floor, unregarded, then she carefully pulled the coverlet from his sleeping form. He slept naked, which was no shock to Talla as her own people took little notice of nudity in general. It would have been of some convenience except that the change in temperature as she removed the warm coverlet was stirring him.

There was no time to lose. She leapt on top of him, pushing him onto his back a bit roughly, and quickly brushed the hair from his left shoulder. She bent down and bit just hard enough to draw a little blood. Then she settled back on her haunches, satisfied, and waited for the venom to do its work.

Chapter Nine

Anton was dreaming in the between places where dreams sometimes become lucid. The dreamer, knowing that he is in dream, could control the progress of the dream to an extent. He had become aware of a woman in his dream. A beautiful enchantress with silvery white hair and large alien white eyes that drew him into their embrace, unknowing whether the journey led to passion, or to death. He was just beginning to become aware, to realise that the woman represented someone he had encountered somewhere in the real world but was somehow forbidden to touch. In the dream, he knew that he could have her, at least for a time.

The cool night air disturbed his dream and the image of the maiden began to fade. He clung as best he could to the vision, willing himself to stay asleep but to no avail. His consciousness all too quickly had become aware that there was an intruder in his bedchamber. His sharp reflexes suddenly let the dream go and fought for full consciousness at the same moment that the intruder leapt on him. But where his muscles would normally respond and fight throwing an attacker off, he found himself unable to move and aware of a sharp pain in his shoulder, very close to his neck. His awareness grew stronger, but his body refused to respond and lay paralysed and helpless. Yet what puzzled him most was the growing realisation that the attacker had bit him.

His innate tendency to analyse things met with some confusion. He had been drugged, there was no question of that, but the only contact had been the bite. Then as the female attacker caressed and stimulated his body he began to understand what was happening. The word floated through his mind...*Succubus*. He was being seduced by the very woman he had dreamed of. He could not open his eyes, yet he knew her through other senses. Her name, Talla, came back to him. He was almost completely awake by now, able to feel and experience every touch, every pleasure that was bestowed upon him. He pitied Latham for his fear as he relaxed into the situation and allowed himself to be taken by her, responding to every caress and yet unable at first to move to respond of his own will.

In her movements he felt the rhythm of the Dance pulsing throughout both of their beings as a celebration of the life force, renewing itself through the energies of the earth as all became one in total harmony with the universe and all that existed within it. His body slowly began to recover its ability to move, but not his strength. The venom, whatever it was, apparently lost its paralysing effects fairly quickly so that his physical responses were freed to react with a degree of spontaneity. He moved his mouth and struggled to recover his ability to speak. When she had finished with him, she replaced the coverlet back over him for warmth and spoke gently in his ear.

'You will be cold and sleepy, but you must send someone. Humans cross the river. They bring trouble to us.'

Anton wanted to sleep. He knew that he was in no condition to respond to an emergency, despite the clarity of his mind.

'Ranalf,' he managed to form the words slowly. 'Two floors down, send him. Use the door.'

Talla understood. She remembered Ranalf, the lovely young human that she would rather have seduced than the oafish Latham. Without stopping to think how she would get the message across, she drew the glamour to herself, slipped back into her dress and walked out of the door. To all appearances she was a human woman again. As long as there were no human women about. All was still quiet in the castle, the possibility of meeting anyone was unlikely at best. She followed the stairs down two floors as Anton had instructed and found a door which would lead to a room directly below Count Anton's bedchamber. There were other doors, but she was sure that he must have meant this one. Slowly she turned the handle and pushed the door open. Despite her care to be silent, the door creaked loudly, waking the vigilant occupant.

'Identify yourself!' demanded a male voice. Her eyes, so accustomed to darkness had seen him tumble out of bed to the right, grab a sword as he spoke so that the sound of his voice would come from that direction, then he deftly feinted to the left so that he was almost beside her in the darkest shadow, sword drawn. The tactic was admirable. A human would have been completely blind in the near total darkness and would probably have attacked to the right, following the voice, and received a sword from the back.

She stood perfectly still, and spoke only his name.

'Ranalf.'

The sword dropped at the sound of the melodic feminine voice. A light seemed to appear from nowhere. Ranalf's mouth hung open as he regarded the woman before him.

'It's you...' he said incredulously. 'I dreamt of you!'

Talla did not understand the words. She decided then that she must learn the human language as soon as possible, but right now she needed to communicate with him somehow. She motioned to him to follow her and pointed up the stairs. With an exaggerated urgency in her voice, she used the only words she knew to direct him.

'Count Anton!' She pointed up the stairs again and repeated, 'Count Anton!'

Ranalf wasted no time. Unlike the Count he slept partially dressed, ready for any eventuality. He bounded up the steps, responding to whatever emergency required his assistance.

Talla saw the faint pre-dawn light beginning to enter the window from Ranalf's room and decided it was time she was gone. She looked quickly out to see that the courtyard was still empty, then swung herself over the edge and climbed down the outside wall. It seemed to be becoming a habit for her. Tracing her path quickly back to the opening to Lirrewot, she ran down the familiar tunnels, grateful for the sound of her own feet flapping against stone.

Anton was finding it difficult to stay awake, but Ranalf was shaking him, demanding to know if he was ill or injured. His mind drifted between total clarity and welcoming sleep, but through the moments of intelligibility he realised the limitations of his ability to act. He also realised that he could hardly give orders to the men of Nodgnirraf to defend the goblins. With some difficulty he managed to get the words out that were needed.

'Ill, yes. Need sleep. Ranalf, southern invaders bring trouble to Nodgnirraf. Need you to warn your clan and bring back word of all that happens to me. Use your initiative, keep peace. Use my name to give orders if you have to, you're audacious enough. Take a horse, they're fast and noisy.'

Anton slipped closer to sleep, wondering if his face reflected the smile he felt as several thoughts occurred to him at once. He had just planted the seeds to turn a direct attack into a situation of chaos, where human would meet human before they ever got a chance to attack the goblins. Talla would surely warn her own kind and they would be ready for the attack this time, even in the unlikely event that the humans could join forces. This would be well out of character for the two human factions as their disapproval of each other reached to the very core of their beliefs. Between these thoughts he began to worry if Ranalf would ask difficult questions if he saw the bite marks on his shoulder. In mid-thought he remembered rather a lot of similar marks on Haghuf, who had refused to speak of them. Missing for several days, like a cat on the prowl…and returning with bites as Talla had given him…goblin mating practices…

Ranalf gave up trying to rouse the Count any further. The man had pulled his own coverlet close to his neck and rolled over into sleep with a slight smile on his face. The illness obviously wasn't so severe as to prevent pleasant dreams. The Count had just given him permission to take one of his fine horses to warn his clan of invasion from the south. This was even better than offering to lend his carriage, even if the carriage might have been slightly faster. Horses were also rare, and mostly only owned by the aristocracy.

His imagination could immediately see the dramatic appeal as he ran down the castle stairs and across the courtyard to the stable. The orders to the sleepy stable boy to saddle his fastest horse rolled out of his mouth quite naturally, as if he were born to hold a position of authority. He also ordered a riding cape, as he had lost his cloak sometime before the party at Count Anton's castle which had led to his position of messenger for the clan. Now he felt more as if he were in the service of Count Anton, which was far more romantic and noble to a young man's imagination.

The strong, black animal that was brought to him was beautiful and very powerful, but it didn't take long in the saddle for Ranalf to realise that he could do with some practice on learning how to control a horse. He had learned enough from tales told by the fireside to know what he was supposed to do; kick with both feet to start, pull left or right on the reins to turn, pull back to stop. It had sounded simple, and he did manage to walk the beast out of the stable well enough to avoid embarrassment in the presence of the stable boy. However, once he was in the road, he was not sure how to make it go faster, or if he was sure he wanted it to.

The distance to the ground seemed much further than he had expected, and his stability in the saddle was in question. The massive hooves, emphasised by the decorative fetters, looked rather dangerous in view of the thought of falling under them. He tried different positions, straightening his legs which he had heard was correct. But that only led to him sliding all over the place. Several times he kicked the horse, trying to get it to break into a gallop. Ranalf had always seemed to communicate well with smaller animals, often feeling as if he could actually touch their minds. He was determined to get the message across to the horse that they must travel fast. On the next kick, he must have got it right because the horse whinnied and shot down the road in a sudden and breathtaking burst of speed.

The clatter of the hooves on the road echoed loudly in the pre-dawn stillness. Ranalf held on for dear life, bending close to the saddle and gripping as hard as he could with every limb. He knew the way well, and managed to get the horse to turn where he wanted it to, although he wasn't sure he would be able to get it to stop when the time came. His thighs quickly began to ache from the unaccustomed strain of gripping the horse with them. It seemed to be the key to staying on.

After several minutes, Ranalf's fear of falling became mixed with the image of himself flying down the road on horseback, cape flying in the wind. By the time he had got to the vicinity of Nodgnirraf, the muscle strain had given in to a form of numbness and he had developed a sense of communion with the horse. He felt a strange elation and nearly wished that the ride could continue endlessly, although his aching body begged for a rest from the unrelenting tension required to stay in the saddle. The light of dawn was just beginning to flood the streets as the pounding of hooves and the strong voice of Ranalf woke the citizens from their peaceful slumber.

'Awake! To battle! Invaders from the south!' he shouted.

Men began to pour out of the houses, questioning their neighbours as to what might be causing so much noise and excitement. Ranalf shouted to many passers-by to explain as best he could. Word flew from mouth to mouth, stirring the clan to defend their homes from armed southern fanatics invading their shores. Gathering anything that could be used as a weapon, they formed an angry mob to block the main road from the river. Like the southerners, they were mostly armed with staves, swords, knives and other sharp instruments as firearms were rare and not often seen among the common rabble.

When all the men were assembled, Ranalf pulled the horse to the front of the mob facing the river and tried his best to sit up straight and look majestic, now that the wild ride had ended.

'Friends and neighbours,' he called above the din of questioning, 'I come directly from Count Anton. He has given orders to deal with the southerners and send them back across the river to their own city.'

'What southerners?' shouted a man in a thin voice, 'I don't see anybody!'

The crowd became quiet, and all turned to look towards the river. There was no one to be seen. Then through the void left by the silence of early dawn and the suddenly hushed men, a sound was heard. It was like the sound of metal hitting rock, as if miners were digging in the middle of the city. It did not come from the river, but from a part of the city behind them, where none would ordinarily go. Ranalf had only been there once, just a few days previously when they had gone on the search for the missing man. Somehow they had been intercepted by Count Anton and taken to his castle for the party. Exactly how this had occurred was not clear in Ranalf's memory. It was only just now that he remembered having seen the dead city at all. Or was it only in the dream...

There was no time now to try to think about it. Ranalf shouted an order to follow and led the men in the direction of the unexpected sound. The echo from deserted houses distorted the direction from which the sound issued, yet Ranalf led the mob right through the streets of the dead city to a place that he remembered only from the dream. Some instinct told him that it would be coming from there.

They arrived to find a gang of men similar in number to their own, but recognisable as southerners by their austere, black clothing. They were using pick axes to dig a hole in the side of a hill. Ranalf tried to think what to do or say. He was still on the horse and would therefore be presumed to be in charge. Part of him badly wanted to climb off the animal, to rest, but he was afraid that he would collapse after the unfamiliar strains of riding. His muscles all felt as if they had been beaten to a pulp. Keeping the horse at a slow trot on the excuse that men on foot had to follow had been partial relief. The southerners heard the horse snort, and stopped their digging long enough to turn and regard the local men who had appeared. Ranalf's men had never seen a large group of southerners this closely. They seemed strange, alien in a way that other clans in the north could not rival. Among them stood a single familiar face.

'Jerrold!' shouted Ranalf. 'What is the meaning of bringing these men into our lands?

For a few seconds, Jerrold just looked at him. He thought of Ranalf as a boy, only just old enough to marry. He was not accustomed to the authoritative tone coming from him or to seeing him lord it over the clan on horseback. Two of the southerners turned back to their work, ignoring the interruption.

'Don't you remember lad?' answered Jerrold at last. 'You was here with the rest. We dug through this hill and found passageways and we chased the demons through them. There was a woman…'

Ranalf ignored the uneasy feeling these words instilled in him. Remembering his purpose, he tried to sound authoritative.

'I forbid you to…'

'We're through!' shouted one of the diggers. Several of his fellows turned and helped pull away rock from the opening that had been created. The northerners forgot their argument with the southerners in their fascination with the discovery of an actual passage beyond the new opening, just as Jerrold had predicted.

Ranalf took the moment when all eyes were away from him to slide off the horse and try his feet. He was a bit unstable at first, but a few quick stretches and walking around for a moment helped to restore his ordinarily confident step. He then pushed his way through the crowd that had formed around the opening and had nearly made it to the front when Jerrold suddenly shouted.

'Look! I saw one of the creatures! You saw it, didn't you?' He looked to the men on either side of him for support but they looked back at him blankly. Whatever Jerrold had seen, they had missed it. He climbed through the uneven opening as he described what he had seen.

'Pointy ears, and big yellow eyes, just like before. It went this way!' He ran down the passageway to the right as several men from both clans climbed through to follow. Ranalf was among them. They ran down the rock corridor, chasing Jerrold blindly after the unknown enemy. Nobody had stopped to think about what they would do when they found it. Ranalf shot a few glances to the enclosing walls as he was swept up in the chase. He felt uneasy. The odd sense of having been there before, and Jerrold's insistence that indeed they had, was disconcerting. Especially in light of his mention of the woman. Something was causing a chill on the back of his neck. His brief encounter with her at Count Anton's castle had been no dream. He intended to look for her when he was able to go back.

The thoughts drifted away as they rounded a curve in the passage and stopped abruptly. It was a dead end, but there was something unmistakably alive crouching in front of them against the wall. The light spilling from the opening in the wall which was behind them now, was just enough to reflect from what could only be a pair of large eyes. In the near darkness, it was impossible to make out the shape of the creature behind them. The yellow eyes shone back at them with a menacing stare. A low, whining growl issued from the creature in the darkness and the men began to slowly back away from the cornered enemy. Fear became a palpable presence as the common men, even the fanatics from across the river, confronted a real creature where only their imaginings had prepared them for such an encounter. They did not know its strength, or how to go about fighting it.

After a couple of tense moments, one man with a pick in his hands charged the creature with weapon upraised and a guttural shout proclaiming his courage. The creature sprang towards him. There was an audible gasp from the crowd as it visibly bit him and then, in a flash of ginger fur, it streaked through the forest of legs and disappeared back down the corridor from which they had come and into the light of the outside world.

'Well there's your demon.' Ranalf's voice mocked the assembly and the slowly releasing tension that they had allowed to build among them. 'Pointed ears, big yellow eyes, massive teeth...sure the nice kitty didn't hurt you fatally?'

The locals burst into laughter, covering their own embarrassment by projecting ridicule onto the invaders. The man who had been bitten by the cat looked dangerously determined as he swung his pick axe back up. He focused his narrowed eyes onto a fresh stretch of wall, and began to hack away at the solid rock.

'Stop!' shouted Ranalf. His confidence had returned. 'I have the authority of Count Anton himself to forbid any further destruction of the few natural places we have on our side of the river. If you people want to chase imaginary demons, go back to your own lands and hack them to pieces!'

The man stopped in mid-swing, and several of the southern men tried to argue at once. They were shouted down by the locals who had decided to cast their loyalty with Ranalf. They knew him too well to believe that he would claim authority from Count Anton falsely. Within a few moments, the crowd had dispersed with a hail of threats and counter threats volleying through the air from each side, neither of them inclined to physically start a fight with each other. The southerners headed back to the river, throwing back promises to hunt down and kill the demons, whatever it took to do so. There were assertions that the local men would see the error of their ways when the planet was invaded by the monsters.

Ranalf was the last to leave the cave. In his ordinary daily life he worked with metal and so found himself examining the rock at the dead end. The patterns he could feel and almost see on the rock face reminded him of melting, as if some great heat had melted solid rock into this path. The cave itself also reminded him of the dream where he had first seen the woman. For just a moment, he wondered to himself about the possibility that any part of it might have been real. Then he turned to leave, trailing behind his fellows. As he rounded the bend towards the daylight, some part of him imagined that he could hear a faint, high pitched giggle echo somewhere within the cave. Or was it imagination? He rubbed the hairs on the back of his neck which had stood up. He walked more quickly to the familiar outside world, and the pleasant light of a warm spring morning.

Talla visited Count Anton that evening. Anton had spent the afternoon with Ranalf. After hearing his report about the dawn events he invited him to stay a couple of days. He could travel back to his clan once a day to collect messages and then return to report again. Count Anton had showed him around the castle himself and they had just finished a game of chess and retired to their bedchambers. The Count was just falling asleep, when he felt the familiar bite followed by a repeat of the previous evening's experience. Only this time, there was no crisis to attend to. This time, the goblin woman stayed a while to speak to him.

It was only after she had questioned him about the human language and he had revealed to her the secret of its relationship to her own language that he realised how the venom worked to render him compliant. He had thought it only a paralysing agent, but that effect wore off fairly quickly. The relaxed, agreeable mood it left him in long afterwards was pleasant and left him feeling at ease, but he had revealed many things to her during their conversation which had previously only been discussed between himself and Haghuf. As he drifted into sleep, vaguely aware of the female figure retreating through his window, he hoped that it would not lead to trouble of any kind.

The following night he found her waiting for him on his bed. He had just finished another game of chess with Ranalf. It had been characterised by an exchange of intense questioning between them. He had tried to subtly draw information from the lad about the mood of the people of his clan and any plans they might have, while Ranalf in turn had grilled him about the mysterious woman whom he had met within the Count's own castle. Anton explained her away as a visiting foreigner from a place with customs very different from their own, and a different language which explained her inability to converse with him. He tried to dissuade the lad from any fancies he had for a match being made between them. He told him that women were held in high esteem among her people and marriage outside of their own kind was highly unlikely. It was as much of the truth as he dared reveal. He did not attempt to explain to him that in fact, marriage didn't exist among her people. It would have been too much to ask him to accept.

Finding her waiting for him afterwards, the Count asked her not to bite him this time. Curious as to what he had in mind, she allowed him to take the initiative and discovered that the mating customs among the humans were very different from what she had known all her life among her own kind. Playing a receptive role felt very strange to her, yet it had some interesting advantages and she found herself intrigued by the differences between the habits of the species. However, it did not occur to her that it could become a habit. Like Anton himself, she liked to experience different perspectives in life and savour the variety that diversity had to offer.

Again, the following night, Talla visited the castle. This time she found the moon shining too brightly on the face of the tower that she would normally ascend and so she climbed round to the other side to the safety of shadow. There were several other windows on the various faces of the tower, but she climbed well clear of them until she reached a height that she reckoned would be close to Count Anton's floor. This brought her to the highest window on the shadow side. She approached it carefully, reaching ahead with her senses to determine whether anyone was in the room beyond. It was empty, she was sure, but she remained alert as she climbed carefully through to the bedchamber beyond.

It was a nicely furnished room, yet it lacked the character of Count Anton's chamber which reflected his personality through it's décor. It was an interesting concept to her, to reflect oneself through the material objects that one chose to collect. This room reminded her of Ranalf's room, although she had only glimpsed it on her way through the window when she had made her escape two nights previously. It appeared that the humans kept extra rooms for visitors, which seemed sensible for a species that kept specific places for individuals rather than the more communal habits of the goblins.

As usual, she had worn a human style dress for her nocturnal visit, just in case she should have to call the glamour to herself to get past any stray human guards. At least she had been able to practice some phrases in their language now, so that she would be able to communicate sufficiently to avoid a repeat scenario of her previous capture. She could express herself as a foreign guest of Count Anton and as long as she avoided any women, could probably convince them to take her directly to him if the situation arose.

Talla noted that the discovery of this room could also be useful. If the Count was elsewhere, she could claim to be staying in it. Her long collected knowledge of human customs would serve her well now. Cautiously, she opened the door just enough to see what lay beyond it. There was a corridor and the door to another room directly across from hers. There was no sign of humans. She drew the glamour to herself anyway, as a precaution, and opened the door wider. She stepped through into the corridor as quietly as only a goblin was able and looked around. There was a stair to the left of the door opposite and more doors to the right. An imperfection in the stone next to the other door told her that she had been here before. It was not just an identical layout to another floor. She was standing opposite Ranalf's door.

She smiled involuntarily as she remembered her attraction to the young human when the bigger one had been dragging her off. The Count was no doubt sleeping in his chamber just up the stairs, but for a moment she was tempted to creep through the door before her. She immediately thought better of it. She remembered the horror on the face of Latham when he realised what she was. Unlike the mushroom potion, her venom did not bring forgetfulness.

She turned and pulled the door behind her, closing it slowly so that it would make no sound. The hinges were well oiled so it moved as silently as she did herself, until the latch caught with an audible clack of metal against metal. She cringed at the echo of the abrasive sound as it vibrated through the silent corridor, but was more startled by the soft human voice from behind her.

'Talla.' She turned to see Ranalf standing in the open door to his room. She was surprised by the fact that he knew her name. She could not know that it was the only piece of information that the lad had been able to wrest from Count Anton over their chess game. She collected herself, composing her posture to that of a human maiden, and curtsied to him. It was something she had never tried doing in the presence of anyone before, but she had apparently done it correctly as he stepped towards her and began speaking to her quickly in courteous tones. She could not follow the words as they came too fast. Eventually she held up the palm of her hand, to indicate that he should stop. With some effort, she translated a few words in her mind and tried to speak to him.

'Speak little. Cannot. Fast.' She saw understanding in his eyes, and was pleased that she had managed to communicate with so little practice. She saw something else in his eyes as well. His desire was palpable as he returned her gaze and took her hand. The words came a little slower, but still too quickly for her to follow completely. She caught 'hope' and 'love me' among the next few sentences. His impetuous declarations were clear enough, yet were in conflict with what she had thought she understood about human courtship. Instinctively, she closed her fingers around the hand that held hers and reached with the other to stroke the side of his face. This seemed to please him. He closed his eyes, enjoying the touch, then gently put his arms around her and pulled her close to him.

Talla felt the beginning rhythms of the earth within her as their bodies pressed against each other and their arms held tightly in the fusion of two which become one in the movement of the Dance. She was sure that she could not mistake his meaning as he kissed her gently first on the forehead, then on her face, and on the side of her neck. She returned the little kisses, grazing his flesh with her sharp teeth when she reached the exposed shoulder where his night shirt fell loosely, exposing the sensitive neck and shoulder skin.

She started to bite, but his convulsive reaction to the intimacy reminded her that the ways of the succubus were known to the humans and feared by most of them. She retracted her bite without breaking skin and soothed the reddened indentations from her teeth with her tongue. His frenzied reaction to this excited her, reminding her of the exhilaration she had shared with Count Anton the previous night when she had allowed him to lead her through this expression of the Dance. She did not resist when Ranalf took her hand again and led her into his room.

Ranalf was caught up in his responses to the woman too far to consider whether there could be consequences of any kind. He had never shared more than polite conversation with a woman, and had only speculated about whose daughter he might marry as soon as he had reached an appropriate age. His fascination for the mysterious foreign woman had clouded his judgement just enough to forget himself and declare his love to her, expecting rebuff from his advances. Much to his delight and surprise, she had responded with gentleness, touching his face in an affectionate manner that compelled him to forget all propriety and reach out to hold her. He could not help himself. He had expected resistance, but she had responded with passion. She nuzzled his neck in ways that no woman of his clan would be likely to do even after marriage, and he lost all sense of decorum.

Ranalf found himself caught up in some sort of rhythm that he could feel coursing through their entwined bodies. Even before he led her into his room, he felt as if they were already making love within some secret enclave of nature, separated from the ordinary world by the call of an ancient power that demanded to be satisfied. In the privacy of his chamber, they were completely alone together in a world that only they could share. Speech was unnecessary, all the communication they needed occurred mind to mind as they gloried in each other's passion and ecstasy.

Afterwards, he held her as they lay together and contemplated what might be necessary to make the woman his own. Perhaps, after what had just occurred, it would be customary among her people that they should be married after all. He would ask Count Anton in the morning about being introduced to her family. He drifted off to sleep, a smile gently touching his lips as he held Talla closely to him in contentment. When he woke in the light of morning, she was gone.

Chapter Ten

Ranalf preferred the position he seemed to have attained at the castle. It wasn't that he minded the work he did normally, it was more a matter of the company. Going among his own people to listen to them alternately grumble about their lives and insist that God most loved those who worked hard, had become an irritation after many nights at the castle enjoying the Count's pleasant humour. He took secret pleasure in noting that the assumption that Count Anton had been attending private services within the castle was a complete myth.

What did he care if the Count never attended Temple? In secret, he had never thought much of the practice himself. In his deepest thoughts he had often questioned the validity of a religion based solely on blind faith. He dared not speak the thoughts among family, but his visits to the castle had afforded opportunities for intimate conversations with the Count on philosophical concepts that he just couldn't discuss among the members of his own community. He looked forward to staying over at the castle as well as to the chess games with the Count. He swore he would win one someday.

Ranalf did not see the woman Talla again. His questions about her only elicited evasive answers from Count Anton. Once he had said that he believed she had gone back among her own people. The introspective frown on the Count's face as he said it discouraged

Ranalf from asking further questions. He suspected that Count Anton may have had an interest in her himself. Ranalf wondered if perhaps that the times he had explained that she was unlikely to marry outside of her own people had been more to convince himself than to explain it to an unworthy young man. He wished he could speak openly about what had passed between himself and Talla. If it had been any other woman, Ranalf felt that he could discuss matters with the Count that his own family would be horrified to learn. But the subject was clearly a sensitive one, so he kept the knowledge to himself and tried to concentrate on the game of chess.

Anton had his mind on another game tonight. So much so that Ranalf had taken several of his pieces before his innate sense of strategy took over and he moved in for the kill. Anton's visits to Haghuf had been as pleasant as ever. Their discussions went on as if nothing had ever happened. It was frustrating however, that his questions as to Talla's welfare only ever met with, 'She is well, as always.'

Haghuf side-stepped his questions so artfully that Anton had been unable to learn anything about her movements. Several months had passed with no further visits from her. Anton understood Haghuf's resistance. He would no doubt discourage any interest from a goblin for a human woman in the same way. The potential trouble it could cause was more important than any man's fancy. Still, he could not put her out of his mind. If he could only see her on odd occasions, or even just one more time…

Something else was bothering him tonight as well. The rhythm felt wrong. Although he could hear nothing, he felt the disturbance of steady drums somewhere, beating a martial rhythm unlike the celebratory pulsation that he had come to know in the Dance. The new beat stirred something in him that was akin to anger, an instinct to fight an unknown enemy.

'Checkmate.' The Count's voice was flat, as if the inevitable win was so commonplace that he could hardly be bothered.

'Crikey, Anton! I didn't even see that coming.' Ranalf saw the familiar wolf smile spread across Anton's face as the brows lowered over his intense eyes. He had seen the expression many times now. It looked predatory and amused at the same time, like a wolf that had cornered its well-earned prey and was about to enjoy a good meal. This was a man who enjoyed outsmarting the opposition.

'Still, at least I gave you a good run, this time,' Ranalf continued. 'Someday, I will win a game against you.'

'Winning is just a matter of keeping the game as a whole in focus rather than getting a myopic view of a single encounter.' The Count spoke casually as he sipped his wine, resisting the effects of the martial rhythm that plagued his senses. 'Tell me Ranalf, what is the gossip among your people?'

The sudden change of subject seemed even more wolfish. It was a term that Ranalf had been applying to Count Anton in his own mind with increasing frequency. As much as the Count was open and friendly, even intimate as a favourite uncle towards him, there was a guarded side to him that Ranalf had not yet fathomed. He collected information constantly. Books, tales and current events among the people were all of intense interest to him. Ranalf knew that his own position served the purpose of bringing information about his clan to the Count's ears, yet he did not see it as a conflict of loyalties of any sort. It was the Count's business to know what passed among them.

'Actually there is something I've been observing the last few days that I think will be of interest to you.' Ranalf had been looking for the right moment to try to explain the turn of events and the shift in attitude towards the Count himself that was growing among his people. The Count moved forward in his chair, giving Ranalf his full attention.

'Latham came to me yesterday and asked me some odd questions. They were about that day when the southerners broke through the rock and found that odd passageway.' He stopped a moment to sip his wine and to think carefully about how to phrase what he would say next. He was beginning to feel a little nervous.

'He specifically asked if I had any memories of being in such a place before or of having dreams about the place the night we all stayed here at the castle.' He met the Count's piercing gaze, feeling very much like a rabbit caught under the wolf's paw. The dark eyes flicked a moment to meet those of a servant whom Ranalf had frequently seen working close to the Count, then back to meet his own gaze. Such unspoken communication had passed between them before, as well as with another of the Count's personal staff. Ranalf often felt as if he were the subject of scrutiny. He partly hoped that he was being considered for more official service to the Count, yet could not understand what the opinion of the other close servants might mean.

'I got the feeling that he had been asking others the same questions so I asked him about it. It seems that several of them had similar dreams, but very vague ones that they had found too fantastic to speak about or that it was bad luck to do so.'

'And did you have such dreams?' The Count's question pierced through him, demanding a completely honest answer.

'I dreamt of Talla,' he said quietly, then dropped his eyes and began fingering one of the captured chess pieces. It was a knight. 'But I didn't tell him that. I said that I didn't remember any such dreams.'

'Perhaps,' said the Count evenly, 'the suggestions of Jerrold affected their memories, which were already rather confused that night because of drink.'

Ranalf looked back up at the Count as he answered.

'Yes sir, I will tell them that.'

Anton considered a moment. It was obvious that Ranalf observed far more than he revealed. He had been watching him for some time... and not just as a useful agent to gather news from his own clan. Dani had gone about his business elsewhere in the room but would of course have been following the conversation intently. Anton took another sip of wine and sat back in his chair, using the movement to distract from another quick meeting of the eyes with Dani. The nod was almost imperceptible.

'Ranalf,' the Count began in a serious tone, 'you do know that I make myself aware of all that affects this land and our people.'

Ranalf nodded.

'And you also know that if anything brought danger to us, from this realm or any other...' He sat forward in the chair again, capturing Ranalf's gaze with his own, 'that I would not hesitate to eliminate the danger.'

Ranalf nodded again. The Count's direct statements spoke only what he knew. His trust in the Count was absolute.

'People do not speak of it aloud,' he replied, 'but it is commonly known that you are a magician. That all of the rulers of the lands are magicians and that is why you are the rulers. You can protect us better than anyone. The faithful don't like to think about what it means for their religion, they prefer to assume you believe in God and attend Temple privately.'

'They?' the Count repeated after him. 'Are you not among the faithful?'

Ranalf hadn't noticed his own slip. It was only then that he began to fully realise that indeed he was not like them.

'Not as such, sir…I don't feel as if I disbelieve, but there has always been something missing in the faith of the people. I feel as if there should be…something more.'

'Perhaps you would care to know others like me.' The Count motioned for Dani to fill the glasses again. As he approached, Anton continued, 'you've already met Jerak and Dani of course.'

Ranalf stopped in mid-motion as he reached for his filled glass, looking directly at the servant a moment. Remembering himself, he nodded to him politely. He had long noticed the unusual closeness of Count Anton's personal servants but had never considered that someone in that position might actually be a magician.

Before the conversation could continue, it was interrupted by a disturbance in the courtyard. The shouts of what sounded like an angry mob quickly grew louder as the courtyard filled with a substantial contingent of men. They were bearing torches that flickered against the darkness of the night. Anton sprang to the window, then with a quick glance at Ranalf and a more meaningful nod to Dani, hurried out of the room.

'It looks as though you will be tested early my young friend.' Dani stared with trepidation from the window at the crowd. For the first time he met Ranalf's eyes directly. 'Come with me, he may need our help.'

Ranalf had never been directly ordered to do anything by a servant before, yet he obeyed without question. There was something in Dani's eyes that was not unlike those of Count Anton himself. Things were moving too fast for him to fully understand, yet he knew that he had just been thrust into a new status that was far beyond what he had hoped for among the castle company.

Count Anton reached the courtyard only a few moments after his first glance at the commotion from the tower window. With no thought of personal danger he strode directly to the centre of the disturbance to learn the cause of it. He was met with a sight more grisly and disturbing than anything he might have expected.

Leading the entourage from its centre were men he recognised as leaders among the southerners. In the hand of the one called Paul was a pike. At the sharp end of it was impaled a severed head. It was blackened with death, but otherwise unrecognisable as anything but the head of a man except for the distinctively pointed ears. As comprehension stole over the face of Count Anton, his expression changed from disbelief to disgust.

'What have you done?' he demanded in an uncharacteristic rasp.

'Count Anton!' replied Paul in a clear, proud voice. 'Our failure to unearth the demons in your lands made it impossible to prove their existence to you, but now with diligence we have searched out and excavated one of their passages in our own part of the city. Here as you see, we have captured one, and brought it to you as proof. Surely now you will deputise several of my men, that we may flush out and destroy such evil creatures from all the land?'

'What have these creatures ever done to harm you?' There was a dangerous glint in Count Anton's eye as he spoke, tearing his eyes away from the countenance of the unknown goblin to meet the fanatical stare in the eyes of Paul. Taken aback by the challenge, Paul fell back on the tactics that had characterised his own speeches.

'They have taken our pubescent girls!' This assertion was too much for Anton. Ranalf and Dani reached the courtyard just in time to witness the anger that few had ever seen displayed by the Count. He seemed to flare all at once into something wild and dangerous. He spoke now with a fury that caused the crowd surrounding him to step back in genuine fear, and dismay that their previous excitement over the discovery might well have been misplaced.

'Your girls run away when they reach puberty because you marry them to men nearly old enough to be their fathers. I dare say that if you look around you may find many of them fostered in villages nearby or married to members of my own household.' Anton's gaze met Ranalf's for a split second, but the expression was unreadable. Then he turned his attention back to Paul. 'It helps diversify the inbreeding that occurs in closed communities like your own which produces the sort of idiots who would commit such acts of prejudice towards a peaceful species just because they look a little different than your own!'

Paul's face fell as he stepped back in the face of Count Anton's unbridled rage. He had never been directly insulted before and decided quickly that he did not like being the subject of such vehemence and ill favour. Still, he remained silent against the tirade for lack of any better thought of what to do.

'The creatures you have hunted out live peacefully and do no harm to humans. They are descended from humans themselves, through many generations past. They have transcended the base territorialism that leads to the sort of conflict you've just created. How do you expect them to react to having one of their number hunted down and brutally killed?'

Paul had not considered this. The idea that the creatures might organise into a real threat simply had not occurred to him. His attitude had been one of hunting down a stupid animal, vermin, and of flushing out the others like rabbits in a warren.

'You disgust me.' The words were spat out by the Count in a way that expressed more abhorrence than the words themselves. 'Take this token away and leave the creatures in peace, if you can. You may have just started an unnecessary war by committing murder, unprovoked.'

In the face of the onslaught, a thought began to occur to Paul. The Count seemed to know rather a lot about these creatures. In fact, it would seem that he had been aware of their existence for some time. Yet never had he told the people about them. What right had he to conceal the fact that demons lived beneath their city and then to become angry when one of them was killed by a good citizen? Paul's eyes narrowed, yet he did not speak against the Count's anger. A wall of castle guards seemed to appear from nowhere, pushing the intruders out of the courtyard the way they had come. Ranalf was as surprised at their sudden appearance as the southern men. He had never noticed so many men among the castle inhabitants. He had not even realised until that moment that Dani was no longer by his side.

Paul acknowledged the Count's authority with a curt bow and motioned to his followers to leave the castle courtyard. Within minutes the courtyard was emptied and returned to peaceful night, yet the tension of the encounter remained. Ranalf met with yet another surprise when he watched the last of the intruders disappear through the gate, followed by the sudden disappearance of most of the guards into thin air.

No more than half a dozen guardsmen had actually done the job. The rest were the illusion of magicians. As Ranalf looked around the darkened courtyard, he saw that Count Anton, Dani and the other servant Jerak were in positions that formed a triangle in the space where the phantom guardsmen had appeared. He began to understand. What he found more difficult to work out was the lack of reaction from the real guardsmen. They seemed to treat the incident as though it were an ordinary occurrence.

'Ranalf,' said the Count's voice, suddenly at Ranalf's elbow. 'Stay with Dani and Jerak, there is something I must do.'

Ranalf turned intending to reply, but the Count was already halfway across the courtyard and nearly invisible in the shadow of the wall.

'Ranalf.' The young man turned to respond to Dani's voice, but something pulled his attention back to the shadow where he had seen the silhouette of the Count. He was just quick enough to catch the fleeting glimpse of a shape running through the gate. However, it did not look human. In fact, it looked rather like a large wolf, and it could run fast. Confused, he looked back again at Dani.

'Come Ranalf. There is much you must learn, in time. But now we cannot be sure that there will *be* time. We must wait for his return.' Ranalf turned and followed Dani back to the tower.

Count Anton ran with the swiftness that only his wolf form could provide. The entrance to Krapneerg was halfway across the city from his castle, yet in this form he could cover it in less than an hour. The black wolf would not draw the attention that a carriage would attract even more at night than during normal waking hours. The danger he ran towards did not escape his attention, yet the actions of the southern men demanded that he must know the response that could be expected from the goblins.

His motives were not entirely unselfish. His position required that he should be aware of any threat to his people, yet he did not deny to himself that his friendship with Haghuf and his concern for Talla drove him towards a direct confrontation. If he were only defending the humans, his knowledge of the goblins and their habits was sufficient that he could order adequate defences from the safety of the castle. He did not stop to think about what he would do if he met with hostility from the closest friend he had.

Meanwhile, Paul was not idle. He would not accept the insults and dismissal that he had received from Count Anton lightly. Rather than retreating to his own side of the city as the Count no doubt expected, he spent the rest of the night parading across the northern city, waking people as he went and showing the goblin head to the common people as he cried out for volunteers to raise a fighting force against the demons. He told his story from one clan to the next of how Count Anton had known about the demons and had ordered him away from the castle, defending the creatures and their evil ways.

Some of the northern people threw things at him from their windows, shouting at him to take his madness back to his own shores and let decent people sleep. Others, a few at a time, came out to join him. Among them was Latham. At one point the swollen company returned to the castle, demanding to speak again with Count Anton. They were told that he was not within the castle grounds. Paul guessed that he had gone to visit his demon friends.

The men broke up into groups and spread out, waiting for his return.

Anton transformed back to man shape as he entered the first gate to the between levels of Krapneerg. He had hardly passed through the doorway when Leap dropped from the ceiling to block his path. The nod of respect before he spoke was a good sign.

'Well met, Anton, we've been expecting you.'

Anton suddenly became aware that they were not alone. He sensed more than he saw, but there was no doubt that several other goblins, mostly unfamiliar ones, were placed strategically throughout the cavern.

'Leap,' Anton acknowledged the goblin with a nod of his own, including his shoulders in the movement to show an even greater respect. 'Where is Haghuf?'

'He was needed elsewhere, but left a message for you.' Leap looked a little uncomfortable as he delivered the prepared message. 'He said that you must not attempt to enter any other enclave of the goblins. Our people are at war with yours and *Those Who Protect* have come from the deep places to guard the entrances. Even Krapneerg must temporarily be closed to you. He said that he will come to you when he can, when it is safe.'

Anton looked around a little more carefully. He could feel the hostility from the unknown goblins, some of whom clung to the walls in springing position while others hid themselves in the same shadows that Anton had once used himself. The underground world he knew had changed all too quickly. He was no longer welcome within its once comforting closeness.

'Anton,' Leap continued, this time speaking for himself, 'the men across the river continue to dig. They do not realise that...' Leap stopped a moment, eyes darting around to those who listened. 'They know not what they do. There is much to fear. We will protect ourselves. I can say no more.'

Anton met Leap's eyes and read the warning that he could not speak. An open battle was forming, one that the humans could not possibly win, although the goblins knew that they could also expect losses. There had been no time to formulate a plan of what to do, but he could be sure of one thing through the turmoil of emotions that assaulted his senses as his world turned upside down.

'Please tell Haghuf...' he began, unsure of his words. 'Tell him I am faithful to this.' He grasped the amulet tied round his neck, so like the one he had given Haghuf. Leap nodded in understanding. Spontaneously, Anton grasped Leap's shoulder with the other hand.

'You are a good friend, Leap.' He nodded to the goblins seen and unseen around the cavern, then retreated back to the surface world. His world, he reminded himself. He was not so sure that he would have chosen it, had the choice been his to make. The rhythm of the deep places, changed as it was, still called to him within the depths of another world that had closed to him.

There were only a few hours before dawn, and he knew that he should be back at the castle well before then, preferably with a plan of action in mind. He could not think of strategy when he was in the form of Wolf. The animal instincts were all he knew in that form, but he took it now to allow himself to cover distance.

As Wolf, he was aware of the disturbance in the air. Somewhere to the south he could hear distant drums, muffled as though the beats issued from within the ground. His paws flew at full speed taking him close to the place that he knew as home. He felt the sense of urgency, though he had forgotten why. He knew only that he must get home as quickly as possible and that there was danger. Danger everywhere. His powerful limbs moved in rhythm with the war drums, using their beating to hold the necessary pace beyond exhaustion. His breaths came heavy but steady as the unwavering undulations of his limbs carried him further and further, until he reached a place he knew and stopped.

He had not run all the way to the castle but had stopped to rest in a sheltered area not far from it. He had visualised the place before transforming, remembering it from his search for Talla so long ago. The memory of her came to him as he changed back into a man, stretching his limbs and trying to recover his breath. Then he remembered why he had chosen to stop here.

There was still time before dawn and a need to formulate a plan of action before issuing orders to those who served him at the castle. These at least, he knew would be loyal to him. He could not be sure of anyone else, human or goblin. Still, he was Count Anton. He must maintain the demeanor which was appropriate to his position, no matter what happened. The world he knew had been thrust into a delicate balance of change where much of the future depended on the most subtle perceptions of those who played a part in the changes as they occurred. A part of the prophecy came to his memory;

'If ignorance is chosen, all will die. The races will pass from the earth and the lands will be ruled only by the small creatures that survive until another Turning shall bring renewed evolution for sentient species. If the knowledge comes too early, only one species will die, and if too late, perhaps both will perish, yet some will survive to start the cycle again.'

It wasn't very promising. Timing was important, but getting the message across to the ignorant would not be easy in any circumstances. He had already tried once, but his words had been ignored by the fanatics. They clung to their ignorance as if it were a lifeline. A part of him felt that they deserved the slaughter they would bring on themselves by attacking the goblins in their own underground world. Yet he knew that leaving the war to play itself out would leave goblins and humans as enemies forever, or at least for his lifetime and beyond. And all for nothing more than an old superstition that should have died out with the last Turning.

He knew that he must not tarry. He was all too close to the entrance to Lirrewot and he had been warned not to enter there long before this trouble. The closeness of the security force to the surface at Krapneerg was probably mirrored in all of the entrances. With things as they were now, it would be reasonable to expect at least guards to patrol the openings, if not whole parties of raiders ready to quash any attempts at human invasion.

The moment it took to get his breath was enough to restore him so that he could finish the journey to the castle, not far away. He abandoned his place of concealment and sent his senses out to locate his guards who should be patrolling this area, the same guards who had captured Talla on her first visit to the castle. Instead, he found strangers in the vicinity, and they were alarmingly close. It took a moment in the darkness to recognise the hostile resonance which emanated from not one, but several small groups of men throughout the grounds. They were southern men.

Anton had no way of knowing why so many of them were posted in groups around his castle but he did not like the look of it. He started to move from one shadow to another, irritated that he felt he had to skulk in secret at the very doorstep of his own home. He considered a moment whether it might be wise to return to wolf form, but before he could finish the thought a man who had been relieving himself in a clump of bushes spotted him in the faint moonlight.

'He's here!' the man shouted to his nearest companions. 'I've found Count Anton!'

Anton cursed himself silently for allowing the distraction of so many men to divert his attention from the more obvious presence of the one so nearby. Another six men immediately surrounded him. He did not recognise any of them personally. Their south-of-the-river origins were clearly marked by their countenances and mode of dress. His quick mind swiftly examined his options. Wolf could probably take them, but there were many others nearby. It was unlikely that they would die quietly. Running for the castle might become possible with some manoeuvring, but again there were others stationed in his path and once he ran, his authority over these people would be lost forever. There was one option left. He stood proudly and addressed the men in the tone of nobility addressing inferiors.

'I had not expected a welcoming party on my return home, what business brings you men to my castle at such an hour?'

Taken aback for a moment by the bravado, the men looked to each other for a response. There was no natural leader among them but the one who had first spotted him eventually spoke.

'Demon business o'course! We know about you now, Count Anton. That you know all about these demons that live in the ground in our own city and never said nuthin to nobody.'

'Of course I never said anything.' Anton replied arrogantly. 'Look at how your people respond! The creatures have never done anything to you, yet you hunt them down and kill them. It doesn't even cross your mind that if they were in fact the demons of legend that you imagine, your pikes would do them no harm. Even in legend demons are creatures of spirit. What you've killed is flesh and blood.'

For a moment the men looked confused. Again, one looked to another for a response. There was no answer to what Anton had said, but the sound of their voices had carried swiftly on the still night air. Voices were raised in anger as another group of men came running towards them from the direction of the castle. There were at least a dozen of them and Anton could see that these were not in the mood for philosophical conversation.

'Explain it to your comrades will you?' he said irritably, then dashed between two of them in the opposite direction up the hill over the entrance to Lirrewot. Behind him he heard shouts of 'Demon lover!' and other accusations. The shouts roused the other groups of men that had been patrolling the area. The Count had not realised how many there were, but from the vantage point of the small hill he could see men running towards him from all directions brandishing sharp weapons and shouting for his blood. He wondered for a moment where his guards were and whether the shouts would alert his own people within the castle. But there was no time. The southerners were closing on him. They were too much of an angry mob to expect other than to be torn limb from limb.

With no other choices before him, he leaped down to the entrance and ran into the moonlit shadows of Lirrewot cavern. His only thought was concealment. If he didn't go too far in, perhaps he would not be noticed. It was possible that some of the men would search until they found the entrance as well, but would they be foolish enough to enter?

He knew the tricks of goblins enough to find an alcove where men would be unlikely to look for him.

Such hiding places were common near the entrances in particular, so that if an enemy entered the caverns they would find goblins both in front and behind them if they came in very far. Anton was grateful that he didn't find a goblin already hiding in this one.

He closed his eyes, acknowledging to himself that he was afraid. It wasn't death that frightened him, but the pain of a violent death at the hands of humans or goblins did not appeal. Given a choice between being ripped apart or eaten alive, he wondered if his magical disciplines would hold in such a situation enough to leave his body and travel into the astral realms before the worst of the violence. Neither promised to be an easy death.

He heard a few men run past his hiding place. Fools indeed. They ran without thought, too caught up in the chase either to notice the concealed prey or to consider the danger they ran towards. He heard the screams as they ran down the first stair, which came to an abrupt halt all too quickly. The goblins were indeed patrolling near the surface. Hopefully the blood-curdling shrieks would be enough to dissuade the others from following. The acoustics of the cavern were like a giant echo chamber which would reverberate the horrifying sounds out through the entrance, chilling the blood of any who stood outside.

Anton waited patiently, but there was no other sound. An eternity seemed to pass, yet there was nothing. At last he was reasonably sure that the men must have given up the chase, perhaps assuming him dead like their comrades. He consciously relaxed his shoulders, releasing the tension that the fear had raised in him. Slowly, he opened his eyes. He hoped to see nothing more than the empty cavern, still lit by the soft moonlight that spilt through the doorway just a few steps away.

Despite his optimism that he had managed to escape, he wasn't entirely surprised to see the shadows before him broken by the reflection of moonlight from two pairs of large yellow eyes, looking directly at him. He almost chuckled as he thought to himself that they were far too big to belong to cats.

Chapter Eleven

Anton's mind raced through his limited options. All of them demanded that he come out of his hiding place willingly. To wait for them to come in after him would mean certain death.

'I am Count Anton,' he said clearly in the goblin language. He hoped that identifying himself would at least make them hesitate to attack, although the two large goblins were certainly of the kind called *Those Who Protect*. They were very unlikely to extend the status of *guest* to him, even in these circumstances. Still, if he could stall their movements by talking to them, he might be able to get into a position where turning into Wolf would allow him to run for the door swiftly enough to escape. He dared not attack them, even in defence. That would be the one move that would make him *goblin enemy* forever, and even Haghuf himself might hunt him down for such a transgression.

'I apologise for invading your realm uninvited,' he continued, holding their gaze as he moved slowly to a more advantageous position, 'but the humans were hunting me, intending to kill me for my friendship with your people…'

Suddenly his breath was knocked out of him by a powerful arm that scooped him unceremoniously into a clinch that defied the act of breathing at all.

'No humans in the caverns!' asserted the very large and muscular goblin who had come up from behind Anton.

Jiggling about like a rag doll in the grip of the goblin as the flapping feet ran down a passage, Anton was so surprised and disoriented that he could not react at first. The journey must have been very short or the goblin's running was very fast. In the few seconds it took him to regain perspective so that he was able to determine which way was up, the goblin had reached his goal. Anton was twisted around once again as the goblin's powerful arms lifted him above his head with no apparent strain, and casually threw him into a fissure.

He was immediately engulfed in complete darkness. In his mind's eye, he remembered the pits that Haghuf had warned him to avoid. He had got the impression before that they were very deep, which was reinforced now as he continued to fall for what seemed an eternity. He supposed that he should count himself lucky that it was a particularly large opening, as all the flailing about that his unruly limbs could manage only met with open air, rather than with potentially very damaging abrasions from the sides of the pit. He tried not to think of the inevitable force of the landing, or what he might be landing on, when at last he reached the bottom. He must have fallen a great distance already, far more than he could expect to survive through the impact when at last he hit solid ground.

He was even more surprised when the fall ended in a sudden rush of changed air in a dimly lit open space and a splash, which held an impact of its own as he plunged deep within the unexpected body of water. Until that moment, he had managed to maintain his equilibrium. Now as he rolled helplessly through the torrents of water caused by his own momentum through its depths, he wondered if the darker conditions within the water would allow just a glimpse of which way the bubbles from his breath floated so that he could determine which direction led to the surface. Whether there was any chance of reaching it before he drowned was another matter.

His will to live had carried him a long way through the series of events that brought him to this juncture, but it was beginning to fade as his attempts to blow bubbles in the dark water only resulted in less air in his lungs and no clue as to which way he should swim. He began to float helplessly, having run out of options…and of air. He had begun to accept that at least drowning was reported to be a peaceful death.

Then he felt something sharp on his ankle and thought he heard a high-pitched sound pierce the water. This was followed by something snaking around his waist yet again. It felt to be about the diameter of an arm, but certainly longer. Anton had a vision of some form of horrifying tentacled beast. *There's something in the water.* He was losing consciousness, but then something engulfed his face and pushed air into his lungs. Instinctively he thrashed and resisted having his face covered by something unknown, perhaps the mouth of some deep creature who would swallow him in the next breath. This confused him. Why was he given breath?

He felt himself moving, propelled by whatever had hold of him through the water. He had given up struggling, having no strength left to fight whatever fate awaited him from the unknown creature. All at once he found himself thrust into airy space and dropped hard onto a rocky surface. The impact knocked water out of his lungs and he rolled onto his stomach to cough up more of it and gasp for welcome breath.

He looked around to see soft, iridescent light in a rocky cavern with stalactites reflecting crystal light over a dark pool of water. Of the creature that had apparently spat him out, he could see nothing. There was only a slightly foamy disturbance far out in the water where something powerful had dived back in. *There's something in the water*. The thought repeated itself, but he was too weak to think further. He collapsed where he lay on the rocky shore and slipped into exhausted sleep.

* * *

Ranalf woke to a gentle tapping on his door. He recognised the pre-dawn light from his window that had plagued his dreams and sat up, instantly awake. Dani had said last night that if the Count had not returned before dawn, they would have to act without further delay. The implication was clear at the time, that such a failure to return could mean disaster for Count Anton.

He leapt up and threw the door open to find Jerak waiting on the other side.

'We must cross the river. How soon can you be ready?' His flat tone and gaunt look suggested that he had been awake all night. Ranalf suddenly felt like a child who had been sent to bed while the grown-ups held a war council.

'Three minutes,' he answered crisply. Then closing the door gently, he began to throw his clothes on as quickly as he was able, ignoring the tears that welled in his eyes. He didn't need to hear the words spoken to know that the household feared that Count Anton was dead. Within his heart, he felt strongly that Anton lived still, but he recognised the possibility that it may only be a vain hope based on his own desire. Count Anton had become closer to him than even his own father or older brother, and had so recently brought him into some form of inner circle. He could not entertain the thought of his loss so quickly, not now.

Ranalf composed himself and opened the door again. Jerak had waited. He led him down the stairs to the courtyard where Dani was issuing instructions to the castle guards as if he were a trained army commander. Ranalf's world was becoming surreal, was it just last night that this man was pouring wine for him as a servant? What confused him more was what they expected to do with a handful of guards against the southern army. They would be hopelessly outnumbered. Jerak had said that they were crossing the river, Ranalf could only surmise that the intention was to attack them on their own ground. The plan seemed mad, or desperate.

Dani turned as Jerak and Ranalf approached.

'We're as ready as we're going to be, let's go,' he said to Jerak, then turned to Ranalf.

'You're going to see some things today that you may not fully understand. Stay close to one of us and we'll guide you. There will be some things you can help with, but it's going to be a steep learning curve.'

Ranalf nodded, accepting his position as…apprentice perhaps?

'The others are waiting by the river.' Jerak said. Ranalf looked at him. *Others*? Dani nodded to Jerak in response and ordered the guards to follow as they all began walking towards the gate. Ranalf kept the barrage of questions that plagued him to himself. He was intelligent enough to realise the importance of whatever they were going to do. The explanations would have to come in due course. Whatever was going to happen, it promised to be an eventful day.

Ranalf had expected to see a few more men by the river waiting, or possibly even a small army. What he didn't expect was a mixed group of men and women. There were about twenty of them altogether, readying the small flat bottomed boats for the crossing. They took little notice of the approaching group, apart from the occasional nod of acknowledgement. They boarded the crafts efficiently, despite the wobbling that characterised the unsteady boats that were commonly found by the river.

'I never thought I would get into another of these,' said an attractive auburn-haired woman. She reminded Ranalf of someone, though he wasn't sure of who. He offered her a helping hand and was guided by Dani to get in as well, followed by himself and Jerak. Four people per boat was as much as they could hold. Ranalf thought that they would have to make several trips across to move everyone. It was then that he noticed the other group of about ten people on the far shore waiting for their companions. Whoever they were, there were a good sized group of them.

'Laura, this is Lana's boy,' said Dani by way of introduction. The woman suddenly looked at Ranalf intently. He wondered what his mother had to do with any of these people, but was too polite to interrupt.

'Ranalf, this is Laura.' Ranalf nodded graciously as Dani spoke. The boat prevented any possibility of standing up for a more formal greeting. 'She is your aunt.'

He looked up sharply, then remembered to close his mouth. The shock of this information had left it forgotten. Laura smiled indulgently. She understood all too well what impact this sudden information would have on the lad.

'Lana crossed the river several years before I did, for the usual reason,' she said sadly. 'I missed her, I was only a child of eight at the time. They promised me to the man she was meant to marry, but my mother insisted that they must wait until I was twelve for the wedding to occur. My father would have planned it for my birthday, but I didn't wait.'

Ranalf didn't know what to say. Jerak rowed the boat steadily. No sound was heard in the early morning light besides the water splashing rhythmically against the oars. Ranalf had worked out that it was indeed his mother that Laura reminded him of, but a much younger version of her. What confused him was that there should only be four years between them according to Laura's story. She looked little older than himself. He contemplated the relationship as the boats moved slowly across the water. If indeed he was related through his mother to the southern fanatics, then there would be others among them that were direct kin to him. Was he now expected to fight them, or even kill some of them?

Meanwhile, the scene which awaited the magicians not far from the river had progressed into full battle since dawn. The dead goblin which had been taken to the Count had been unearthed at Y'smonreb. Literally unearthed. Such vehicles as carriages were even less common on the south side of the river, but some of the southern men had discovered and repaired a large machine in one of the abandoned factories which existed from before the last Turning. It was called a digger. There had been no fuel for it, but one of the men had heard an old rumour that distillated potato water could be used in some machinery. They had chosen a spot to test its use randomly, but then they found passages under the ground much like those they had encountered during the demon hunt months before. Some men had been sent to gather weapons while others continued to dig. The goblin they had found was unfortunate to be too close to the digging site and far outnumbered before his enclave could be alerted.

Paul and his close lieutenants had been very disappointed in Count Anton's response to the evidence they had provided. They had hoped for authorisation to mount a full scale digging expedition. After the Count had disappeared into one of the demons' secret caves they had returned and organised it without his permission. It was after all, their own side of the river and the Count had largely left them alone in the past.

This time, however, armed men were waiting before the digging started. As was customary, the operation had been planned for the crack of dawn. Paul might have decided to start sooner, but there was little moonlight and it was impractical to use the machine in insufficient light. Besides, he was sure that the demons could see better in darkness. It was the way of such creatures.

What he didn't expect was that the goblins might attack in the darkness of pre-dawn, or that the battle would be silent. He had pictured a hoard of marauding, raiding goblins screaming as they ran out of their underground hiding place en masse. He only realised that the battle had already begun when he climbed the machine to have a word with the man who had been chosen to operate the digger and found him sitting dead in the operator's seat, his throat cut.

Paul shouted to the company below in warning and instantly the sound of clashing metal rose from the field. The open battle was begun.

The various small groups of demon hunters gathered on the field had been more than a little surprised when the warning came. They had seen nothing, but even as they turned to look in the direction of the excavation the demons appeared from the shadows all around them. More alarming still was that the creatures all carried proper swords, and seemed to know how to use them. The men were inadequate against them with their pikes and staves, although some were fairly handy with a knife.

A goblin suddenly sprang up right in the middle of a group of four men. A quick spin and kick and two human heads rolled away as a third body crumpled to the ground. The remaining man ran, but the goblin caught up with him quickly and despatched him with a sword through the ribs. In another slightly larger group the men put up a fairly good fight despite the surprise attack from the shadow next to them. For a moment, they thought they were winning as they battered the goblin with various instruments that passed as weaponry. The sharpest of them was a pike, but the close quarters fighting was too limiting to get an advantage with the weapon. The goblin appeared to be fighting a losing battle, but then the men noticed the drops of blood dripping from his blade. One of them crumpled, quickly followed by another. The remaining men would have checked themselves for wounds if the goblin hadn't been joined by one of his companions. The effect of taking serious wounds unknowingly, even when they appeared to be winning, was almost as terrifying as the blood on the goblin's sword. The men fought less skilfully, and before long it was only the largest pockets of men that managed to hold their ground at all.

The sun rose over a scene of desperate battle. The men fought for their lives even as they remembered that they were supposed to be fighting a holy war. Many of their companions were found dead in the shadows where they had been despatched before they had learned that the demons were among them. The renewed hatred that these discoveries elicited was enough to add an element of fervour to the fighting skills of the outraged men and the battle began to become more evenly matched. It might have ended quickly if it wasn't for the sheer numbers on both sides.

Paul's eyes narrowed as he surveyed the carnage below him. He was not well acquainted with the workings of the digger, but he understood some of its basic controls so that he could manage to turn it on and make it move. The rest he could work out as he went along. He pushed the body out of the seat, sending it with a sickening thud to the ground. There was no time for sentiment.

The machine had been rigged so that the push of a button would start its engine. This he did, and the unnatural roar of machinery thundering through the sounds of battle. The distraction caused some deaths on both sides as some fighters both human and goblin turned to see what was causing the tumult. Others, thinking more quickly, grabbed the opportunity to take advantage of their opponents. The digger itself did not have to move far as it had been digging on the site so recently, but Paul did not intend to dig further at present. It had occurred to him that the source of reinforcements was the underground caverns and that by closing them he could cut off an easy escape for the fighting demons, as the sun rose higher in the sky.

The strategy soon became apparent and several of the goblins turned from the battle and tried to climb the digger as it moved. The men they had been fighting followed them, attempting to protect their leader by chasing the demons down and stabbing them in the back as they tried to climb. Some escaped long enough to climb halfway up the machine, followed by human pursuers. By a fluke, Paul found a lever that would spin the cab of the machine and sent goblins and men flying in all directions.

Despite their superior weapons and fighting skills, the battle was beginning to turn against the goblins. The sun blinded them as it grew stronger, and they had been vastly outnumbered from the start. The digger, freed of interference, collapsed the excavation. Paul had succeeded in cutting off access to an escape route as well as reinforcements for the goblins. Those who were still above ground had begun to accept their fate, that they would not survive the day. It was something that *Those Who Protect* assumed any time they were called to battle, that many of them would not return.

The outcome of the battle was seemingly inevitable. Even the most head-blind southern humans could feel the change in the struggle. They were heartened by the taste of victory to come. Paul climbed down from the digger to join the fighting. He wanted to kill at least one demon himself before the battle ended, to taste the thrill of the conqueror. He had not thought ahead as to what the men would do when the demons they had trapped above ground had been despatched. He knew that this was only one battle, that there were many more demons hiding under the ground, but for the moment he could only think of the combat at hand.

The feel of the battle changed again as more humans began spilling onto the scene. Suddenly the clouds darkened and covered the sun. The fighting goblins began to pluck up courage once more as the enemy became easier to see. There was carnage everywhere. Weapons of all sorts dripped with blood. The goblins observed the newcomers with curiosity as they were apparently unarmed, yet they took a stance of authority as they gathered on an incline above the scene of the battle. They could not understand the words that the humans spoke, but the goblins recognised that it was they who had darkened the sun. For some of *Those Who Protect*, it was the first time that they had ever seen human magicians.

'Stop!' Dani shouted though a cone-shaped device which amplified his voice over the crowd. 'This conflict is not authorised. All men retreat from battle and gather here at the foot of the hill. In the name of Count Anton, you are forbidden to provoke further hostilities. Retreat!'

During this speech, the other magicians had been performing some sort of dance, with slow movements and low chanting. A sort of paralysis descended over the combatants, so that both human and goblin were unable to raise their weapons to each other. Yet the humans were able to move to obey the command to retreat and gather in the designated area. The goblins naturally regrouped closer to the site where they knew their own goblin diggers would be working on re-opening the passage to the deep places.

Paul was livid. How dare these godless magicians interfere in such a holy purpose, and in the name of the traitor, Count Anton? They were demon lovers, all of them. The power that they had exerted over his fighting men was the power of evil, but he would vanquish it and see these traitors slaughtered as well. He had no weapon in his hands. The paralysis had been directed at the weapons themselves, so Paul was free to move where he wished, despite his anger and intent to put a stop to this interference. He strode up the incline to their leader, whom he recognised as a servant of Count Anton. It was time the people learned the truth about their precious nobleman.

* * *

Anton woke to the feeling of a million small rocks pressing uncomfortably into his flesh. He did not move. Somewhere in his memory, he knew that he had been in danger. His waking senses immediately told him that he wasn't alone. He reached carefully with his awareness and sensed someone sitting next to him. Carefully, he opened one eye just enough to see a knobbly foot, with greenish flesh. There was no doubt that his companion was goblin. Memory flooded back in all of its terrifying detail. He quieted his mind as much as possible, knowing the senses of the creatures to be even more acute than his own. Having one of *Those Who Protect* recognise his wakefulness would not be to his advantage.

'You asked me once what we do with our dead.' Anton recognised Haghuf's voice with relief. 'Now you know.'

He tried then to move, very slowly, as he took stock of each of his limbs and their condition.

'Where are we?' asked the Count.

'Someplace where no human should be,' Haghuf answered flatly. 'We need to move as soon as you are able.'

Anton managed to sit up a little and look around at his surroundings. Through the haze of his tired vision he could see the opening in the ceiling of the cavern that he must have fallen through. It was surrounded with the iridescent stalactites that were everywhere in the cavern, glowing with an eerie purplish light. This was reflected off the dark blue pool of water. The water itself looked to be clear, but dark. Flickers of movement could be seen within its depths. But the darkness itself prevented human eyes from seeing what moved within its secret abysm. He noticed that his boot had been removed from his right foot and remembered the sudden pain he had felt before hearing the high pitched sound in the water that preceded his tentacled ride and expulsion onto land. There were marks on the foot. An even crescent of needle-like punctures, but they were not deep. In fact, they appeared to have all but healed over very cleanly. Still, they looked very much as if something had started to take a bite out of him. He glanced again at the flickers of movement in the pool.

'There's something in the water,' Anton said aloud this time.

Haghuf looked uncomfortable and refused to meet Anton's eyes as he answered.

'The deep places have many such pools and secret places. How do you think my ancestors survived without dying from thirst?' Despite himself, he turned and looked at the water for a moment before he continued. The shimmery flickers that reflected within the water made him feel anxious. They seemed to have become more active since Anton's waking. He turned to the Count, this time locking his gaze to emphasise the importance of his words.

'All bodies of water have creatures that live within them. In the deep places, it is better not to ask too many questions. Some secrets are buried very deeply indeed. We must leave. Now.'

'Leave to where?' Anton asked as he bent carefully to recover his boot. He had become completely disoriented in the underground world. He had lost all sense of time and knew nothing of the battle that raged on the surface world. Too many things had changed too quickly.

'Your people have attacked mine at Y'smonreb. They have a machine that digs. Many of us have retreated to the deep places to preserve the species, while *Those Who Protect* guard the entrances.'

Haghuf's explanation brought back the memory of the goblins who had thrown him down the pit, apparently expecting that whatever lived within the deep waters would finish him off. He took in the events that Haghuf had explained as he pulled the boot on. Much was happening in both worlds.

'What of Talla?' Anton asked. He had to know.

'She refuses to go to safety. She has...ties with the surface world,' he continued quickly, not wishing for Anton to think too much about what those ties might be.

'Your magicians have crossed the river. Even now they are nearing the battle. I don't know their intentions, but I think they may need your wisdom. We must leave. Quickly.'

Haghuf's eyes kept darting towards the water as he spoke. Anton noted it, but did not ask further questions. He could see that Haghuf knew more about what lived in the water than he told, but he had never seen him show fear about anything before, and logic told him that his friend's anxiousness to leave was probably well founded despite his own feeling toward the water. Whatever was in it felt calm, even loving. Somewhere in the back of his consciousness, he thought that he heard gentle singing from an entrancing female voice. Had he been alone, he might well have entered the water again to look for the source.

'Anton!'

Haghuf's voice jerked him back to the present. Anton was surprised to find that he had actually taken a few steps in the direction of the water. He had been slipping into some form of trance.

'Anton, you must promise me that you will never try to find this place, or any of the others like it.' Anton nodded in agreement. The danger was all too apparent, but he would question Haghuf about it later.

'I know ways that you must not try to remember,' Haghuf said. 'They will bring us to a place near the battle, near enough to get there quickly without coming into the middle of it without knowing how the tide turns.'

Haghuf hesitated a moment before asking the question that had been turning over in his mind.

'Anton, we have never spoken of it openly. You have an ability that even few of your other magicians share.'

Anton knew immediately what he meant. Shape shifter. Wolf. He had never actually changed in front of the goblins, but he hadn't been very careful to remain unobserved by them either. He had felt that it would help separate him from other humans in their minds if they knew.

'We need to travel quickly.' Haghuf finished.

Much of what was said by goblins was left to implication, but Anton understood clearly. Immediately, he began to sink into the consciousness that was Wolf. He felt himself becoming more aware of his most primal instincts. Hunger, safety…scents. He scented danger in the cavern. But from the goblin he sensed only a well trusted friend. There was urgency, a need to move away from this place. The goblin needed to be transported.

Haghuf couldn't help but think that the powerful creature was surprisingly large compared to Anton's human form. He had never been so close to him in this form before. The black fur made him difficult to discern clearly in the dark, even to goblin eyes.

Wolf crouched next to Haghuf, looking at him expectantly. The goblin climbed onto his back carefully, watching for any sign of a negative reaction. There was none. As soon as Haghuf was securely seated, Wolf leapt forward, ready to travel. He stopped in mid-stride, waiting for instructions. Haghuf leaned forward, knowing the first passage was going to be a tight fit. Grasping the body of the animal with his knees, he pointed to a dark opening ahead that could have been easily overlooked.

'That way.' He said, then hung onto the heavy scruff of Wolf's nape as they lunged together through the opening and into the dark labyrinth of caverns that formed a part of the secret ways. No human had ever entered them before, not even Anton.

Wolf ran as swiftly as the limited space in the passages would allow. He was guided by the goblin on his back. A nudge of the knee from one side or the other determined which path he would take in the labyrinth. The goblin knew the way. They worked together as a single unit. Wolf could provide the speed that the goblin needed, and the goblin provided direction. Wolf would have been completely lost on his own in this warren of passages with no distinctive scents to mark one from another, but he trusted the goblin completely. They shared a single goal, a single destination. Wolf could not remember what that was or why, but he gave himself over completely to the goblin, because he knew. All Wolf had to think about was getting there as quickly as possible.

They seemed to climb forever upward along paths that sloped slightly, yet twisted and turned in all directions. The correct path was far from obvious whenever they reached a junction of more than one passage. Once a steeper path looked as though it might lead to the surface more quickly, but the goblin didn't choose this one. The goblin didn't hesitated for a moment. Eventually the scents changed and Wolf could smell sunlight and grass, trees and other things that grew in the surface world. He whined ever so slightly when the goblin directed him away from a path that smelled strongly of these things in favour of another path that actually sloped downward and smelt more musty. A little later, Wolf smelled these things again and the goblin seemed to spur him on to run freely towards the growing light.

Suddenly they burst into the sunlight and the goblin buried his face in the wolf's fur. Wolf knew that the sunlight hurt the goblin's eyes, but he also knew where he was now and where he was going. He knew all of these lands well, and had travelled them many times both as Wolf and as man. He was able to run at full speed now, crossing natural country under his own guidance while the goblin friend only clung to him as baggage. The weight was nothing to Wolf. His powerful muscles undulated freely, paws flying so quickly that an observer would not have been able to make out their detail.

All too suddenly the sun was darkened by clouds which had not been there a moment before. The goblin looked up a little, still keeping his head low to Wolf so that he would not break the wind as they flew towards their destination. Wolf recognised that the change was unnatural, but knew it as the work of magicians. Urgency spurred him on even faster. At some level, he knew that magicians only changed the natural world in times of dire need. Whatever was happening, he was needed.

The battlefield came into sight. Wolf's keen eyes could see the magicians on the hill, but there was a struggle. A man that Wolf instinctively sensed as enemy was physically struggling with one he knew well as one of his own pack. He was trying to take something from him, both men shouting to the waiting men below them. There were goblins as well, a group of them standing away from the men, but many of them were disappearing into an opening in the ground. The men seemed unaware of the movements of the goblins. The goblins dispersed silently as the attention of the men was on the struggle before them, between those of their own kind.

Goblins parted to let the wolf run through as he sped towards the altercation. Somewhere along the way the friend-goblin on his back slid off. Anton began to become aware of himself. He was beginning to understand the words. Wolf had nearly reached the struggling men when suddenly the woman was there, shouting above the two men, and another man leapt up to protect her. No Ranalf! Suddenly they were all on him. Anton knew the boy's words put him in danger. Wolf leapt to the attack, scattering those who assaulted one of his own.

Haghuf watched as the wolf threw the human altercation into greater confusion. He saw the magicians drop their spell and scatter. The clouds they had raised would take some time to disperse, but those humans who were nearest the goblins discovered that they could lift their weapons again and Haghuf was glad to be among what was left of the fighting goblins. One of the larger goblins had been fighting with two swords, but handed one to Haghuf.

Two of the humans rushed at him, seeing a smaller goblin that they thought might make easier prey. The few other goblins that had not gone back underground were busied with attackers themselves. There was no choice but to take these two alone.

Haghuf grinned and heard the sinister note in his own laugh as it escaped his lips. He swept circles to the right and left with the sword to try its weight and fell into the remembered stance. It was one of the things he had never told Anton about. There was a time when Haghuf had been a fighting goblin, much like the marauders of the human legends. He had killed humans in battle with the best of them. He was no stranger to sword fighting.

One of the humans had a proper sword. He didn't seem particularly adept at using it, but it was a weapon not to be ashamed of. The other swung a pike towards Haghuf and tried to charge him. It was a small matter to step aside and pull the man by his grip on the weapon onto the blade of his own sword. The soft flesh, the momentary resistance followed by the blade penetrating deeply and the blood spurting touched a very old memory. Haghuf felt *goblin* again. He had been spending far too much time sympathising with humans of late.

The sword wielding human took a clumsy swing at Haghuf. Blade rang on blade in close combat. Again Haghuf heard himself chuckle as he was seeing himself through the head-blind human's eyes. The man saw a goblin from his own twisted perception of creatures of Hell, his evil laugh a mockery of respect for human life.

If the man were to live, the image would damage any chance of peace. But Haghuf was not concerned. He saw the human's thoughts all too clearly. Each move he made as they parried and thrust at each other was known to Haghuf before it occurred. If he hadn't been enjoying playing with the prey the fight might have ended at any time. Then he heard Talla's cry. Haghuf's sensitive goblin hearing recognised even the faint sound of her voice coming from the churning maelstrom of humans. He thrust the killing stroke to end the altercation.

He hadn't seen her among the humans before. Somehow she was there and was in trouble. He dropped the sword and began to run, hoping that he would be fast enough.

Chapter Twelve

Ranalf smelt the sickening stench of spilled blood as the magicians approached the battlefield. He had never seen death close up before. To see so much of it all at once, and the randomness of it that characterised battle, was enough to make him hope that he would never have to see it again. He was glad that he had eaten nothing more than a lump of fruited bread on the journey across.

The magicians acted quickly as if co-ordinating their movements had been planned and drilled over months of practice rather than decided on the fly. They spread out into a circle over a convenient rise overlooking the battle. Immediately Ranalf felt something pass through the unit they created. It was a sort of force, or energy, that took him up with it and brought him into the fold. He suddenly felt intimate with each person in the circle as if they were close family that he had known all his life. Most of them hadn't even been introduced to him yet.

Laura stayed close to him and mouthed the words of the chant with exaggerated expression so that he could take it up and join with them. He found his participation in the ritual all too natural, much to his own confusion. Strange as it was he felt completely at home among them. Whatever was happening to him, it felt good. His attention wavered for a moment when the sun darkened rapidly.

Then the energy he felt was captured and concentrated by someone within the group that he could sense but not see and directed to the battlefield. The fighting stopped. The combatants simply lowered their weapons all at once, giving in to some sort of paralysis that Ranalf could perceive emanating from his own group. The feeling of absolute power thrilled him, even as it perplexed him. What had he actually been doing to contribute to this magic? He obviously had much to learn.

Dani was outside of the circle speaking to the people, ordering them to retreat. It was a truly impressive sight. Such power, without raising a weapon, was something he knew he would have to learn more about as soon as this was over. He saw the magicians clearly for the first time. They were not at all as the people of his clan had portrayed them in superstitious whispers. Ranalf had little time to speculate on this, when suddenly the leader of the southern men was there, challenging Dani and trying to wrest the megaphone out of his hand to argue his own case to the people.

'Listen to me!' Paul shouted through the device. 'These creatures have killed your brothers, they bring weapons to kill us all!'

'No!' returned Dani, wresting the device back from Paul. 'They defend themselves because you are digging into their homes and cutting them down like animals! Wouldn't you do the same?' Dani caught another breath before Paul lunged at him again, trying to take away the megaphone once more. Ranalf wondered if he should help and was in fact preparing to spring when Dani wrested it back and addressed the field in a gentler tone.

'Look at them,' Dani continued, with a sweeping gesture of his arm. The people were suddenly reminded that the goblins were standing and watching them from just a short distance away. 'They gather in defence, not in attack. They look much like other men, except for the pointed ears and the colour of their skin. In fact, you all share common ancestors with them. They are descended from men like yourselves. They are not animals, they are your brothers. They protect themselves as you would do yourselves if another settlement attacked you.'

Paul lunged at the megaphone, grabbing it roughly from Dani's hands.

'No! He lies! Look at the green monsters, at their broad feet and hands. These are not men!'

Ranalf had noticed that the horde of goblins was slowly growing smaller during this, no doubt taking the opportunity to disperse many of their number back underground. Then suddenly without warning, Talla was there in the fray with Dani and Paul, holding a bundle. Ranalf didn't know how or when she had made her way to the front of the crowd, but she appeared so suddenly that Paul was taken unawares. Even with only one hand available she took the speaking device from him without difficulty. More confusing than her sudden presence was her green skin and pointed ears. Ranalf had never seen her in her true form, but she made no effort to hide it now. She stood before them proudly, as goblin. Ranalf saw the face of the woman he loved through the greenish complexion. He wanted only to reach out and hold her.

'It's true!' Talla shouted clearly through the megaphone. Her command of the human language had grown during her absence from the surface world. 'Your people and mine are closely akin. We have always known this. And here is proof! My daughter, born of my own body. Only creatures of a kind can breed in nature, you all know this. My child bears the attributes of the human who seeded her, one of your own people.'

Dropping the megaphone, she unwrapped the bundle and held up a perfectly formed baby girl, wiggling and pink like any human infant. The assembled company gasped in unison. The impact of the revelation took them by such force that they forgot any thoughts of conflict for a moment. One by one, they began to question much of what they thought they knew. Some began to see that they had been driven by prejudice rather than by actual events. It was true that there had been no trouble from the goblins before the humans had invaded their world. They felt anger at the loss of their companions mixed with guilt and confusion.

Paul swept up the discarded megaphone and took advantage of the sudden silence. Pushing Talla back so hard that she nearly dropped the baby, he leapt in front of her and addressed the crowd again.

'The demon bitch lies! The child is clearly human, a changeling, stolen from its cot in the night! Who among you has lost a child?'

Paul knew the rate of crib deaths among his people. It was highly likely that several of them would have lost infants of the right age to support his assertion. Everyone knew that demons stole children and replaced them with their own ugly brats, leaving them to die in the healthy infant's place. It did not occur to him that there could be anyone who would support the demon woman's story.

'She speaks the truth!' Ranalf shouted, projecting his voice with the power that had been flowing through him. He needed no megaphone. In the distance, he saw the wolf running towards him. A wolf he knew. A goblin had been riding it, but it slipped off the back of the animal in mid-stride and joined its own people. Heartened by the return of the Count and driven by a protective instinct to place himself in front of the woman he loved and her child...his child...he continued.

‘This child is of my making, she is my daughter. Human and goblin can breed, and so are of a kind. Do not act in ignorance!’

Paul was visibly horrified by this revelation. His face contorted into an expression of disgust at the thought of a human joining with a goblin woman, and worse, producing offspring from the union out of wedlock.

‘Demon fornicator!’ he shouted again through the megaphone. ‘Such creatures are not suitable for marriage, but you lie with them in the night and create such abominations!’

This was too much for the superstitious humans. Their prejudices could not so easily fade. The violation of their religion with its stringent sexual taboos in addition to the alien appearance of the goblins could not make them easily accept the mental imagery of an unmarried young man among them lying with one of the creatures. Many were outraged by the thought. They rushed towards him, picking up rocks as they came. Some threw them at him, others used them as weapons to smash into the skull of the demon fornicator.

Talla’s instinct was to force her way forward and fight, but she was burdened with the baby in her arms. Even as the press of attackers first assaulted Ranalf, Paul’s closest companions pushed in. Talla found each of her arms held by a man as another took the baby. Someone put a sack over her head. She protested and squirmed, but even her goblin strength was no match for so many. A cloth was tied around her mouth to gag her through the sack and she felt herself lifted as several pairs of arms carried her away.

The magicians also broke their circle and hurried to defend their companion, but they were outside of the main body of attackers and could only fight those who formed the outer circle of the foray. The angry mob was so intent on their revenge that they did not see the wolf running and leaping until he was among them. Some ran at the sight of the monster, while others were grabbed by powerful jaws and thrown aside. Even the magicians fell back under the vehemence of the familiar animal's rescue charge.

The sudden carnage was so shocking that no one saw which way the Hellhound escaped after its brief but vicious attack, or from which direction Count Anton suddenly appeared. Despite their recent doubts of him they were relieved to see that he had returned among them. The habit of respect was such that the crowd immediately fell away, leaving Ranalf alone in the Count's care as he tenderly approached the fallen lad. He took him into his arms like a broken child. Some of them suddenly remembered that the lad was one of their own. But it was too late. Ranalf was dead.

Latham stood in the front of the remaining mob. A blood-stained rock fell from his fingers as the Count lifted the slight body of Ranalf, confronting his killers with the evidence of their foul deed. His dark, fierce eyes seemed to bore into each of them individually as his gaze swept the faces both known and unknown.

'See what your prejudice brings?' His menacing voice was controlled, almost subdued in its tone, and yet rang clearly through the open field. His grief for the boy eliminated any thoughts of jealousy that he had lain with the woman that they both loved. The child, he knew, might be either of theirs. Possibly even someone else's. Goblins had no social custom of monogamy and Talla was her own woman. The thought that they had both known her intimately only increased the closeness he felt to Ranalf, though he lay dead now.

'You have murdered one of your own, a mere lad. Some of you are kin to him. Yet his blood is still wet on your hands.'

Several people shifted from one foot to another uneasily, unable to look directly at the Count under his accusing eyes. One man openly began to cry. He had been of Ranalf's own kin. Slowly they began to speak quietly among themselves of the lad's parents. They had refused to join the escalating mob as Paul had gathered recruits in the night. Someone must bring them the news of his death. Count Anton was just about to take the responsibility himself when he felt a gentle hand on his arm and looked up to see Laura.

'Anton,' Laura said, with both sadness and urgency in her voice. Her eyes met his, saying what she dare not speak with so many people about. 'They have taken the goblin woman and the baby, some of the other goblins have followed but they may not be quick enough. They were moving towards the river.'

Anton felt the urgency. His impulse was to leap to the chase, but he hesitated a moment, looking down at the body of the boy in his arms.

'I will care for my kinsman.' There was an old sadness in her voice. 'It is time I met my sister again.'

Anton nodded, then tenderly handed the boy over to her. With a single tear glistening from his cheek, he took a last look at the lad that he had known like a favourite nephew, then sprung into the chase. There was no time to mourn the dead now. The other humans, unsure of what was happening, divided into those who quietly returned to their homes in the south of the city and those who followed. The northerners would have to cross the river anyway, but some of the southern men joined them to see what would happen next. None of them saw the Count after he disappeared through some brush well ahead of them, or the wolf who emerged from the other side and bolted along the path that Paul and his men had followed, leaving their scent for wolf nostrils to follow.

Wolf's paws flew faster than ever before. He did not need his man consciousness to work out that the man Paul meant danger, or that the woman needed protection from him. He was only vaguely aware that suddenly the goblin was on his back again. He did not remember where the creature had been or how he came to be there, but his weight did not slow the pace so it did not matter. He was *friend*, and it was good to have allies in any fight. He Knew that the man Paul intended to harm the woman. He salivated at the thought that he would have his throat out the minute he saw him.

Then there was water. Wolf saw the river before him and had no choice but to stop. His frustration was unbearable. The men were out of reach on the water. He pulled up short at the river's edge and began an embittered howl that ended in a plaintive human voice crying one word, 'Talla!'

There were three boats close together on the river. Three men occupied each of the boats on either side, and in the centre one was Paul with two of his men and Talla, squirming and upsetting the unsteady boat. Paul held the baby in his arms himself, but not as closely as one would normally hold an infant. He looked as though he might drop it at any second. The Count stood on the bank of the river searching frantically for a way to reach the boats. Haghuf had been unceremoniously dumped on the ground during the change. He didn't mind as he had been grateful that their paths had crossed in the chase and he had managed to leap onto the wolf's back and travel more quickly. Now he pulled Anton back as he started to wade into the water, determined to swim if he had to.

'No Anton,' Haghuf shouted insistently, 'This is no time to be in the water. You must not!'

Anton pulled against the restraining arms, but to no avail. Goblin arms were strong.

'They'll kill Talla.' Anton tried desperately to make Haghuf see the obvious, to understand that he must let him go to the rescue. 'And the baby, that child may be mine!' He turned and took Haghuf's shoulders in his hands as he said it, willing the meaning of the words to travel through the intensity of eye contact to make him understand. He must let him go to her!

'Never say that to her, Anton,' Haghuf replied calmly, 'Among us, a child belongs only to its mother, and then only until it is weaned.' Haghuf thought of the news that had recently spread throughout his underground world, that a rare winged goblin child had been born in Nacibrab. In some ways he could understand the human pride in the male contribution to the creation of their young, but a lifetime of conditioning and closeness to nature had taught him that a mother nurtured her child. The male only fertilised.

Anton looked at Haghuf as if he had gone mad. How could he speak of parenting customs as the madmen in the boat prepared to kill an innocent baby? Paul held the child up, shouting prayers to their sterile god to accept the child as appeasement for the sin that had brought about her existence. Another man tore the gag and hood from Talla's head so that she could see the scene. Her hands were bound securely behind her, but her eyes were wide with panic as she saw the intent of the savage men. Anton lurched forward once again unable to free himself of the goblin's powerful grip as Paul threw the baby over the side of the boat, into the river. Talla screamed.

'No!' Anton shouted, wailing the word across the expanse that separated him from the horrifying scene.

His cry was joined by others, as many of the other humans had begun appearing behind them. Northerners and southerners alike were shocked and sickened as the water splashed and swallowed up the helpless infant. Its parentage suddenly meant nothing to people who treasured life and every birth among them. Only Paul and his closest men seemed anaesthetised to their own abominable actions.

Then Talla was pushed roughly forward as the man who had unhooded her took her bound hands and the other tried to take her feet, grasping desperately as she struggled hard against them. Her sharp teeth gnashed at Paul, just nicking his arm before she was lifted helplessly. He swore and ordered the men to fling her over the side. As they swung her once, then twice, Anton pleaded with Haghuf to release him and struggled to get loose, even starting to change to Wolf again at one point. But he could not concentrate enough to make the change. Among the babbled words that he refused to listen to from Haghuf was an odd phrase that sounded like that Talla could take care of herself. Anton rejected it with the rest of the protestations as on the third swing Talla was let loose and flew well over the water from the boat and into the sparkles of the reflected sun on the water.

Anton lunged once again as her bound body splashed with a note of unconscionable finality. And once again, Haghuf held him securely.

'I'll kill him the minute he comes back to shore,' Anton growled, 'he will be hung as a murderer. Haghuf, let me go!' Such a thing had not been done in the Count's lifetime, or his father before him. But then there had been no murders for many generations.

Haghuf continued his iron grip, but whispered in Anton's ear, 'Anton, look into the water. You've seen those lights before.'

Anton looked and saw that indeed, not all of the sparkles of light glittered off the water's surface. Subtly, beneath the choppy water, there were other reflections darting to and fro. He hadn't quite worked out what to make of them when the first thump hit the bottom of Paul's boat, upsetting it so that all of the occupants suddenly swayed and grabbed onto the side.

Then something hit the boat to the right with similar force and a second hit nearly upended Paul's craft. Suddenly all three boats were being attacked from something below and Paul's boat was flipped over, sending its occupants into the river. This was closely followed by the other two boats. Immediately the water bubbled and foamed in a way that reminded Anton of stories he had heard of shark attacks in the deep sea. *There's something in the water.*

Red blood floated to the surface. Horrified, the humans on the shore fell back gasping and muttering about the river being unsafe and that they would not be able to return to their homes. Anton turned to Haghuf, a question in his eyes. He had been swimming in the river for all of his life without encountering any danger. He was even sure that he had seen such reflections beneath the water before and yet had come to no harm.

'Come Anton,' said Haghuf, pulling him gently away from the waters edge. 'You can do nothing more here.'

Anton allowed himself to be led by Haghuf, but thought again of Haghuf's words a few moments before. *Talla can take care of herself. Things are not always as they seem among our kind.*

The actual phrase hadn't registered before, but the memory of the words was clear in his mind now. He stopped a moment, pulling back on the arm that led him so anxiously away.

‘Haghuf, what did you mean, that Talla can take care of herself? Is there a chance that she is alive? Do you know something you aren’t telling me?’

Haghuf hesitated a few seconds, deciding how he could answer the direct question honestly without breaking the habit of keeping the nature and existence of the *Kol’ksu* a secret from the humans, even Anton. There was no time for long explanations.

‘I have no knowledge, Anton. Talla may be dead or she may not. I know only that what befell those men on the river will never be Talla’s fate.’

He turned away and tugged on Anton’s arm again, relieved that he didn’t press further for answers. He was not even sure of the accuracy of his reply. The *Kol’ksu* did not waste meat. If one of their own died, their remains would meet the same natural disposal as any other body found in the river or one of the underground pools. As for Talla, she needed to breathe air like any other land dwelling goblin. She had disappeared under the water, yet the *Kol’ksu* had their ways. Many cycles before, Talla’s mother had tried to keep her among the water goblins despite her inability to breathe in their element. Even Haghuf didn’t know how she had managed until the decision to give her up to the land dwellers had torn them apart. All he knew for sure was that he had no more answers to give.

The humans on the riverbank gave no resistance as the goblin led their leader through the crowd. It was curious being so close to a creature that until now had only been depicted in stories for children. Some of them were close enough to touch him as they passed. The crowd had swelled as the drama had unfolded on the water. Not only men now, but wives and children of the southern men had begun to appear as well. Those who had gone home had spread the gossip of events thus far, and the families of those who had not yet returned had come to the battlefield to bring supplies and look for their menfolk who might have fallen. They found the battle had ended, apart from what they had witnessed. Some had found the bodies of their husbands and fathers. The others had followed the path to the river with renewed hope.

One child, a small girl, held tightly to her father's hand as the goblin and the infamous Count Anton passed. On a whim, she reached out and stroked the greenish skin of Haghuf's arm as it brushed by. The goblin stopped and turned, regarding the young girl child for a moment. Then he caught the father's icy stare. Some hatreds did not die easily. On impulse, Haghuf bowed deeply and formally to the child, in honour of her innocence and femininity. Count Anton followed suit, concealing a wan smile, and even kissed the girl's hand as if she were a noble lady. They then continued on their way as the child stayed behind, blinking her eyes in confusion, or perhaps in pain. Her father was holding her hand very tightly.

Haghuf continued to lead Anton well away from the riverside, yet they didn't seem to be going exactly back to the battlefield. They had gone a little way when Anton began to think clearly again and to realise that normally he would have stayed with his people and helped them work out how to cross the river safely to their homes. The conflict between the species had become a complete debacle. He searched his mind for any scrap of insight of how he might have been able to prevent events from unfolding as they had. But there was only the ignorance of humans to blame. It was the one major difference that he found between goblins and his fellow humans. Many of the humans insisted on clinging vehemently to their ignorance.

'Haghuf, where are you taking me?' Anton pulled back involuntarily from the cave opening that had suddenly appeared as Haghuf led him. Consciously he reminded himself that he had made innumerable visits to the underground world over the years, yet the trauma of his most recent experience was still fresh. He knew that the passages would still be filled with *Those Who Protect*. Haghuf turned to him, and with the slight inclination of the head that formalised the invitation, spoke the ritual formula.

'You are *guest*. From this moment until next you see the sunlight, none of my people will lay hand on you or offer insult at pain of banishment from our world forever.'

Anton returned the gesture that was more than a nod, yet less than a bow, touched by the inviolable liturgy that no goblin would dare to dishonour. Haghuf had used the formal words only once before in Anton's presence. It had been the first time he had taken him into the passages of Krapneerg. He hadn't even understood the words in the goblin language then. After that, it had been left as an implication. Strictly speaking it would not apply once he had returned to the surface, but it had been honoured just the same. Now, in another place where there were no doubt many who would object, Haghuf had offered Anton absolute protection.

As they descended through the secret passage Anton had the distinct feeling that they were moving towards the battle area now, but to a very deep place beneath it. He tried to maintain his sense of direction through the twisting and turning paths. They had not gone far when he was distracted by the rhythms pulsating through the walls of the passages. It was the steady beat that preceded the Dance. The beat that began close to the end of a storytelling. Haghuf was taking a big risk by bringing him into the midst of goblin kind at this of all times. His own life would depend on the solidity of the code of honour that held their otherwise anarchistic society together.

Anton saw no other goblins as they descended towards what he thought must be the very bowels of the earth, but he knew that there were eyes that watched. It was difficult to gauge the mood of beings who chose to remain unseen. At least no one offered them challenge. The drumming grew louder as their path took them deeper to the soul of its rhythm. It reached a crescendo at a crossing in the paths that Anton surmised would be the way to the largest cavern, where the goblins would convene for the Dance when the Storytelling was ended.

The rhythm took him, blocking out the images of the horrible events of the day and clearing his mind in a way that was not oblivion, but greater knowledge, as he became aware of the inter-relationship of all of life and existence. He would never be able to say for sure whether he actually danced as they passed the passage, swept up as he was in the complete release and almost erotic ecstasy of that rhythm. It was during those few moments that he *knew*, without knowing how or why, that Talla lived still, as did his child. Only in that moment did he know for sure that the child had been conceived from his own seed.

They continued downwards through the serpentine passages. All of Anton's sense of direction had been abandoned, but Haghuf led confidently. He knew the way. The drumbeats receded quickly, but the rhythm issued much deeper, from the earth itself. It retained its hold on the spirit of a man who had first braved the depths of the earth in answer to its call. Still they saw no others, until they reached the cavern where many were gathered for the storytelling. As they passed through the opening, instead of challenge they were handed the customary bowls of food. But for a moment, even that was an unavoidable confrontation. The goblin at the door was one of *Those Who Protect*. Worse, the goblin was familiar.

'I threw you to the *Kol'ksu*!' the massive creature said in surprise and obvious displeasure. Anton couldn't help but notice that the goblin reminded him a bit of Latham, rather big and not overly bright, ready to fight at little provocation.

'But they didn't eat him,' Haghuf replied softly. 'He is *guest*.' The big goblin's eyes widened as the combined implications reached through his oppositional mood. He stepped aside and even bent noticeably at the waist to show respect to Count Anton. The sudden change in demeanor raised Anton's assessment of the brutish creature considerably. Apparently he was far more intelligent than Latham after all. Anton's presence here indicated that he hadn't been devoured by the creatures in the water. Having that detail pointed out to him resulted in a change of attitude in the goblin rather than the swaggering measure of ego that his human equivalent would no doubt serve up in a defensive stance. If anything, his admiration for the goblin society increased as their adaptability never ceased to amaze him.

Anton tried to seize the opportune moment as they sat with their food.

'Haghuf, who or what are the *Kol*...'

'Don't ask me that, Anton.' Haghuf cut him off sharply. 'I cannot speak of it.'

Anton didn't push further. He knew this mood of Haghuf's now, there were limits to what he would ever tell of his people. Anton would never stop being inquisitive, but this was not the time to press as he sat as *guest* among a people who would otherwise kill him for invading their sacred Storytelling. He began to pick at the collection of fruits and vegetables in his bowl, grateful that at least this time, there was no meat. He would not want to have to speculate on its origin so close to a battlefield. He picked up a small, yellowish apple and bit into it. He found himself surprised by a particularly sweet and cinnamon-like flavour. He wondered briefly how the goblins managed to gather such perfectly ripe fruit in the cold season, but his musings were soon interrupted by a call for another story.

'Haghuf!' shouted an unknown voice. 'Will you grace us with a story of the *Foringen*? Tell us the one about their first meeting with the deep dwellers!'

Anton could not see the speaker, but Haghuf stood up, as if he was about to comply, then turned to Anton before answering. He gave him a shrewd look, as if he was assessing how best to use the moment.

'That is no tale for a foreign *guest*,' he said calmly, projecting his voice throughout the cavern. Many pairs of eyes seemed suddenly to see that a human was sitting among them. Anton wondered whether Haghuf's assessment of the tale's suitability meant that it was inappropriate because he would be bored, or because it would tell him yet more of the things that Haghuf wished to keep among his own kind. He had never heard mention of *Foringen*, any more than the word '*Kol'ksu*' had reached his ears before the big goblin had so casually said it.

'I wonder,' continued Haghuf, 'if we can persuade our visitor to tell us the tale of how the humans developed a society where one man serves another.'

Anton smiled genuinely for the first time since the struggle on the river. Haghuf had long ago expressed an interest in this aspect of human society and he had often promised to tell the tale someday. He stood up as dozens of feet stamped on the stone floor, encouraging him to come forward. Finally he felt that he was in his own element. It was time that more open communication was used to dissolve the boundaries between their species, and this was a way to take a first step and amuse them at the same time. He just hoped that his own family's part in the story wouldn't get back to the humans on the surface, especially the men south of the river. His position among them was already more than a little precarious.

Anton walked among the hulking bodies of the goblins known as *Those Who Protect*, even leaning on the occasional shoulder to keep his footing as he pushed towards the front of the cavern to take the place of Storyteller. There were almost no familiar faces among them, but he did catch a glimpse of Leap nodding encouragement to him as he passed. An hour ago, these goblins would have torn him apart. Now they waited to be entertained. As Anton turned to face them from the front, they reminded him of a military camp from the books of history that he kept in his tower. Rather than a local grotto of goblins well known to each other, he looked on a gathering of fighters who had come from places he would probably never know, joined by a common cause.

Again he smiled as he reflected on the similarity to the men in the story that he was about to unfold, a tale of men who defended their own homes but then fell into a way of life that was uniquely human. Anton forced a more serious expression as he began to relate a tale that would start as it would finish, and which held the secret of his own family legacy.

Chapter Thirteen

The first thing Talla saw as the water engulfed her was the teeth of the *Kol'ksu.* They seemed to be everywhere at once, ripping and tearing flesh. Blood turned the water red. As her vision faded through lack of air and the foaming of the water from so much activity, the teeth she could just see heading straight for her face were the final reason to give in to welcome unconsciousness. However, the end was not going to be quite so easy.

She felt the mouth of the *Kol'ksu* form a seal over her own mouth and nose, and then there was air. It was not the pure oxygen she needed, but the exhalation of another's breath. It robbed her of the easy escape and left her with enough consciousness to remember that her baby had been drowned as well. But she wasn't to be allowed to die. The strong arms which held her were unrelenting in their grasp. It was a male *Kol'ksu* who held her and he was taking her somewhere.

Her consciousness rose and fell repeatedly in what seemed an endless sensation of rushing water. At one point she was aware of rock walls close to her, yet she was completely submerged throughout this journey, wherever it was taking her. Slowly she remembered that the *Kol'ksu* were her friends. They had not come to kill her along with the humans. They were not going to let her die, even if she wished it. The image of her baby being thrown in the water haunted her, making her eyes sting with tears that were immediately washed away.

Then all at once she felt cool air surrounding her and an uncomfortable thump as she was unceremoniously dropped on the ground. The thump made her cough up water as she felt herself turned on her side and her body struck and squeezed alternately to encourage her to spit out as much as possible. When the deep breaths came and the tormenting ceased, she felt no comfort in her renewed grasp of life. She was miserable in a way that she had never known was possible.

Slowly her eyes focused and she was able to see the *Kol'ksu* who had rescued her and brought her here, wherever 'here' was. The fact that it had indeed been a rescue came to her slowly as his face came into focus. She didn't know him personally, yet his concern for her was evident in his expression and the gentle way in which he stroked her with his taloned hand. Perhaps he meant to make up for having to be so rough with her in order to get her to breathe.

She was unsure what to say to her strange rescuer. She hardly had the strength to speak at all, or to move, apart from the violent shaking that her body refused to allow her to control. She hoped he would speak first. It looked as though he might when the encounter was interrupted by an almost imperceptible sound of singing, the melody that hung on the edge of hearing and calmed the soul…the song of the *Kol'ksu*. She looked up to find another being in the cavern, a female *Kol'ksu*. She noticed for the first time that she was within a rocky cavern with a dark pool through which she had apparently been brought.

The *Kol'ksu* woman looked at her curiously, turning her head from side to side as if she were examining an alien. In fact, she would have looked more alien herself to most goblins with her white hair and eyes and the iridescent scales which covered her body. Talla looked into the large white eyes, so like her own apart from their slit pupils that resembled those of the dragon statue she had given Count Anton. She didn't need anyone to tell her into whose presence she had been brought.

'Mother…' she gasped weakly.

The woman walked towards her awkwardly in the way that the *Kol'ksu* did when moving slowly on land.

'Don't try to speak yet, just breathe,' she said. Her claws parted and the webbed hands unwrapped from a bundle she held closely. As the bundle was placed in Talla's arms, the long webbed fingers wrapped around Talla who was still shaking. In Talla's embrace, her child slept peacefully. Her sharp and frequent breaths were clearly audible in the stillness of the cavern. The webbed hands moved again as Le-ina encircled her daughter with her arms, still helping her to hold the baby securely. The male *Kol'ksu* had slipped away into the pool silently, so that Talla didn't even notice that he had gone to leave her alone with her mother and daughter.

*   *   *

'A very long time ago, even long before the last Turning, men lived in small groups much as they do now.' Anton was surprised by the confident tone of his own voice as it boomed over the sea of unfamiliar faces. Faces of trolls he thought to himself. *Those Who Protect* were very different from the goblins he had known in Krapneerg. He could not help but compare the company before him to the more homely gathering of the anarchic society that had characterised his previous experience of a Storytelling. There had been a wider variety of goblins there. Even some women, and a few children. This looked more like a military assembly.

'Because it is in the nature of humankind to lead or to follow, the small groups developed leaders who were much as your respected ones. Only sometimes they became the leaders by superior strength, rather than by wisdom.' Anton paused a moment, letting the words sink into the hulking specimens before him. He controlled a shudder as he thought what life on earth would be like if *Those Who Protect* sought to lead the goblins. He continued.

'They called the leaders chiefs and by other names in different cultures, and groups of men often fought each other and many died because they would follow the will of the chief, even when they knew that he had not the wisdom to make sensible choices. Over time, the position became hereditary and would pass to the oldest male heir of the chief's family.'

A voice shouted in disbelief from somewhere in the front of the gathering.

'That is stupid, how would a male chief know if a child was of his making or not? Were there no female chiefs?'

Anton smiled indulgently, oddly enjoying the opportunity to demonstrate the vast gulf of cultural difference that separated their species.

'There is some evidence of societies ruled by females, but many more were reigned over by males. So to insure the line of succession they developed a system of marriage, where a woman was given to a man as wife, mating only with him and bearing his children.'

'They made breeding slaves of their females?' shouted another voice incredulously.

'Effectively, yes,' answered Anton before continuing his story.

'The humans bred freely and populated much of the lands of the earth, until they began to claim borders of lands that they considered their own.' This time he kept the pause short, just long enough for breath so that he could continue without interruption. The heads shaking in his audience said enough.

'They fought over land and food supplies. Eventually instead of one chief they set up hierarchies of authority to help keep so many people under control. They were led by Kings or Emperors, whose wives were called Queens or Empresses. Variations on these words were used in different languages.' He used the human language words, as there were no equivalents in the goblin tongue.

'These ruled over other officials, with titles like; Count and Countess, Duke and Duchess, Earl, Baron, and even down to minor authority figures like Sheriff. There were others, and again variations in different languages because the humans spoke many languages in different parts of the earth.' Again Anton paused only for a breath, and continued.

'After a very, very long time, the rulers bred only among themselves and thought themselves too important to breed with the common people and so became inbred. They began to behave irrationally and sometimes the people would rebel. They took away the privileges of the ruling families and began to set up governments where they elected someone to hold the position of authority.'

'Why did they need authority at all?' The question was from the same goblin who had interrupted the first time. Anton smiled indulgently again, and answered calmly, 'The groups were so large now that co-operative societies had become...difficult. Also, they had become used to having someone take responsibility for dealing with other countries and organising resources. As is the nature of humans, this was not done fairly and evenly, but there were always some who had privilege.'

'Like *Those Who Provide*?' asked the goblin in the front.

'Not exactly,' answered Haghuf from the back, '*Those Who Provide* take a share of the food they gather to sustain them on their excursions.' Haghuf nodded to Anton to continue. Anton guessed that this information was part of what he was not meant to know, but the offhand comment from the goblin had forced some explanation. He let the indiscretion pass, and carried on with the story, noting it for later contemplation.

'The elected leaders of the humans took what was best, as had the kings before them, while those less privileged did the work.' Anton watched the goblins look at each other in disbelief around the room as he prepared to tell them the part he hoped they would find most amusing.

'After many, many seasons of this way of doing things, some of the humans began to have romantic thoughts about the days of hereditary rulers. The elected rulers spent so much time and energy on fighting to be elected or overthrowing a previous official that the hereditary titles took on a mystique. The titles themselves still existed in some families, but they were effectively meaningless.

As the population grew ever larger and the power of the rulers the humans had set up for themselves became too difficult to oppose, many of the humans began to retreat into fantasy and played games of simpler times, like children. They took on titles during the games, and called the activity 'role-playing', so that the real holders of these titles could take no offence. They dressed up in bright costumes, inspired by the fashions of history, yet often added decoration to the costumes to make them even more exciting.

Sub-culture societies grew from these games and groups of humans as large as the early populations themselves would sometimes gather and role-play in their shared fantasy worlds. Some of them were even real magicians.'

Anton paused again and looked around at the sea of faces, now rapt with attention. Goblins understood playing. No one interrupted.

'Then the last Turning occurred. As you know, most of the surface population was wiped out. The political leaders were unable to save themselves. You all know the ravages of a Turning.'

There was a general shudder as the goblins imagined all too clearly the devastation, when a planet shifts on its axis and throws everything into total uncontrollable chaos. Even a goblin could not hide from such a cataclysm.

'In the aftermath of the Turning, the pockets of humans who had survived formed their own small societies. Some, like those who live south of the river in my own world, immediately elected a leader of their small group. They went about looking for other survivors to join them and rebuild what they could of the lives they knew. Others, like my own ancestors, saw the change as an opportunity to start afresh and to build a new world, having learned from the mistakes of the past.'

'So why do you have an old title if they were avoiding the mistakes of the past?' shouted the goblin in the front. Anton had to suppress an urge to laugh now, as he was just getting to the part that revealed his own family secrets.

'Those who were like my ancestors at first organised into co-operative societies, much like yours. They sought food and shelter first of all. Many more buildings survived the Turning than we might have predicted. Among them were many of the old castles that had stood the test of time. Some, more than others, had been kept in good repair and used as educational sites so that the people could see their own history in the stones laid by their ancestors. These were the structures that survived best.

When they were found by these humans seeking shelter, it seemed only natural to move in. If the group were among those who had played the fantasy games, they immediately began to play them within the castle. Once the practicalities of survival had been seen to, they began again calling themselves by their adopted titles and the others pretended to serve them. Thus it was with my own ancestor, Count Victor.' A murmur travelled through the audience now along with a few chuckles of laughter from those quickest to comprehend where the story was leading. Anton sought the face of Haghuf, to gauge his reaction to the story unfolding before him at last. But he was difficult to find among the sea of larger goblins.

'Victor worked by the side of his men in the gardens planted within the castle grounds. They did not forget that the deference was only a game, but in imitation of their ancestors who actually held titled positions his pretend servants would bow to him. Humans bow to show subservience rather than as a polite gesture of respect as it is among goblins. Yet they did it in jest, just as part of the game. Or so it was until the others found them.' The goblins who had been laughing all stopped now and had their attention riveted on Count Anton's story. There was more to come.

'Groups of other humans who had held together in the days after the Turning began to find their way to the castles, only to find them already occupied. They might have offered challenge or sought to be brought into the groups already established within, but an odd thing happened. There was no communication from one castle to another. The expeditions that would find each other would come later. Yet many reacted in the same way when others found them. Most of the castles had been avoided by people, except by the magicians and role-players who did not hesitate to fill them with their merry bands.

You see, the ideas of nobility, royalty and living in castles still held a certain mystique among humans. Within just a few seasons of the Turning, the role-players had developed the game into a reality of sorts, although they had not actually forgotten who they really were. But when homeless and hungry strangers hailed from the castle gates, something in their instincts prompted them to answer 'in role' and to give the strangers a front of established power. You see, they were actually afraid. Humans, like those who attacked your people so recently, are just as capable of attacking other groups of humans to take away their homes and food supplies.'

For a moment Anton fidgeted, wondering if it were wise to remind the goblins of the recent battle and his own position as a human among them. But the murmuring of outrage that reached his ears was not directed at him. For the moment at least, he seemed to have been accepted as something different than the humans that had killed so many of their kind. The rhythm of the drums from the nearby cavern was beginning to invade the mood, and they looked to him instead to finish the story.

'The bravado paid off immediately. When the strangers were treated formally and only their leader allowed under guard to have audience with Count Victor, they complied and began to fall into a role of their own, as supplicants. It would not have lasted of course, had Victor sent them away to fend for themselves. These people had survived cataclysm first hand. They wanted leadership, but more than that they wanted security. Victor gave it to them.

It was Victor who granted them the lands south of the river. He lent his men to help them get some of the surviving buildings into shape for habitation, and to plant gardens. They had wisely saved extra seed from their own agricultural efforts for a full season before the others had found them. They planted fruit trees and shared some of their stores of food to tide the strangers over their first season. There were few of them then. The co-operative efforts of Count Victor's household had provided well for their own comforts and needs. There was plenty to share.'

The rhythm of the dance was invading the story now, creating a cadence that spoke of the natural cycle of chaos that had occurred at the time of its making. The events that had shaped the society he knew had fit a pattern, as if by design. Now the goblins who had their own history were caught up with him, feeling the turn of events that had made his family the leaders of men who had a need to follow.

'Victor had a natural wisdom and, most importantly, a cool head. He could find solutions to any problem and others would follow his direction simply because he was the Count. Before long he had organised men into work parties to explore and repair what could be salvaged, or to strip resources from whatever remained of the old world they had known.

Over time, others appeared and encountered an established society, where the Count ruled as well as provided for what had become his people. The ragtag groups of survivors gladly joined the new civilisation that they found. Count Victor walked among these people and occasionally recruited likely candidates to join his own household, especially if other magicians wandered in among the survivor groups. Others were directed into some form of co-operative work to benefit the society as a whole. Victor had a talent for assessing the individual talents of people and for listening to them. They often chose the occupation for themselves, Victor only helped direct them and to determine where there was need.'

Anton suddenly realised two things. One, that in many ways, he was much like his ancestor. It was not only his title that held the respect of his people, it was the ability to listen and to organise that he had inherited from Victor. The other thing was that he was moving. The Dance was taking him, as well as the others. Their attention was riveted on him, but the movement and the surging blood of instinct begged for release into primal expression.

'And so the people followed Victor, and looked to him for authority in all things. Then to his descendants after him. They fell into a natural rhythm of their own, those of greatest skill gravitating towards the castle and life among the magicians. They played at the façade of servitude for the benefit of the real servants, the commoners left outside. So still is the game played today as I fill the shoes of my ancestor, surrounded by my closest companions in such guise. Magicians among the people.'

The note of finality in his last sentence acted as a signal, and all leapt up at once, stamping their feet in appreciation of the entertainment. The stamping quickly took on the rhythm that was already throbbing through the earth. Many of the goblins roared in a primal call of completely free expression. It might have been for a hunt, or for joy or anguish, but this time the roar was for the release of the Dance. The crowd surged towards the door, scores of goblin feet flapping down the corridor to the larger cavern where the drums beat loudly in rhythm with the earth. The Dance had begun.

Anton too was caught up in the swell of pure emotion, yet he retained an awareness that noted the raw manifestation of vented emotion he had just witnessed. A single spark could ignite such uninhibited power, so that they could easily have turned on him and torn him apart had he said anything to upset them. Instead, they had been clearly amused. Now the Dance called them to express their joy in the way that was most familiar to them. He had the feeling that rather than being insulted by the sudden exodus, he should be complimented by the fervour of their reaction.

As the dispersing crowd thinned, his eyes fell on Haghuf at last. He waited near the cavern opening and appeared to be speaking with someone that Anton could not at first see through the shifting throngs of charging goblins. When enough of them had disgorged through the passage, he was able to move closer to where Haghuf stood pressed against the wall. Soon he was able to see better and saw that the two goblins were huddled together in some sort of deep conversation that seemed to involve rather a lot of body language. Anton made yet another mental note. The continued roar and stamping of the goblins would prohibit ordinary speech. Formulating non-verbal communication for such times would make perfect sense.

The other goblin was odd-looking, if it was possible to be even more odd considering the diversity of physical types among goblins. He was small, certainly not one of *Those Who Protect*. What could be seen of him beneath the heavy cloak he wore was dark and rough skinned in a way that resembled overly roasted meat. Anton wondered for a moment if the goblin had suffered some sort of horrible accident, but he moved comfortably, even gracefully as his arms gestured in conjunction with his body postures and expressions. As Anton drew close to them the goblin turned to him suddenly and the hood fell back to reveal a completely hairless creature whose face and head was much like the roughened skin on his arms. It was dark and leathery, obviously from nature rather than misadventure as anyone charred so completely would not be behaving naturally, or even able to live in such a state.

The goblin held something wrapped in leather. From what creature Anton preferred not to speculate. It too was dark. The object was long. As the creature quickly unwrapped it and offered it to Anton with a sweeping undulation of his body that seemed very much like a bow of respect. Then Anton saw that it was a gleaming sword, like those the goblins had used in battle not very long ago.

'Take it, Anton,' said Haghuf urgently in the human tongue. 'It would be deep insult to refuse.'

Anton nodded respectfully to the dark goblin and took the sword with both hands formally, nodding again his appreciation. The creature backed away, making a gesture with his hands and arms and a shift of his body weight that Anton did not understand. Then he disappeared through the cavern opening so rapidly that he might have been a puff of smoke. Anton looked at the weapon in his hands, confused by both the unexpected gift and the odd writing that was scrolled artistically on the blade. The throng had dispersed sufficiently now that voices could be heard easily again. Haghuf seemed to gather his words a moment and to translate to himself through gestures like the other goblin had made before he began to speak.

'Some who live very deep in the earth have little air, they do not waste it on speech. What you look upon is a written language that has no verbal translation.'

Anton could almost see the process working through Haghuf's mind as he chose which information to give and what to keep back. He obviously did not want to explain about the creature, yet was put in a position where he must explain the significance of the gift. A part of Anton was amused by watching his friend struggle with the conflict, while another part felt sympathy for his dilemma. The call of the Dance added difficulty to any attempt to think logically. The drums seemed to echo in Anton's ears, moving him with a rhythm in tune with his own heartbeat, enticing him to simply accept that which is, rather than to question the dark goblin's motives.

'The sword of a goblin has never been given to a human in all of our history. You are the first.' Haghuf looked up at Anton as he spoke, looking for comprehension of the magnitude of what had just occurred.

'You see, Anton, you have been accepted by something that...I have not the words to explain.' Haghuf shook his head a moment, then gestured towards the writing on the shining blade.

'These words translate to something in your language that would literally read as *Not the Leader* or *First Among Equals*. Very high titles indeed from a species that does not use titles.'

Haghuf shook his head again, and Anton realised that his friend was in a state of unprecedented bewilderment. Haghuf was trying to explain something that had obviously surpassed his understanding of his own people.

'What did he communicate with his motions as he was leaving?' Anton asked despite his desire to give in to the drumming. The call of life expressed itself in movement that would join his spirit with those of these creatures with which he had so much affinity, despite their differences. Haghuf seemed to think a moment and to move his own body in similar motions, but less exaggerated, in some form of personal translation process.

'As I told you, they do not use words. It can be difficult to translate exactly. The emotions expressed were of great respect and a wish that you will use the weapon wisely in battles to come.' Haghuf looked up at him seriously again. 'It was not a general blessing. It spoke of things that will be in the future, more than one, and yet they provide a sword that could never be used against goblin kind.' Haghuf shook his head once again. 'I do not understand. There was something about leading your kind, yet the gift itself would indicate that it is your own kind you will fight. I know no more.'

Anton wrapped the blade again and held it safely under his arm. He reached to place his hand on his friend's shoulder, reassuring him and bringing him out of his reverie.

'Come my friend,' he said with his accustomed humour to Haghuf, 'Let's dance.'

Their eyes met, and as the smiles spread across their faces simultaneously, a primal scream joined their voices as one, and they charged down the corridor to the place of celebration. Anton placed his parcel on a rock formation that formed a natural shelf and joined the Dance. There was no question of it being disturbed. Haghuf was already lost in the crowd in the time it had taken just to lay the parcel down. There was no need to seek him. They were all one in the Dance. Anton gave himself over fully to the beat of the music and the ecstatic release of physical expression of all of life and pure joy. He danced freely, without inhibition among those who shared this rite in a place without any concept of the restrictions of human authority.

As he felt his own heartbeat adjust to join in the rhythm reflected through the earth by the drummers, only one analytical thought invaded his complete abandon to the expression of pure emotion; Haghuf had used the word 'they'. The dark goblin had to be one of a race yet unknown to him. There was much about goblins that he might never fully know.

Chapter Fourteen

Anton awoke slowly, wondering where he was. As his eyes began to focus he recognised cavern walls and the softness of fur caressing his naked body. Apparently he had slept among the goblins last night. He tried to remember...he had been absorbed completely by the Dance and somewhere along the line he had rested a moment. Someone had given him a small wooden goblet of some sort of liqueur. It had tasted of apples...and of cinnamon. Sweet, but not sickly. It warmed him and when someone else handed him another goblet, he had accepted it gladly.

Alcohol? He wondered, but he had no headache or other signs of hangover this morning. Was it morning? He didn't know. Somehow he felt that it must be. As a surface dweller he was very much attuned to the movements of the sun, even here where he could not see it. The goblins were not so affected, but surely they would all need to sleep after so much revelry?

He was grateful to find no one else with him among the furs. There were some scraps of memory that he preferred to explore when he was more awake. The goblin who had given him the second drink appeared in his mind. It had been a pretty one, the sort that might have been dubbed fairy or elf in the surface world. He had wondered why such a one danced among so many of *Those Who Protect*. He had not been able to determine whether it had been a male or female, so refined and androgynous were its features. But he had a nagging feeling…a memory of pleasure…that suggested to him that he may have found out sometime during the celebration.

He sat up a little at this thought and looked around to see if anyone shared this particular cavern with him. Indeed, there was a figure sitting quietly against the wall near the opening to the passages. She rocked gently, softly singing to herself and to the bundle she held in her lap. It was Talla.

'Good, you are awake,' she said without looking up. Anton was disappointed that the singing had stopped, but glad to hear her melodic voice. She looked up at him then and he was captivated by the familiar white irised eyes that still drew him in, and by the squirming of the baby as it reacted to its mother's movement.

'Blood calls to blood, you knew it was you who seeded her even before I did. I thought you might like to see her.'

'Then she really is mine?' he asked innocently as he crawled over beside them, ignoring his own nakedness. Talla looked at him with an expression of mixed horror and confusion.

'A child belongs to no one, surely you will not speak to me of human concepts of child ownership!' Suddenly she held her baby close to her chest. For a moment she bared her teeth. He knew that if he reached out for the child just then she might well kill him. He backed away a little, longing to reach out and touch them both but not daring to breach the animal protectiveness of its young.

'Haghuf said that among you a child belongs to its mother, but among my people those who make her would share in her upbringing. As you said, blood calls to blood.' He tried to explain calmly. He recognised the instincts that hormonal states would arouse in a new mother. Especially among those who lived so close to nature. Talla relaxed as she consciously made herself understand that he offered no threat.

'Haghuf seeks to protect me. He knows how important it is that she stays in the care of her mother until she is weaned.' She recognised her inherent defensiveness, so recently aroused by the long held sadness and feeling of loss that she had shared with her own mother. The wound had still not healed from when Le-ina had been separated from her daughter before time. They had spoken at length after Talla had rested. Le-ina had told her of the guilt she had felt. She spoke of her attempts to care for her baby who could not breathe in water. Her determination to care for her child had led to her development of the method of sharing air by encompassing the face of an air breather with the flexible *Kol'ksu* mouth, but it hadn't been enough. The growing child was awkward to carry through the water long after a time when *Kol'ksu* young would have been swimming independently. Still, it was this method that had so recently saved the lives of both Talla and her own infant.

The *Kol'ksu* were less accustomed to separation as children grew because of the nature of their life in the water, but Talla could explain none of this to Anton. Instead she tried to explain to him the customs of the goblins.

'Among the land-dwelling goblins, those who seed the young are often unaware that they have done so. Especially those who move from one place to another. Once the child is weaned, it becomes a member of the community and all care for it until it is old enough to care for itself and choose its own way. You would still think them children at such an age. Our customs are very different from yours. We do not own our young ones. We only help them to grow.'

'But surely,' he asked in his curious way, noting her reference to land-dwelling goblins as if there were others. 'One who knows that he has seeded a child must have feelings of connection to the offspring? Many animals in nature have this.'

'In nature there are some animals who will kill their offspring, especially other young males, to eliminate competition,' she answered teasingly, then relented. 'But you are right. Those who know themselves so connected to a young one will have such feelings, yet they will also care for those that are not of their making in the grotto. Some will not know for sure whether or not they will have seeded a particular child. Still they will treat it as if it was so anyway. The only way to know for sure if a young one is seeded by a particular male would be to imitate your ways, to make breeding slaves of females. But some know through instinct, and others imagine they know. Your instincts Anton, are greater than some among us. It is one of the reasons that Haghuf has so much curiosity about you.'

She looked up at him again then and held the baby up to him.

'Do you wish to hold her for a moment?'

Anton immediately slid close to Talla, feeling her close and welcoming presence as he took the baby in his arms. He was amazed that the child had not cried or fussed but seemed very calm in the presence of her parents. He took her into his arms and held her as if he was well accustomed to holding infants, much to Talla's surprise. She had to remember that they were far more abundant among humans. She did not ask where he would have had occasion to handle one of them.

Anton looked into the eyes of his daughter. They were shaped much like the large almond eyes of her mother, but the colour…exploding starburst rainbow was the way that Dani had described them once...was very much like his own eyes. There could be no doubt who had fathered her and given her those eyes. What amazed him was the intelligence and curiosity that emanated from them. She was not very old. He was not sure exactly how many days, but surely she was too small to manage to focus her eyes, much less to look as though the wisdom of the ages hid behind the silent and innocent features. But it was the resemblance of the rest of her to his own species that worried him.

'Talla, what possessed you to bring her onto a battle field?' he asked gently. He did not want to challenge her but only to understand.

'I overestimated your species,' she answered sadly. 'Among our kind, a mother is sacred. No one would raise a hand to harm her. I believed that the humans would value life as we do. I sought only to prove what you and I know to be true, that we come from common ancestors. It was foolish perhaps to have faith in the nature of humans. My people have hidden from them for so long because of their murderous ways, but I knew you and Ranalf. You are not like those who sought to kill me and an innocent baby who looks as one of their own.'

'She looks so human. Will it become difficult or even dangerous living among the goblins?' As he spoke he handed the child back, knowing that he must choose his words carefully and avoid any hint of seeming to want to come between them as he expressed his concerns.

'The goblins are her people,' she answered. 'She does not smell human, any goblin would know the difference. There is no other place we *could* live.' She thought of the worlds open to her as a member of her species; the water, the deep places where Haghuf came from, the other pockets of goblin society that she knew. No place seemed to be practical except the caverns that she had lived in herself, although she was sure that the child would explore others as she grew older.

'You could live in the castle, be my Countess.' It was a spontaneous suggestion that he knew he had not thought through, but it was said now.

'And be slave to a man like your human women? Do you think your other humans would have a goblin Countess to rule over them, or do you expect me to stay in glamour all the time and exhaust myself? Besides, what would they think when they find their Countess entering their rooms at night and seducing men as they sleep next to their wives? And what if there were other children, there is no guarantee that they would look human and not goblin.'

Anton winced at her reproving tone. She was right of course. Getting the people to accept the existence of the goblins was going to be difficult enough without expecting them to have one by their ruler's side. Talla was what she was. He had made up his mind that he had to bring a peace between the species, regardless of what danger he put himself into during the process. Still, the desire to have his daughter near him would not relinquish its hold on him so easily.

'But she *looks* human, won't she encounter prejudice among the goblins?'

'Do you think that all goblins look alike, or even like the same species? Look at me Anton, do I look like other goblins to you?'

He had to admit to himself that she did not. There was an ethereal quality to her that went beyond the white hair and eyes - an alien nature to her features that spoke of another kind of life form. Yet he could not place what she seemed to remind him of, or to remember seeing any other goblins that were like her. Surely she must have parents among the goblins of her grotto, at least a mother? Or had the mother been seeded by something unknown to him, perhaps something from the deep places that he was unlikely ever to travel? And how did such a creature breed with a betweener, who probably spent most of her life close to the surface? There was still much that he did not know about these creatures, and especially of Talla.

'I understand,' he said genuinely. 'But if she encounters any problems later, long after she is weaned and growing, you know that she would be welcome to live in the castle. That I would care for her.' He stopped abruptly, not wishing to push too far as Talla shook her head.

'And what if she did live among humans, learned their ways, even became property to one of your males? What would happen to her if she brought forth a child with green skin and pointed ears?'

Anton blanched. He had not thought so far ahead. The result of such an occurrence was unthinkable...and it was a distinct possibility.

'There is no other way Anton. She must live among her mother's people. No goblin infant can be separated from its mother. And a girl child as you know is rare and treasured. It would not be allowed. The consequences would be too terrible to contemplate. She is goblin, whatever her skin and features say. Her kind will know her. The stories already spread of her making.'

Anton could not escape Talla's simple logic. There was more than the animal instinct to protect its young in what she said. His desire to be near this child of his making had caused him to forget for a moment the restrictive life that a human child would have compared to life among the goblins. And also that a girl child was of great value to these creatures who bred but sparingly. Either way, her breeding abilities would affect her place in society. At least here she would be honoured for it, rather than enslaved. He reached out, gently stroking first the side of Talla's familiar face, then the head of the child.

'Will I be able to see her?' he asked, remembering how difficult it had been to see Talla herself for so long.

'So long as you promise that you will not speak to her of human concepts of ownership by he who seeded. I do not object. I think...' Talla stopped a moment, recognising the inner sight that came upon her on rare occasions. Her mother's legacy. When she continued speaking, she knew that she spoke truth of the future.

'I see a time when she has come to know you as she knows those who care for her in the grotto. She looks forward to your visits and to showing you all that she learns. She will know your people through you, and bring understanding of your world to some who object that she tells you too much.' Suddenly she gasped and her hand flew to her mouth to stifle whatever sound would have come next. Her eyes had become focused on a vision.

'Talla, what did you see?' he asked anxiously. He realised that she was using the *second sight*. It was a talent he had seen in more than one of the young women among his own magicians, but he had never seen Talla use it before.

She did not answer immediately but calmed herself and held the palm of her hand towards him to gesture that he should wait a moment. The quick glimpse she had seen was nothing to become alarmed about, but she could not explain it to Anton. She had heard, as had many, that one of the rare winged goblins had been born in another grotto. The vision that had passed before her eyes had disappeared too quickly to interpret its meaning clearly. She had seen only her daughter grown, Anton with silver streaks in his hair, a flash of a goblin sword and the winged creature. She had already known that one way or another, Haghuf's child would affect many lives someday just by being what he was. There was no reason to alarm Anton with these visions. Explaining it to a human would be too difficult. She would ask her mother later.

'You must go back to your people now Anton.' She said instead. 'They have crossed the river safely, but in needless fear. They are confused and will need your leadership now more than ever.'

'If they will follow,' he said as he got up and began to dress. 'It seems that many of them have realised that I am only a man after all.' He wondered for a moment how she knew that their fear was needless. He did not ask, as he had worked out that there was no point asking about what was in the water that attacked the men in the boats. He thought of the southern men lying in wait for him around his castle and the complete lack of respect that Paul had taught them. It brought out the doubts that he realised now had haunted him for a lifetime. Talla stood up also. She laid a gentle hand on his shoulder for reassurance. She stroked his bare arm, admiring a tattoo that she remembered seeing there before. She had thought that such skin decorations were only known among the goblins. She had meant to ask about it, but this was not the time.

'I heard you speak at the Storytelling. I know that you have the will and the courage to inspire them and to guide them well.' Anton was just a little surprised to hear that she had been there. He had seen no sign of her, but he knew he should be used to that among the goblins.

'If you heard my story, then you know that I am a fraud. My whole family was a fraud from the beginning.

Just a group of game players who bluffed their way through a sticky encounter.'

'But you are not a fraud,' she said evenly. 'You are like your ancestor, Count Victor. You lead them through wisdom and courage. They follow your lead as we follow the guidance of our respected ones. You are to them like Haghuf is to us. You have answers when there is crisis. It is not your false title that they follow, but your spirit and endurance. You calm them when they panic and counsel them wisely when they need direction, like now.'

The baby wriggled and Talla took her hand back to shift her hold on the restless infant. Anton began to reach for his ruffled shirt, part of his façade in his role as the Count, then instead reached for the bundle that lay neatly wrapped by the side of the wall. Whatever he had done during the revelries, he had retained enough of his faculties to look after the precious gift. Talla's eyes were on the baby as he began to unwrap the sword. She did not look up as she asked a question that had troubled her.

'Anton, you spoke of your title passing from each male to the male offspring of his making. You are young even as the humans count such things, what happened to those who made you?'

Anton smiled as he answered casually.

'Oh, my father and mother still live in the castle grounds, they run the blacksmith shop.' He speculated a moment whether it would be worth explaining about the way in which his father had chosen to change his role among the people and the travels of his grandparents, but just then he finished unwrapping the goblin sword. Talla's eyes glanced up from the baby and fell on its gleaming surface.

'*Foringen!*' she gasped as she took a step backwards. Her eyes became very wide, her expression unreadable.

Anton could not resist stroking the blade appreciatively for a moment before re-wrapping it. He had some knowledge of swords, both of their making and of their use. He had received training in swordplay early in life.

'Talla, what does that word mean, *Foringen*?' But it was a deeper voice that answered him.

'It is a name for the goblins like the one who brought that to you.' Anton turned to find Haghuf standing in the opening to the cave with another unknown goblin. He was more amazed to receive what sounded like a direct answer from Haghuf than at suddenly finding him there.

'I brought you a guide.' Haghuf continued. 'I thought you might be wanting to see the sun by now.' One who knew Haghuf less well might not have caught the note of teasing in his voice. Anton smiled again, accepting that his friend knew him all too well and could often predict his movements. He had been grateful for that talent when Haghuf had found him by the underground pool. Ironically, it was Anton's similar knowledge of his own people that made it easy to predict where they would be today.

'How close can I come before we break surface to the large human Temple?' The young looking goblin by Haghuf's side suddenly grinned, showing rows of sharp teeth as he answered.

'I can keep you unseen until you come out in the rafters if you like.' The glint in his eye told Anton that he was not just teasing, this was obviously one of the goblins who took sport in hiding from humans right under their very noses. He returned the grin and finished putting on his shirt. He tucked his parcel under his arm, then turned and impulsively kissed Talla on the cheek and the baby on the forehead.

'Let's be off then, I wouldn't want to miss the service.' He winked at Haghuf, knowing he would appreciate the joke. He quickly followed his guide who was already running down the passage in his excitement for the adventure.

Talla, left alone with Haghuf, decided to ask him about the tattoo. Haghuf was so often knowledgeable about such things that she was not surprised when he answered right away.

'What was that symbol on his arm?'

'It was a bit of a joke in its time,' Haghuf answered without hesitation. 'The Rose and Chaosphere…taken from an earlier group of men who called themselves the Brotherhood of the Rose and Cross. Many Turnings ago, those of the First Time preserved their knowledge of the *heka* for those who would come after. This you already know. But it is the way with humans, they fight for territory, like cats, and many of them broke away from the First Ones and found their way to the lands that were separated after their time.

Before the last Turning, those who kept the knowledge were eventually conquered by a people who imposed a belief system on the Art. They all but forgot the importance of the balance of male and female in the creation of the *heka*, because they had developed a society where their females were made little more than slaves and forbidden to use their magic, as the humans call it. The knowledge passed again to others, who also lacked the spirit of *heka*. Yet they became obsessive in their quest to master the Art of the Ancients. The sons of man first sought gold, the material that gave them what they called wealth. It was nothing more than the accumulation of more gold. Many forged successes, only a few remembered that which was lacking.

Then, when only a very few among even the most famous of them could find any success, they turned to spiritual alchemy and sought to 'purify' themselves in spirit, without the test of the physical transmutations. But what they thought was 'pure' was based on a faulty belief system that denied nature.

By then, humans had developed religions that attributed all magic to an imaginary god whom they believed was an all-powerful ruler of the universe and all that was in it. It was a sterile belief, for a sterile god who despised all pleasure. Many of the humans believed that purity was attained through denial of the mating instinct. So in their quest to become completely pure, they denied the essential spark of life to their experiments and thus failed completely. Some of the followers of this false god preserved the writing and the symbols and thought themselves very pure indeed. It was they who used the symbols of the rose and the cross.

Then, during the twenty-first cycle before the last Turning, there were some who called themselves magicians. They recognised the folly of a people who had become enslaved by a superstition, one that depended on blind faith from its followers to survive. Many began to see the lie and those who perceived the spirit of *heka* adopted a symbol with eight rays. It was similar to the cross in design, yet completely different in meaning. As a joke, some of them formed an Order, as the humans called such groups of themselves. They gave it the symbols of the rose and chaosphere to reflect the knowledge that they had rediscovered, that which the earlier group had thought themselves to possess.

It is from this group that Count Anton has come to us. That is why he understands the Dance.'

Talla looked thoughtful. Haghuf had slipped into the tone of a Storytelling, but in doing so had explained a concept that helped her to understand the humans a bit better. She could see now that those who had sought to harm her were the victims of superstition, the blind belief that could easily drive a human to acts of madness. Then she caught her breath, suddenly realising what it was that Anton intended to do. He was on his way this very moment to confront his people in the Temple where such superstitions were given strength. He was going to ride the balance of chaos that could tip one way or the other. It might lead to his death at their hands like Ranalf, or he could grasp control of their collective belief and become like a god to them.

'There is no need to worry for him Talla. 'Haghuf's ability to guess her thoughts and allay her unspoken fears was often a comfort to Talla.

'Nala and his people will look after him.' Talla saw the glint of goblin mischief in Haghuf's eye. Then she realised that Nala, the guide he had sent with Anton, was one of *Those Who Provide*. Anton, though unaware of his escort, would be far from alone on his mission.

Chapter Fifteen

Nala set a fast pace, staying just ahead of Anton so that he was constantly trying to catch up with the flapping feet of the goblin. Anton was completely unable to initiate any conversation. After a short time, he worked out that the little goblin could have run faster if he wished. He was deliberately adjusting his speed for the human to keep up. It was a technique that Anton knew from his own training, adjusting speed for the slowest but keeping the group at as fast a run as possible. Anton guessed that the little goblin played a role in their society that required leading group raids, something he had heard of in legend.

Anton began to tire after a while, but Nala still didn't stop. He adjusted his pace so that the weak human could walk a while rather than running the whole way, but he didn't show any hint of impatience. He stopped only once, when they had to cross a brief span of open territory and human voices could be heard beyond their secret tunnel. Instinctively, they both pressed themselves against the rock wall and remained still.

Then Anton saw something that surprised him more than anything he had learned about goblins for a long time. Nala changed colour, blending into the wall behind him so that a casual passer-by would be able to look straight at him without seeing him. It was an ability that was known to exist in some reptiles and sea creatures, but Anton had never seen it done by the goblins before.

He wondered if it was a universal talent among them or if only certain types of them were able to do it. Certainly it would be useful for any who habitually trespassed into human territory. A nearly forgotten term that he had overheard once came to him, 'the rock glamour'. He wondered if this was what was meant by it.

Then he thought of Talla and her ability to appear human for a time. Suddenly it made sense. A practised ability to change her skin to hues appropriate for human flesh...perhaps some shading in the tops of her ears to make them appear rounded. Add a healthy dose of pheromones released to entice the males of the humans so that they saw in her their own fantasy of a woman and her glamour was easily explainable without resorting to magic. That would explain why it did not work on human women. Without the effect of the pheromones, the changes in appearance were not sufficient to maintain the disguise. The release of these scent particles he knew to be among their mating habits as he had experienced it first hand.

Anton was more impressed with the goblins and their ability to adapt than he would have been had he discovered a magical technique. However, there was no time to dwell on it. The humans had passed and they were moving again. Nala quickly dropped the colour change and was easier to follow in his usual greenish hue.

The journey seemed to go on for a long time and yet it seemed too soon when at last they emerged from the inside of a large tree onto the roof of the Temple itself. It was far too easy to breach into the heart of the human world. Anton was grateful that the goblins had actually never wished his people any harm.

Nala led him through a few more secret ways in the building that only someone who had visited the place often could have found so easily. They emerged quite literally in the rafters. Anton could see the entire main room of the Temple clearly. It held hundreds of people and appeared to be filled to capacity which in itself amazed him. Despite prolific breeding, only a few generations had passed since the last Turning and all of Anton's people together would only half fill the Temple at best. There was only one way that so many could be in attendance today. The southerners had crossed the river and come to the Temple as well.

The service had begun and the congregation were singing a placid and spiritless hymn that was thankfully coming to a close. It occurred to Anton then that much of what gives a people their spirit came from their music. He could not imagine this gathering of solemn and drably dressed people letting themselves soar free in the complete release of the Dance. Yet it was what they needed more than the droning of some priest telling them what miserable specimens of humanity they were. After a few words of the sermon that started up right at the close of the song, Anton realised that there was no ordinary diatribe about sin and suffering to be had today. The term *eavesdropping* took on a new and literal meaning as he listened to words of memorial, of a cry to war, and of betrayal of himself and of all of the magicians that he might have to protect against his own people. It was time to leave his guide.

'Today we remember our fallen, the husbands, fathers and sons who fought valiantly to protect their families against the demon threat.' The voice of the priest urged on in a tone of outrage. Too much outrage for one who had never left the Temple. 'For too long have we obeyed the magicians who shun our place of worship. And now we find that they have protected the creatures of our destruction!'

Shouts of agreement echoed from the Temple walls as Anton began to climb down, stopping only to listen to Nala's instructions as he whispered in his ear of the best route. Once again, he was astonished at the cleverness of the little creature. He did not argue when Nala suggested leaving the wrapped sword in his care as it would be awkward to carry it while climbing narrow struts. Anton hurried to scramble along the ways that the goblin had indicated. The priest continued.

'Too many are dead, yet the demon creatures still live just beneath the ground on which we walk. And where is the Count when these vermin attack us? Among his malignant friends!'

'But isn't it the Count who has protected us from them?' shouted a woman's voice from somewhere among the congregation.

'Yes,' shouted a man's voice from another part of the room. 'The Count has always solved problems and taken care of his people, perhaps he kept this knowledge from us to protect us!'

The priest's eyes darted from one face to another as the people began to murmur among themselves, remembering incidents when Count Anton and his father before him had solved one crisis after another for the benefit of the people. Even some of those from south of the river remembered his generosities and his special talent for bringing wisdom and solutions to any situation that arose.

'A clear head does not guarantee a pure heart.' The priest growled in his most commanding voice. 'Tell me, any one of you, how we can be protected by having information about these demons hidden from us! What possible reason could there be for keeping it from us?'

'To protect you from your own ignorance.' Count Anton's words rang clearly throughout the main room of the Temple, echoing off the walls in a way that caused the congregation to look around for its source. When they turned back to the front, it was to see that he was standing within arms reach of the priest on the main stage. He, like the priest, was well aware of the acoustics of the building and how to pitch his voice at the right angle to put them to the most effective use.

There was a slight swagger to his step as he walked slowly across the stage, looking from face to face. His intense gaze challenged each person who met his eyes to disagree with him, but all were silent and in awe. Only the slow rhythm of the Count's boots echoing from the wooden floor of the stage could be heard for a moment, until he spoke again.

'It is in your ignorance that you have attacked creatures that have lived peacefully beside you for nearly as long as this planet has known human life. You have sought them out to slaughter them without reason. Then you have the audacity to become outraged when they defend their families, as you would defend yours. Is there a woman or child among you who has been harmed by them, or is there one among the fallen or injured?'

He stopped a moment again, allowing them to think and realise that there were none.

'And yet one of those who considered himself holier than even our cloistered priest here was seen by many of you throwing an infant into the river to drown.' His eyes blazed at the memory, unsoftened by the knowledge that his daughter and Talla were now safe. The cruel deed was not changed by their unexplained survival. He could be certain that it was not the humans who had arranged it.

'You seek a battle you cannot win. These are creatures of nature, called by your ancestors *fairies*, *elves* or just *the little people* for centuries and treated with a healthy respect. They use the term *goblin* for themselves. They can walk among you unseen as those who fell today learned all too well. Yet you need not fear them if you do not attack them. They wish us no harm.'

'Liar!' exclaimed a deep voice from near the front. The speaker pushed his way forward. It was Latham. 'Those were not fairies we fought! Where were you when men were being killed by these creatures you say we should accept?'

'Being fed to the fishes by some who were protecting their homes from unthinking murderers! Invaders that would hunt down an animal and then complain when it turns and bites!' Anton spat back. Latham was not so easily distracted.

'Then why are you still here?'

'Because they spat me out,' Anton replied in angry tones. Suddenly, forgotten visions of webbed fingers and something that felt all too human swam through his memory. 'They spat me out,' he repeated, more gently. The revived memory would need examining later, alone.

'No doubt to send you here to betray your own kind.' Latham's hostile accusation angered Anton, but he kept his composure for the benefit of others who would hear.

'No, but to save them. Do you think any man would be left alive in an all out war with the goblins? But they want only peace.'

'You defend these demons, fight their cause, and allow human blood to be spilled so that you can consort with the vile creatures of Hell! You defy the will of God and practise the black arts of magic with others like you and recruit innocent souls like Ranalf! He *died* because of your demon friends!'

'No goblin ever raised a hand or weapon to Ranalf.' Anton's voice was pitched low and menacing, yet projected clearly throughout the Temple. 'In fact, I saw his blood wet on the stone in *your* hand, Latham. A mob of his own brethren, hysterical in their bigotry, stoned him to death for his love of a goblin woman whom you once tried to ravish yourself.'

Anton was not surprised when Latham snarled and leapt up onto the stage, charging towards him in an attack. In fact, he welcomed the opportunity to strike out at the larger man for his part in the assault on Ranalf and for his attempted rape of Talla. All the built-up anger that he felt towards the brutish man for his part in stirring up the people against the goblins coalesced into a simmering, yet controlled rage that begged for release. Anton felt, rather than heard, his own heart beating loudly. He recognised the union that it had formed with the rhythm of the earth, the natural pulse that usually led to the Dance. His movements took up that rhythm, yet this was no dance of celebration. This was a rhythm that acknowledged life in all its aspects, and this time, it expressed itself in a dance of battle.

The training of his childhood and adolescence came back to him as he automatically fell into form. He dropped his centre of gravity low to allow balanced movement of the spiral patterns of the fighting art that he had practised daily for most of his life. Latham's first charge as much as passed by him as he manoeuvred his body so that a swing of the waist spun his upper torso like a swinging door or a bullfighter's cape. One arm swung round like a wet towel and finished in a punch which sent Latham flying onto his face on the stage.

He came back up quickly, even more enraged. He looked around quickly for a weapon and grabbed a standing candelabra to use as a staff. Anton knew he could take it, but started to wish that he had brought his sword down with him. He kept his intense eyes on the enemy as he moved carefully and lightly, shifting his weight into one side of his body at a time so that he could move a foot and feel for obstacles before shifting weight onto that side. The walking pattern he had learned in his training allowed him to keep his eyes on the enemy at all times while moving quickly and confidently, all the while maintaining the connection to the thrumming of the earth's forces. His upper body moved independently in supple, swirling motions that gracefully swooped and concentrated power into a movement that sent Latham's second charge with his weapon in hand flying head over heels so that he dropped the candelabra in mid-flight. It clattered out of the way to the feet of the priest who had backed away at the first sign of a fight. He pressed himself against the altar for safety.

Latham had landed near the altar as well, but he abandoned the candelabra as a weapon when he scrambled back onto his feet. His eye fell on the ceremonial sword which adorned the altar. His eyes met those of the priest for a split second, just long enough for the priest to nod assent. The sword was in Latham's hand instantly. This time instead of charging, he approached Anton more carefully, swinging the sword menacingly.

Anton took his position, feeling the natural rhythm course through him as he watched the motions of the blade, taking in their pattern. An unexpected upward spin just as the blade rose would do it. He waited for that extra heartbeat to allow Latham to come just a little closer. In that moment there was a glimpse of something that appeared to Anton as a slight distortion of the air that passed him. Something had been pressed into his hand as it passed. He closed his grip on the hilt of the sword, recognising it, and expertly swung the weapon up into the arch of trajectory that he had been about to follow. Every part of his body moved in concert with the spiral pattern of the fighting form.

Blade rang on blade, the distraction had thrown off his timing just a fraction. But still it had been an uneven fight from the beginning and now he was in his best element. Anton had always thoroughly enjoyed his lessons in swordplay. The two men fell into a pattern of parries and thrusts as Anton got the feel of the sword's balance. Latham was no swordsman. Anton was effectively playing with him while he settled into the pattern and contemplated how the goblin had managed to cross the stage so completely unseen. This was more than fading into a background and a sword would not change colour like a goblin's skin. He would have to get to the bottom of it later.

The people sat breathlessly watching the battle, but no one interfered. If any had thought of it the sudden appearance of a sword in the magician's hand had dissuaded any such ideas. Latham's movements were sloppy at best and the sword in his hand flailed randomly. At one point he dropped the blade at the wrong moment so that it bounced off Anton's sword and flew up, just scratching Anton's right cheek. Blood flowed down the side of his face and at that moment he fell into perfect unity with the sword, with the earth, and with the rhythm of the battle.

Anton felt the pulsation of the earth match his heartbeat and flow through his being, calling Wolf to just below the surface of consciousness so that there was no physical change. But the animal instincts joined with the human consciousness in a complete balance of all that he was and all that he knew of the natural patterns of the world that he inhabited. It was time to move in for the kill.

Man and blade worked in perfect unison, beating back the attacker and his impotent weapon mercilessly. Anton's body flowed through movements like water that gently caressed the contours of the moving patterns of the Dance he followed in battle. He gave the opponent no opportunity to counter the closing stance. Latham's blade crashed uselessly against the sweep of the goblin sword that swirled before him. His attention was so fully riveted on the blade that he didn't even notice that Anton himself had come very, very close to him.

Latham's blade swung upwards again, only to meet with a parry to the left so that Anton's sword swept the offending blade in a circle and down to the ground, pinning it to the floor. In that split second Anton shifted his weight perfectly so that with the force of a circular motion of his waist, he formed a complete circuit of energy through his left leg. He pushed off the earth in an angle that passed through his centre of gravity. It flowed through his right arm as it released the two handed grip on the sword and came up elbow first, unfolding through each joint. It finished with the heel of Anton's hand completing the straight line into the earth through his entire body and connecting with Latham's jaw.

The larger man flew off the ground, his sword clattering uselessly to the floor. The force of the punch sent him beyond the edge of the stage so that he seemed to fall endlessly. At last he hit the ground and in that moment, it felt as if the whole planet hit him back. Latham started to move, then thought better of it. The slight movement was enough for Anton to see that the man still lived, but he was beaten. Anton took no joy in the victory. It would solve nothing. This single combat would not change the minds and hearts of the people.

Anton was still attuned to the rhythms of the earth. He felt, rather than heard, the movement behind him and ducked instinctively just as the priest threw the heavy candelabra at his head. It flew into the crowd. The people parted abruptly, allowing the impromptu weapon to fall harmlessly to the floor between the pews. In the sudden jostling a man was pushed into a woman holding a small baby, smashing her into another man next to her. Despite her instinct to hold onto the infant, her arms flailed up helplessly and the baby flew into the air.

Time seemed to move in slow motion as the baby fell towards the back of the church pew where surely its head would be smashed. The people closest to the terrifying scene tried to respond but the fallen candelabra blocked their path. It was all too apparent that none would reach the falling baby in time. The mother screamed.

Anton sprang off the stage towards the crisis helplessly. He knew that he was too far away and could not possibly reach the infant in time, even as Wolf. Yet his trained eyes saw the whisper of greenish shadow that others did not as it rose from under the pew and he felt hope.

The baby landed neatly into the arms of the little goblin that seemed to appear from nowhere. There was a general gasp from the crowd, but no one moved. Anton didn't recognise him. It wasn't Nala. The creature resembled a gargoyle more than anything else as it perched on the back of the pew, holding onto it with his back toes like a bird perched on a limb of a tree. He smiled up at Anton and gave him a quick nod, then scrambled across the pews towards the infant's mother. He held the baby lovingly as he bowed to the mother with a complete undulation of the goblin's whole body. Then he held the bundled infant up and presented it to her. The baby hadn't even cried.

The mother hesitated, then reached for her child despite the shock of seeing it in the arms of such a strange little creature. As she took the baby the little goblin undulated a second time and scrambled directly down under the pew where it had stood. It had disappeared again.

'Find it!' Shouted the priest from the stage, 'We must hunt the vile creatures down!'

There was a moment of confusion as some of the people moved to obey the priest, attempting to look under pews and jostling among those who reacted by trying to back away in shock at the command. But none had much room to move as they were crowded in amidst the pews. Anton stood before them in front of the congregation, but on their level now rather than standing above them on a stage like the priest. Once again he pitched his voice for maximum effect.

'Look what you do! A goblin saves a child among you, and you seek him out to kill him as thanks!'

Ignoring Anton's words, the priest stepped forward to the end of the stage. He encouraged the people to obey him as the emissary of God instead of their inherited ruler.

'It's only one goblin, surely you can flush it out!'

The sound of whistling passed through the edges of Anton's hearing, perceptible only through his wolf senses. It sounded like a signal of long and short trills that might be used by a hunting party. Anton felt the expression of the earth's rhythm thrum through him as goblins began to appear from hiding places within the Temple. They seemed to appear in waves that kept rhythm. The size of the gathering grew dramatically as each heartbeat of the Dance permeated the congregation and brought the room alive. Anton saw his own people begin to almost imperceptibly move to an unheard rhythm that only he and the goblins could consciously feel.

Once again everything was confusion. Anton made a real effort not to look as awe-struck as the other people as dozens of goblins appeared from both likely and unlikely places. Some of them scrambled up from beneath the pews as the other little goblin had done, while others seemed to appear out of the walls and filled the aisles. Some also appeared in the high places, melting out of the thinnest beams and sconces and even from around the altar itself at the feet of the disconcerted priest. All of them moved subtly to the delicate rhythm that pervaded the gathering so that they appeared to move gracefully in the way of dancers who are completely aware of the balance and motions of their bodies.

The variety of them alone was shocking. Some were little and grotesque much as the gargoyle-like one before, while others were actually pretty in an alien, yet ethereal way. These reminded Anton more of Talla. He had never seen such a variety of goblins. They were all goblin-like in various ways, green and pointy-eared rather than quite like the fairies of legend. Yet the Temple almost looked like a wooded glade with all the creatures of fantasy gathering together. They were backlit by scenes in stained glass which included the trees in which one would expect to find such a fanciful gathering. Many years of collecting notes on goblins suddenly seemed inadequate in the face of an encounter with those he did not know among them. And with the memories of other creatures that he had come upon all too recently. He did not know the meaning of their sudden appearance and a part of him was afraid. Yet he knew that if he, who knew the goblins fairly well, could be frightened by their ability to manifest unseen in such numbers without trace or warning, then the other humans must be truly terrified of the implications of such a skill.

Anton turned and met the eyes of the priest. He glared back at him accusingly. No matter what happened, this one was clearly going to be an enemy in the future. Latham, another one to watch, was beginning to stir from his place on the floor. Anton walked over to him and offered him his hand to help him stand. There was a moment of hesitation as Latham looked around and took in the developments in the Temple. He saw the massive collection of goblins and, like the other humans, decided that it would not be wise to make a fuss just then. He accepted Anton's hand and pulled himself up and very close to Anton, speaking to him in low tones.

'Those were not the goblins we fought. They were bigger. Much bigger.'

Anton resisted the grin that wanted to manifest on his face. Instead he maintained a serious expression as he answered Latham. Only the twinkle in his eyes betrayed his amusement at the big man's discomfiture.

'As long as these little ones are safe, the big ones have no reason to come to the surface.' The implied threat brought a twitch to the corner of Latham's mouth, but he remained silent.

There was a tense moment that was felt throughout the Temple as the people watched the encounter. They could not hear the words, but tuned as they were to the pulsing rhythm of the planet they could not help but feel the unease that passed between the two men. Then suddenly the mood was broken by the sounds of laughter. Everyone turned to see the source of the merry sounds and saw a group of children dancing in glee, playing among themselves as they leapt about completely oblivious to the adults around them. Then some of the parents froze in shock as they realised that two of the children were not human. They were goblins.

The young goblins appeared to Anton to be about of ten years old and were performing various antics to amuse the younger human children. Some of them would run up a wall and backflip off to land within their impromptu circle, while others performed sleight-of-hand magic tricks or made faces. All the while they kept the rhythm of the Dance in their movements, both human and goblin children alike. The adults witnessing the spectacle were wholly unaware of their own gentle swaying in tune with the pulsating force that pervaded the assembly. They interpreted the tribal movements of the goblins that surrounded them as some sort of affectation of the species.

Anton recognised that this was the opportune moment to take control of the situation and stepped forward to speak to the congregation.

'Do you see? There is no instinct greater than that of a child. Let those who will join me come to the castle and celebrate life. There has been too much death already. Many of their own have fallen and yet they offer no harm to us. They live for pleasure and exist in harmony with nature. Revenge is a human trait, one that has been the cause of the destruction of civilisations many times over. But the goblins live on in peace and harmony, taking little notice of us and our mistakes.'

Suddenly Anton was distracted by Nala who appeared at his side, offering up the re-wrapped goblin sword that Anton had left on the stage. He bent down and whispered to the little goblin. Nala nodded and then emitted a few sharp whistles into the room. The goblins disappeared. The departure was so quick that many would think that they just vanished on the spot, but in fact they scrambled out as they had appeared, efficiently as only goblins could. The children who had been playing with the young goblins would always remember the cute bow that their two companions had made before scrambling right up the side of the walls and disappearing into the Temple rafters. Anton wished he could join them, knowing that they went to celebrate the Dance in their own realms. Nala and the sword had also gone. The humans were left alone. Anton knew the role he must play now and repeated his invitation as if nothing had occurred.

'Who will join me at the castle to celebrate life? Let our dead be remembered with honour and affection, but let us celebrate new beginnings, and freedom from fear. Our dead are not forgotten, but mourning takes many forms. Let us learn to glory in the simple joy of being alive.'

The priest again looked as if he would refute the words of Count Anton, but the voice of the woman whose baby had been rescued by the goblin was quicker to call out.

'All praise to Count Anton, protector of the people!'

Her words were echoed first by the people nearest to her and then taken up throughout the Temple so that cheers for Count Anton quickly became deafening. Anton turned to the priest and Latham. They had drifted close to each other, both glaring their disapproval back at Anton. He smiled playfully back at them and turned to the crowd, shouting as best he could over the din of applause in his honour.

'To the castle!'

Few actually heard his words, but the crowd followed him as he leapt out of the door at the side of the Temple. They moved as one in the direction of the castle. They had already lost sight of the Count who had run ahead. None saw the shadow of a wolf which sped to the castle to give orders for a massive party and for music that would mirror the heartbeat of the Dance.

It took several minutes for the people to file out of the Temple doors, but there were two who stayed behind. The priest, cloistered as always, took Latham aside and asked if they might speak.

Chapter Sixteen

Haghuf looked casually across the rows of books. It was getting difficult to find anything he hadn't read now. His visits to Count Anton's tower library had continued to be very frequent, regardless of the doings of creatures outside. Humans slept at night and none looked for a shadow to climb the tower wall from the outside. Even among Anton's own household, only the Count himself knew that a goblin had this ability. Not that they would have begrudged him access anyway, but stealth was an old habit to be maintained. Anton wouldn't live forever after all.

After a few minutes he lost interest in scanning the titles for something yet unread. Anton occasionally procured new books, but Haghuf had kept up with them and there just didn't seem to be any new material for him. Instead, he started looking around the rest of the room for any interesting features. Old castles were supposed to have secret passages in the walls or hidden treasures besides the books themselves. He half expected to find the goblin sword stashed away safely, but was not surprised that he did not. Anton would probably keep it close to himself.

Haghuf shook his head again at the memory of the *Foringen* and the unexpected gift. Sometimes it seemed as though even his own people were a mystery to him. That such a treasure could be awarded to a human, any human, was beyond his comprehension. Perhaps, as a magician, Anton might be one who could discover its 'special' qualities in time without having to learn from one of the *Foringen.* Or possibly, Haghuf wondered, they actually intended to send one of their kind to the surface to bring the knowledge to Anton. The fleeting thought that they might have himself in mind was dismissed almost at once. It had been too long since he lived among his mother's people. Surely they would send someone who was still one of them, if they sent anyone at all. Once more he shook his head in confusion. He could not work it out. Haghuf speculated that the thing to do would be to travel to the deeper levels and ask them...if he could stand the heat long enough.

His inquisitive eye scanned the room until at last it fell on something out of place. It was only a bit of fringe on the rug that spanned most of the room. Rather than falling sideways as a bit that had been trodden on or kicked, it had been flipped up in a way that suggested that the entire corner of the rug had been turned over. Haghuf immediately moved to investigate. He lifted a good portion of the rug, revealing the artificial stone floor beneath. It was not difficult in this substance to spot cracks that were far too straight to be natural fissures. The easy discovery of the secret compartment piqued his curiosity. What could Anton have to hide in this most inaccessible of rooms?

The answer was yet another book. Only this one had no title on the cover. It was rather large and leather-bound, hand-made by craftsmen who knew the binding art well. Haghuf took it out of the secret compartment and sat down to have a good look at it. It quickly became apparent that the book had originally been bound with blank pages and that the writing within had been added over several generations as information had become available to record. It was a book of notes about the goblins.

Most of the handwriting was clearly done by Anton himself, but bits of it preceded his writings. The first pages revealed that it had been started by Count Victor. It had been passed down through his family until it came to Anton. Haghuf was a little surprised to learn that Victor had known about the goblins at all, as none of the authors had made a serious study of his people before Count Anton. Most of what they had recorded were odd tales and psychic impressions which occurred when goblins were in the vicinity. This seemed to happen most often when the magicians met out of doors and had their own dances.

'So,' Haghuf said aloud to himself, 'I was not the first of my kind to be drawn to the Dance by the humans.' It was a revelation to him. He would have expected to hear of such things, but according to the book these dances had occurred far from the cities of men and from his own usual travels. Haghuf was beginning to think that it was time that he travelled a bit further, to learn what else he could about men and goblins from afar. It might be useful to know what other grottos under the human cities did to avoid discovery, or in the event of it happening as it had here. Despite all of his travels between different levels of his world, it had never occurred to him to travel far through the networks of those who lived close to the surface in other places. He preferred the deep places, which were his natural home.

He began to flip through the pages randomly to see what knowledge had been accrued over the generations. The pages were organised in an orderly fashion with a heading on each, and only as much writing as there was knowledge available. Space was left for later writers to add new information or corrections. His eye fell on a page that started with unknown handwriting, but had been continued by Anton. The original entry recorded a tale that demons cannot cross water. It had been followed by Anton's hand. He had written a speculation that perhaps goblins simply did not swim as he had never seen one enter the water. This was again followed by a separate entry, more recent, that noted that there was something in the water, something that the goblins knew about yet would not speak of. At the end of the entry was written a question, "*Water Goblins?*" Haghuf frowned. It was far too close to the truth. The goblins did sometimes refer to the *Kol'ksu* as water goblins, although he was sure that Anton could not have fully guessed their nature as yet.

Haghuf continued browsing the pages, recognising many of his own contributions through Anton. Much of it was disturbingly accurate, such as the entry about where goblins slept. Anton had written;

"*Goblins cling to a territory to some extent, but are not actually territorial. This is reflected in their sleeping habits. They will establish a habitual sleeping-place, but after a Dance may well sleep in any convenient hollow within the network of caverns where they happen to be at the time. They do not seem to sleep together, apart from in communal rooms towards the end of a celebration when the few stragglers cannot be bothered to look for a more private place. Mating couples are virtually unknown as they do not practise monogamy. A male and female sharing a sleeping-place for one occasion is not unknown, but is not frequent. Despite their mastery of communal living, goblins are individually very solitary people. This may be why it works.*"

Haghuf frowned, disturbed by the accuracy of the entry and yet fully aware that every detail of it had been provided by himself in various conversations shared with

Anton in the past. He smiled again as he turned the page and found the entry for goblin eating habits. He, like the other goblins, had teased Anton mercilessly about this.

"Goblins do not have a set routine of meal times, but basically eat when they are hungry or when food is available. Many times they have replied to my questions about what they eat with the phrase, 'Whatever comes to us'. I surmise that what they mean by this is that they are mostly meat eaters and will eat any creature, yet I have been served a bowl of completely meat-free food on one occasion. It may be that food 'comes to them' through a variety of methods, but this is not openly spoken of to an inquisitive human. I have not yet determined for certain whether they practise cannibalism. Hints have been dropped as to what they do with their dead and whether humans wandering into the cavern end up as dinner, but definite commitment to this information has been artfully avoided. The cat I found wandering among them was clearly in no danger, and yet I wonder if food was scarce, whether that would hold true."

Haghuf chuckled, remembering so many times that he had baited Anton about the goblins' eating habits. There had been a time, long before the last Turning, when allowing humans to believe that they would be eaten by goblins had helped to protect them. But of course they ate very little meat. Many were completely vegetarian. They did not like to kill things. Even *Those Who Protect* left cleaning up the bodies to the *Kol'ksu*, who were entirely carnivorous.

It was the result of the choices made by all their ancestors, who, like some of Anton's magicians, had been shape-shifters. Those who learned to live underground often had to learn this art to survive...to become like the other creatures who survived in such conditions. With some species, the nature of the creatures they became remained in the bloodlines. There were sharks that were brothers to the *Kol'ksu*. Sometimes literally, as novice shape-shifters were not always able to change back. But still it was a way of survival.

Haghuf ruminated on his own ancestry and the random accident of heredity that had made him as he was, rather than scaled or able to tolerate extremes of heat like his closest kin. Perhaps it was why he understood Talla better than most. It was something that they had in common. There was a difference though, in that he had been able to stay with his mother's people until well after weaning and had only sought cooler climes at an age when most goblin youngsters chose their place in the scheme of things.

Haghuf shook away the ancient memories and continued turning the pages until his eye fell on a very brief entry in Count Victor's now recognisable handwriting. It was under the heading, *Changelings*. He was actually surprised to see that no information had been added to the old superstitions of the humans. Yet he couldn't remember discussing the subject with Anton in all their conversations. The superstition had been hard learned by the goblins, yet there it was, staring at him in faded black ink.

"The old tales speak of Changelings, of human babies who are stolen in the night and replaced with the infants of fairies who are ugly and sickly. In later centuries some speculated that it was an excuse made by mothers who had sickly babies, or babies who did not resemble their husbands. Yet the tales are sufficiently widespread to surmise that changes might have been made by these invisible beings. The reasons are not known. Most tales say that it was because the little people preferred pretty human children to their own ugly offspring, yet common

sense tells me that all creatures find their own young pleasing. Perhaps my descendants will learn the truth, as I see a time when communication may arise between us and them. These days so soon after the Turning are filled with turmoil, and yet welcome change as the ravages of technology have been all but wiped out in our world. At least the planet is not irradiated as it might have been through warfare, and there will be children to make our future."

Haghuf ignored the unknown term *irradiated.* Whatever it was had been avoided and so it was of no consequence. The tale itself brought back uncomfortable memories and he found himself shifting his sitting position several times. Victor had left out the detail of how the humans reacted to changelings, that they left them out exposed or pinched them and tormented them, until their own child was brought back. The goblins had learned then of human pride and how much of what they called love for their children was actually conceit in seeing their likeness reproduced. The goblins, living close to nature as they did, were more like the other animals. A mother would protect her young with her life until it was weaned, but then the young one was encouraged towards independence as it grew. By the time it was half the adult's height it would follow its own path in life. The love and recognition of one of their own never stopped, but this concept of owning one's offspring was a purely human concept.

Haghuf put the book down a moment and stood up to pace the floor. A lot of time had passed and the planet had changed since, but he would never forget the last changeling. The humans had tortured the infant until he was near to death. Then the mother had rescued him and replaced the human baby. The baby had been brought to him, as it was beyond natural healing and the mother had sought Haghuf's magic. It had taken a lot of effort and sufficient time for the mother to eventually conceive again within his own grotto. She left the healing child to Haghuf's care, knowing that he would be safe now. He had eventually been assimilated into the grotto as one of their own and the close relationship that had developed between them over time and constant care had naturally led to the young goblin learning much of Haghuf's Arts himself. Leap would make a good successor some day.

Haghuf's eye fell on a quill and ink that stood on the desk not far from where he had left the book. It was a common item that had always been there, but now it gave him an idea. He picked up the articles and returned to the floor by the book. Looking briefly at samples of Anton's writing on the other pages, Haghuf opened the ink bottle, dipped the pen, and began to write under the previous entry in his best imitation of Anton's handwriting.

"*Changelings were a gift from the goblins who sought to rectify the damage done by too much inbreeding among both species*."

Haghuf ruminated a moment. It had been a practice during the time when many humans lived in small villages and did not travel very far. Some of those goblins who lived near the surface were appalled by the mutations that occurred among the humans and a discussion was held with the deeper dwellers of the time as to the eventual effects on the goblin species if there was not more diversity. Haghuf continued writing.

"*A mother cannot be left with empty arms and has an instinct to bond with her own progeny, but some who were generous volunteered to trade infants with the humans. They knew that they would be comforted to have a baby at their breast, and could follow the progress of their own until it was past weaning. Some of them were trained by Those Who Provi...*"

Haghuf stopped at this point and scratched out the last phrase. This he was not prepared to see in writing where the information could be discovered by other humans in later generations. He made sure that the last few words were completely obliterated but intentionally left the part up to "*trained by*" slightly visible. He chuckled to himself again as he knew how it would torture Anton when he eventually came across the entry in his own handwriting. Then he continued on a new line.

"*The humans were cruel and did not appreciate the gift. They tortured the infant goblins and left them exposed to the elements until they were again replaced by their own offspring. Some of the abused babies nearly died as a result and it was then that the goblins realised the arrogance of humans and their ways of projecting their own immortality through their young.*"

Haghuf hesitated a moment, wondering if he should add that they might have achieved more longevity by avoiding the sunlight that aged them so quickly. But in the end he decided to leave it, as it was too much of a digression from the subject of changelings. Besides, the humans liked their sunlight. Let them glory in its damaging rays, as they had been left to live with their own damaged children. For a moment, Haghuf felt the disgust that the thought of humans generally created in him. But then he smiled to himself as he visualised Anton's face when he found the unremembered entry in his precious book of goblin knowledge.

Haghuf had seen enough of the book for now. He would look forward to reading more of it on other occasions, now that he knew its hiding place. Many of the notations had seemed a bit odd as they were of ordinary customs such as the traditions of accenting speech or showing respect through body language. He assumed that the fact that they were noted meant that humans had different customs. He blew on the ink until it was completely dry, then replaced the book in its secret location and turned the rug carefully over it.

He had only just replaced the book when he heard footfalls on the steps. It could only be Count Anton coming to the tower. Haghuf took a book from a shelf at random and sat near a wall in a reading position, maintaining absolute stillness. He had been uneasy about the notation in the book about the goblin's ability to change colour. Nala had been careless to allow Anton to witness this skill, but of course one of his kind would have done it instinctively without conscious thought. He probably hadn't even been aware of doing it.

Anton's speculations as to how this ability related to the succubus glamour were well off the mark, much to Haghuf's amusement. On this, Haghuf would not be providing the explanation. Unable to change himself, Haghuf remained as still as a statue as the door opened with a creak of the hinges.

Anton seemed distracted, even agitated as he crossed the room to the window and gazed out at the clear, starry sky. The moonlight spilled into the room with sufficient light that human eyes could see well enough to move about, but not to read as Haghuf could manage in far less illumination. Anton sighed, then seemed to pull himself away from the window. He lit a candle on the desk next to where Haghuf had replaced the ink and quill exactly as he had found them. Apparently he had not noticed Haghuf sitting so close to the desk.

He turned then and started directly towards the corner of the rug where the secret journal lay hidden. Haghuf guessed that he intended to retrieve the book, but he could not allow him to do so now if he was to retain the secret of his own knowledge of its existence.

'How was your party, Anton?'

Anton spun around quickly towards the sound of the familiar gravelly voice. Haghuf moved a bit to draw his eye. The characteristic amused grin spread across Anton's face as he perceived that not only was his friend here to visit, but also that the goblins could still surprise him unawares. It was a quirk of the goblins that no human could accomplish and one that never failed to beguile him.

'As well as could be expected,' Anton answered coolly. He was not the least bit disconcerted to find Haghuf sitting casually in his supposedly inaccessible tower. 'The humans attempt to dance, and some find a close rhythm. They gossip and chatter though, distracted by things peculiar to their species that would not trouble a goblin.'

'Like whose girl-child will win the privilege of becoming wife-slave to the Count?' Haghuf teased. Anton laughed in response.

'Yes, they continue to push their daughters at me, hoping I will dance with them. Sometimes I do.' Anton moved towards the window again. He didn't need to explain again to Haghuf how little he could converse with the teenage daughters of common people. Too many of them couldn't even be bothered to learn to read.

'Actually Haghuf, I've decided to take a Countess.'

This did surprise the goblin, but he did not display a reaction. He waited for Anton to continue.

'She is one of the magicians, the Lady Ariane. You may not have noticed her among the others…that day. She does not draw attention to herself.'

Haghuf remembered immediately one of the females who cloaked herself in darkness. Tall, yet dark, and hidden among shadows that she seemed to generate herself. He had noted her in passing and had thought that apart from Anton, she was one who was closest to goblin kind in the spirit she projected.

'After all,' Anton continued, 'I shall have to produce an heir in case I ever want to relinquish my position and disappear into obscurity like my father.' Anton winked as the grin returned and sat casually with one leg thrown over the arm of an ornate chair next to the window. Haghuf returned the grin, knowing full well that Anton had no desire to give up his position and was not likely to want to do so for a very long time. Anton's tone turned more serious when he continued.

'You should come and meet the magicians Haghuf. I think you might find them…interesting.'

Haghuf was surprised to find that the idea actually appealed to him, but he was not going to show an interest in such a large group of humans so easily. He scowled at Anton, making his best effort to look disagreeable before he answered.

'Perhaps I will. When I'm ready. When do they meet?'

Anton sat forward in the chair, excited that Haghuf was showing curiosity about the humans at last.

'In three nights time, by the full moon.'

'Bah!' Haghuf all but spat. Anton knew full well that goblins did not measure time by the movements of the sun and moon.

'Oh you'll know the time Haghuf, you'll feel us Dance.' The playful grin was back, mocking Haghuf's attempt at being churlish.

'And we're meeting here in the city. Come, I'll show you on a map.' Anton sprang towards the desk and pulled a small book out of a drawer. The pages were all covered in maps of the streets of the city, but they had little meaning to Haghuf who had only seen such a thing once before.

'Here it is.' Anton pointed to one of the pages. Just in these woods, near the pond. It isn't much of a walk from the opening to Daetsmah.'

Haghuf studied the map more carefully now. It was plain enough. He did not usually travel as far as the grotto at Daetsmah. It was far to the north, yet still in the city of humans. Not many goblins wandered there, apart from *Those Who Provide* who would be likely to have gardens of their own around such a wooded area. That the magicians had been meeting in a wood so close to goblin places piqued his curiosity. Had the magicians actually been joining in the Dance all along right above their heads without drawing attention from the goblins?

Haghuf could see that he and Anton would have a long night ahead of them discussing the ways of this kind of human. It occurred to him for the first time that in all their discussions, they had spoken mostly of the ways of goblins. He had asked Anton little about human affairs, assuming Anton to be an anomaly even though he knew that there were others of his group. He had dismissed them too easily…because they were humans.

'Yes, I think I can find your merry band, Anton.' Haghuf still tried to sound gruff, although he was aware that it didn't actually fool Anton. Anton just continued grinning at him as Haghuf struggled to maintain his scowl as he finished speaking.

'I'll just follow the man-stink.'

All characters and events in this book are fictitious. Any resemblance to persons living or dead is strictly coincidental. Apart from Count Anton, who walks among us and drew the arch for the back cover. And of course, Lucky the cat.

***The Jaq D Hawkins Website is at*:**
http://www.jaqdhawkins.com